D0405609

HIDE and SEEK

ALSO BY JANE CASEY

Bet Your Life
How to Fall

FOR OLDER READERS

The Missing
The Burning
The Reckoning
The Last Girl
The Stranger You Know
The Kill

HIDE
and
SEEK

JANE CASEY

ST. MARTIN'S GRIFFIN
New York

This is a work of fiction. All of the characters, organizations, and events portrayed in this novel are either products of the author's imagination or are used fictitiously.

HIDE AND SEEK. Copyright © 2015 by Jane Casey. All rights reserved. Printed in the United States of America. For information, address St. Martin's Press, 175 Fifth Avenue, New York, N.Y. 10010.

www.stmartins.com

The Library of Congress Cataloging-in-Publication Data is available upon request.

ISBN 978-1-250-04067-1 (hardcover)
ISBN 978-1-4668-3627-3 (e-book)

St. Martin's Griffin books may be purchased for educational, business, or promotional use. For information on bulk purchases, please contact the Macmillan Corporate and Premium Sales Department at 1-800-221-7945, extension 5442, or write to specialmarkets@macmillan.com.

Originally published in Great Britain by Corgi Books, an imprint of Random House Children's Publishers UK, a Random House Company

First U.S. Edition: August 2015

10 9 8 7 6 5 4 3 2 1

For Lauren Buckland, best of editors

HIDE and SEEK

1

As parties went, it was a fairly typical Port Sentinel night out: too many people crammed into a large, expensive house, most of them in some sort of costume, all of them determined to have fun. If there was one thing I'd learned in the five months I'd been living in Port Sentinel, it was that any excuse for a party would do. The mere fact that it was Friday night counted. When it was only a week until the end of term and the start of the Christmas break, a party was inevitable, and it couldn't be anything other than Christmas-themed. There was fake snow dappling the picture windows that overlooked Port Sentinel's pretty bay. Fairy lights decorated the mantelpiece of the feature fireplace, and a twelve-foot Christmas tree stood at the foot of the stairs, rocking slightly as people pressed against it on their way to the kitchen.

"Jess." The hostess appeared in front of me and wrapped her arms around my neck. Her eyes weren't completely focused and her mouth was stained pink: one too many Christmas cocktails. "Thanks for coming."

"I wouldn't have missed it." I patted her back, wondering if and when she would let go. "How are things, Claudia?"

"Oh, you know." She looked around vaguely. "Everyone *seems* to be having fun, but you can't tell."

"Everyone is having a great time," I assured her. It was true. The music was louder than God's heartbeat, there was more than enough to drink, and I'd just seen a reindeer kissing a very pretty snowflake. It was the point in the evening before things started to go wrong, I found myself thinking, and told myself off for being so cynical. There was no reason to think that anyone was going to cause trouble—except that it was as much a part of Port Sentinel's social scene as music. Port Sentinel was a small town full of rich, spoiled kids, and arguments blossomed as easily as love affairs. It was hard to avoid people you didn't want to see. It was proving impossible to stay out of trouble for long, if you were me.

Claudia sagged against me, shedding glitter from her fairy-on-the-Christmas-tree costume. I straightened her wings for her. "*Such* a relief," she whispered. "I don't know what I was thinking, having a party tonight. The *pressure*."

"I can imagine."

"This is it, you know?" She leaned sideways to take a gulp from her glass, still clinging to me. "The last big party of the year. Everyone's away for Christmas and New Year."

"Not everyone," I said. "I'm not going away."

"You know what I mean." She flapped a hand at me. "Everyone important."

2

"Thank you very much, Claudia." I unwound her arms from my neck. "You can do your own standing up."

"Don't take offense," she protested. "Loads of people."

"Loads," I agreed.

"Barbados and St. Lucia, mainly." Claudia frowned. "I told Daddy. I *said* it was the Caribbean this year. He went and booked bloody Cape Town."

"Shocking," I said.

"*No one* is going to Cape Town. Oh, apart from Sam and Belinda and George, but they're doing the Garden Route first." She sighed. "I mean, I'll make the best of it. At least I'll get a decent tan."

"Thank goodness. Otherwise, what's the point?"

"Exactly." Claudia was looking over my shoulder and her eyes narrowed. "Oh my God, who let *her* in?"

I turned to see a slender angel with lots of dark eyeliner straightening her halo self-consciously. "Immy? Are you two still fighting?"

"She hasn't apologized yet."

I couldn't remember exactly why Claudia and Immy were fighting this time. They were always falling out with one another over the stupidest things, but argue with one of them and you argued with both. I'd learned a lot from getting to know them—that appearances could be deceptive, that being wealthy didn't mean you were happy or popular or anything other than rich. And I'd learned not to write people off just because they were privileged. They couldn't help it.

"Maybe it's time to forgive and forget," I said. "It's almost Christmas."

3

Claudia gave me a long disapproving look. "I don't see why *I* should be the one who has to make the effort. It was *her* fault."

"I know," I said, having absolutely no idea if that was true or not. "But she's here now."

"I'm going to throw her out." Claudia looked as intimidating as it was possible for a Christmas fairy to look.

"She's your best friend, Claude."

"She *was*."

"And she will be again." I patted her arm. "Go on. Make friends."

"Why do you even care?"

I shrugged. "Life's too short to fight." I'd seen the things people did to one another in the name of hatred. I'd seen the things they did in the name of love too. Sometimes it was hard to know which was worse.

Claudia raised one eyebrow and squinted at me. "That's not like you."

"I don't fight with anyone," I said primly. "Sometimes people fight with me—"

"And regret it," Claudia finished.

"I don't go looking for trouble."

"But trouble finds you anyway."

"Not for ages," I protested. "Nothing serious, anyway."

"And you miss it."

"No I don't." But even as I said it, I wondered if I meant it. I didn't like other people's pain—truly I didn't. The fact that I kept getting involved in trying to solve other people's problems was an accident, really. My cousin Freya's death was a mystery I'd had to solve, for her sake and for my own peace of mind. And I'd had little choice about trying to work out who

4

had left Seb Dawson half-dead when his little sister begged me to help. Since then, I'd been keeping my head down. Life had been quiet. Quiet and predictable. Restful.

Boring.

But I really couldn't allow myself to think that way.

Claudia's attention wandered back to Immy. "I'd better go and speak to her anyway."

"Be nice," I said, and watched her weave across the room toward Immy, who was furiously ignoring her. Before I could see how it played out, a voice spoke in my ear.

"I'm disappointed, Miss Tennant. What sort of a Christmas outfit is that?"

I looked up into Ryan Denton's very blue, very mocking eyes, then looked down at my dress, which was brief and black. "Ah, you haven't seen the back."

He turned me round so that he could look at the silver star Darcy had glued on for me in her self-appointed role as chief fashion designer for all her friends. I had inherited Darcy from my dead cousin, along with so much else. She had been Freya's best friend, and now she was mine.

"The night sky?" he guessed.

"A Christmas star."

"I was hoping for an elf costume."

"Never mind. Maybe Father Christmas will bring you one."

"That wasn't what I meant."

"I know," I said. "Anyway, you're not in a position to criticize my choice of outfit."

"I had antlers." Ryan looked around as if he was expecting them to materialize in front of him. "Someone nicked them."

5

I thought of the reindeer I'd noticed earlier. "I think I saw them disappearing upstairs with a snowflake."

He shrugged. "I wasn't really committed to it as a look."

"I'm sure they looked dashing," I said. "And prancing."

He grinned. "If I was a reindeer, I'd be more of a Dancer. Hey, you can be my Vixen if you like."

"I don't think so."

"Is Will here?" He said it carelessly, as if the answer didn't matter, and maybe it didn't any more. It was a long time since Ryan had told me he cared about me—at least five girlfriends ago, if I'd managed to keep track accurately.

And it was a good thing if he had given up, because I could admire his eyes and his cheekbones and his perfect mouth all day and all night without my heart missing a beat, but even the mention of Will's name thrilled through every nerve-ending in my body.

I took a sip of my drink, hoping I hadn't given myself away. How I felt about Will was between me and him, and since he was away at boarding school, it was something we shared by text and e-mail and phone call and any other way we could stay in touch with one another without actually getting to touch. It made me feel as if Will was a figment of my imagination, as if I had invented the whole relationship, and thinking about him coming back made me nervous as well as excited. But I wasn't about to mention any of that to Ryan. "He's still at school until next week."

"Shame," Ryan said, not sounding as if he meant it. "So how about that dance?"

"Not this second." I'd seen what he hadn't: his current girlfriend, Yolanda, on a course that would have her arriving at Ryan's side in *three . . . two . . . one . . .*

"Baby, I'm bored." She nuzzled his neck while giving me a hostile look. "Can we go?"

"It's too early."

She pouted, long eyelashes fluttering on her cheeks. "You never do what *I* want."

"That's not true, Yoyo." Ryan wound a lock of long dark hair around his fingers, drawing her toward him for a kiss. She grabbed hold of him and kissed him back, pressing her body into his. One of his hands slid down her back, his fingers spreading, digging into her flesh.

"Oh my God, get a room," Darcy murmured, cannoning into me, off balance thanks to her ludicrous platform shoes. "Are you going to stay and watch or do you want to go somewhere else?"

"Anywhere else," I said, grateful for an excuse to walk off. I had a fairly shrewd idea that Ryan and Yolanda spent their time making each other jealous, and I didn't want to play any part in it. I started to follow Darcy through the crowd, dodging a wild elbow from one of the dancers. "Where are we actually going, though?"

"Somewhere we can sit down," Darcy said over her shoulder. "My feet are killing me."

"You could take your shoes off," I called.

"No way. I'd lose them. Someone would nick them."

"It's kind of hard to hide glittery red platform heels. There are limited occasions when you can wear them. And also, you have teeny tiny feet."

7

"Trotters," Darcy agreed cheerfully. "No one can ever wear my shoes."

"So . . ."

"Still no. If I'm sitting down, I can still pose in them." She pushed open a door. "Ta-dah!"

It was a small snug, a room with an L-shaped sofa filling most of it and a wall-size television opposite the sofa. The lights were off. Someone had put on *Die Hard* with the sound turned down, and the room flickered as the characters on the screen moved. There was a group of girls gathered round one end of the sofa in a tight little knot, but in the half-light from the television screen I couldn't tell what was going on— though as their heads turned one by one I felt, very strongly, that we were intruding.

"Thank God." Darcy beetled across to the sofa and flung herself down, oblivious to the atmosphere in the room. "I was seriously about to cry." She held out a foot and stared at it mournfully. "I love you so much, shoe, but you have to meet me halfway. You can't torture me like this."

"Do you mind?" It was Abigail Norris who spoke, her voice sharp. I didn't know her well, but she was in my year. She ran her fingers down her long honey-blond hair, checking that it was still straight and sleek, a gesture I'd seen countless times. "We're using this room."

"I didn't see a sign on the door," Darcy said, crossing her legs.

"Take the hint and go." Abigail's expression was fierce. In the center of the group, one of the girls moved, pushing past her and heading in the direction of the door. Dark hair curling around a small, sulky face: Gilly Poynter, the quietest girl in my history class. Abigail grabbed her arm as she passed her. "We're not finished."

"Leave me alone." Gilly's voice was a whisper.

I reached behind me and felt along the wall until I found the light switch. The main light flared brightly, and I blinked along with everyone else. As Gilly's face came into focus, I saw that she hadn't been crying, as I'd somehow expected. She was flushed but she looked angry, not tearful. She stood completely still, head down, waiting for Abigail to loosen her hold on her arm.

"Gilly?" I said. "Are you all right?"

She nodded, but she wouldn't look at me. Her eyes were fixed on the wine glass she held, cupping the bowl of it with both hands.

This was the point when a normal person would have taken the hint and found somewhere else to be. I wasn't that person, as I'd proved before and would probably prove again before too long.

"Abigail," I said. "I think you should let her go."

"We were having a conversation."

"Why don't you just get lost?" Louise Manning was Abigail's fair-haired best friend. She propped her hands on her hips, sneering at me. "You're always poking your nose where it doesn't belong, Jess. This is none of your business."

"Gilly?" I said again.

"It was a friendly conversation," Abigail insisted. Behind her, the other two girls were nodding enthusiastically, but that was nothing new: Stephanie Walton and Min Owen were both the sort to agree with the loudest person in their vicinity. And Abigail's voice *was* loud—loud and shrill. Loud enough to attract attention, even at a party. I was aware of the doorway filling with curious onlookers. Some of them spilled into the room, pushed from behind by other partygoers who wanted to see what was going on.

"Oh God, no." Someone said it under their breath, but it was a whisper that carried past me. I looked to see who had spoken, but I couldn't pick a face out of the crowd: everyone seemed to look tense, curious and not a little perplexed, but no one appeared distraught. As I turned back, Gilly's hands clenched on the drink she held, her knuckles shining white. I watched her without understanding what she was doing, until the thin glass shattered into a handful of long curved shards.

There was an exclamation from everyone who had seen what had happened, and a general surge toward her. Gilly looked up slowly. She seemed to be in a dream as she tightened her grip on the broken glass. Liquid started to seep between her fingers—wine mixed with oozing red blood that trickled down the backs of her hands and slid along her forearms, branching out as if her veins were suddenly, shockingly, on the outside of her body.

Everyone had stopped dead, frozen in shock. It took me a second but I stepped forward, reaching out for her wrists. Nessa Mullen got there first, flashing past me. I shouldn't have been surprised. Nessa and Gilly were generally inseparable. Sullen Mullen, the boys called her, and I only knew that she was small and spiky and devoted to Gilly. Nessa held onto her friend, peeling open her fingers and letting the glass fall to the floor. She looked at the other girl's palms. "Gilly—oh my God, what have you done? What have you done?"

"Leave me alone," Gilly said through gritted teeth. She tried to pull away from Nessa, but the other girl held on tighter. They were about the same height, but Nessa had been a gymnast when she was younger and she had far more strength than Gilly. The blood smeared on Gilly's forearms as they struggled. But all of a sudden the fight went out of her and she leaned in to Nessa, putting her head on her shoulder.

"I didn't mean to."

"I'm sorry," Nessa said, and it didn't occur to me until later that it didn't seem to make any sense for *her* to be apologizing.

The only answer Gilly gave was to shake her head, and it seemed to mean something to Nessa, even if it wasn't how she wanted her to respond. Nessa bit her lip. "Come on." She guided Gilly out past me, snapping, "Stand back."

Most people did move to allow the pair to pass, but I could see them murmuring comments, their faces avid with curiosity and alive with the strange kind of excitement that came from being near, but not involved in, Trouble with a capital T. Gilly had dropped her head again to avoid meeting anyone's gaze. As she disappeared from view, the onlookers started to drift away, the noise level rising as the party began to take off once more. I turned back to stare at Abigail, who stroked her hair again.

"I don't know what you're looking at. I don't know why Gilly did that. I don't know anything at all." Her voice was high and defiant.

"Yeah, that's what I've heard about you," I couldn't resist saying.

She glowered. "I didn't make Gilly hurt herself. You saw her. She chose to do that herself."

"What were you talking about?"

"Nothing. Life. Love." She turned and threw a look in the direction of her three associates, who nodded supportively.

"Well, I can certainly see why you didn't want an audience for that." I allowed plenty of sarcasm into my voice, so much that even they couldn't miss it. Darcy raised one eyebrow at me. She was still sitting on the sofa, swinging her leg as if nothing had happened.

"If you hadn't come in, nothing would have happened," Abigail snarled at me. "You made her behave that way, not us." She pushed past me, followed at high speed by the others.

Gilly hadn't been upset when I came in, it was true, but I hadn't caused her to injure herself. When I played it back in my mind, it seemed to me that it was the comment from behind me that had upset her: *Oh God, no.* I wished I knew who had spoken, but I couldn't even guess. It was a whisper, unidentifiable, anonymous.

Darcy came to stand beside me. "I thought Gilly and Nessa were friends."

"They were," I said.

"So what was going on between them?"

"I've got no idea."

"And what was going on with Abigail and Gilly?"

"Again, I've got no idea."

Darcy wriggled her shoulders. "Drama, anyway."

"All the best parties have it."

She slung an arm around my shoulders. "Let's go and make some of our own."

I went with her. I smiled and chatted, danced a little, drank some Christmas punch that reeked of cloves, and abandoned my cup as soon as possible. I looked as if I was having a good time, I think. But one sentence was playing in my mind, over and over again.

If you hadn't come in, nothing would have happened.

Abigail was just trying to upset me. But there were times later when I thought about that remark and how weirdly right she had been without knowing it. Because if I hadn't walked into that room at that moment, maybe everything would have worked out differently.

Maybe everything would have been all right after all.

2

Jess, are you listening?"

I hadn't the least idea what my history teacher had just said.

"Sorry, yes." *By which I mean no.*

"So I don't have to repeat myself." Mr. Lowell raised his eyebrows.

"Absolutely not."

"Because you know exactly what I said."

I just wasn't going to get away with this. "Maybe a quick recap?"

"I thought as much. Pay attention, please." Mr. Lowell gave me a long, hard look that gradually became a smile. He was the kind of teacher who wanted to be strict but needed to be popular with his students. He tried a little too hard to win us over, but it was useful when, as now, I'd drifted into a daydream. It wasn't entirely my fault. It was hard to concentrate during the last class on a Tuesday afternoon at the best of times.

In the last week of the term it was practically impossible. I'd been watching the day burning itself to a spectacular death behind bare trees outside the window, the branches soot black against a pink and orange sky. Now the clouds were the color of ash and I'd run out of excuses. An apology seemed in order.

"Sorry, sir. What did I miss?"

"I was allocating study partners for this project. You need to sort out who is doing what before the end of the term so that you can do the research over the holidays." Mr. Lowell held out a box. "Pick a name."

I reached in and took out a slip of paper. "*Sam Milner*," I read.

"And here's your topic." He handed me another slip of paper from the stack he had in his other hand.

"*Animals and their role on the battlefield.*" Why did I think that was going to be depressing?

"Go and sit with Sam, please."

I got up and carried my books to the back of the classroom, where Sam was sitting. He was playing on his phone under the desk and didn't even look up when I sat down. This was going to be interesting. I'd never actually seen Sam read a book. But if he thought I was going to do all the work on our project, he had another think coming.

The classroom was humming with conversations as everyone tuned out, rightly judging that being allocated a work partner was only interesting when it was your turn to pick or be picked. I was one of the only people watching Mr. Lowell, who had moved on to Max Thurston. "Come on, man. Wake up. Pick a name."

Max did as he was told, then unfolded the paper. Instantly his ears went red. He mumbled something.

"Gilly?" Mr. Lowell turned round. "Gilly, Max picked you. Come and sit with him."

I leaned forward. Gilly was sitting a few desks in front and to the right of me. Her head dropped a little, her shoulders hunching as if she could feel people looking at her and hated the sensation of being watched. She had her hands in her lap so the bandaging wasn't really visible, but I knew it was there. She'd been absent on Monday, walking back into school on Tuesday with her head down, looking neither left nor right, acknowledging no one. I hadn't gone near her. Obviously I was curious, and just as obviously that was something I was going to have to live with. I'd earned my reputation for interfering in other people's business, but generally speaking, like a vampire, I had to be invited in.

"Gilly?" Mr. Lowell backed up so that he could see her. He crouched down by her desk and knocked lightly on the wood. "Gilly, did you hear me?"

She gave a tiny shake of her head, but not because she hadn't heard him. She said something to him; something that made him look surprised. He glanced up at Max, then back at Gilly.

"Well, I could change it."

Gilly whispered something else. Max folded his arms, shifting in his seat as if he was suppressing the urge to stand up. I could see the side of his face, the tightness in his jaw that told me he was clenching his teeth. Embarrassment? Anger? I couldn't work it out. Max was tall and broad-shouldered but gawky, as if he still had to grow into his frame. I knew him as one of Ryan's friends, but Ryan had a lot of friends, and I couldn't actually recall ever hearing Max speak outside class. I didn't really know him at all.

16

Gilly was sniffing now, in between bursts of inaudible words. Mr. Lowell looked from her to Max, his forehead furrowed with concern. Max shrugged. His body language was conveying that he wanted to be anywhere but in that classroom at that moment. Anyone might have felt the same, but my interest sharpened.

"All right, Gilly . . ." Mr. Lowell said slowly. "Why don't I swap Max and Jess? You can work with Jess. Max can work with Sam."

I'd been right about Max wanting to get up, but wrong about him wishing himself elsewhere. He jumped out of his seat instantly, but not to swap places with me. "Sir, that's not fair."

"It's a random allocation, Max. You might have picked Sam out of the hat first if Jess hadn't picked his name already."

"Yeah, but I didn't. I picked Gilly."

Mr. Lowell walked up to him, lowering his voice. He was a bit shorter than Max so he had to tilt his head back to look up at him. "She would rather work with a girl."

"Why?"

"I don't have to explain it to you. Take it from me, she feels strongly about it."

"You wouldn't let anyone else change."

"That's enough." Mr. Lowell glared up at Max. "I want people in my class to be happy. Gilly wasn't happy. I've asked you and now I'm telling you to swap with Jess. You aren't working with Gilly. You've got Sam to deal with."

"Oh, thanks very much." Sam looked up from his phone for a second. "Like it's a punishment or something."

"You said it," Mr. Lowell said. He was back to being friendly but firm. "Go on, Max. I'm waiting. Jess, get a move on."

He dropped a topic slip on Gilly's desk, then walked away, immaculate in pressed chinos and blue shirt. I wondered if he had ever, for the briefest moment, been cool. Then I gathered my things again and went past Max to sit beside Gilly. She was still flushed, her eyelashes spiky with unshed tears, but she looked essentially normal. Certainly she wasn't the blank-eyed self-sacrificing victim I'd seen at the party. She glanced at me then looked away again.

If people didn't start being pleased to see me, I was going to become paranoid. I risked a look back over my shoulder and saw Max scowling in my direction, which was hardly fair.

Mr. Lowell turned from the whiteboard. "You four will probably have noticed that the majority of your classmates are already discussing the topic they're going to tackle, so you might like to catch up."

The majority of our classmates were *supposed* to be discussing the history project, but I doubted whether anyone was doing much work. I glanced sideways at Gilly, who had turned away from me a little, as if trying to discourage me from talking to her. She'd picked the wrong person if she thought that would be enough to put me off. But I didn't want to treat her like a freak show either. I'd already told myself not to see the fact that Gilly and I were going to work on the project together as a sign. There were a lot of questions I wanted to ask her, like *What happened the other night?* and *Why don't you want to work with a boy?* and *What's going on between you and Nessa?* I knew that asking any of them would be a quick way to guarantee Gilly never spoke to me again, project or no project.

I picked up the slip of paper Mr. Lowell had left us.

"*Weapons of war—new military technology in the First World War*," I read.

"Sir, can't me and Max do that one?" Sam asked.

"Nope."

"Oh, sir, I know loads about machine guns and chlorine gas, though. Jess and Gilly won't know anything."

"Then they have lots to find out." Mr. Lowell folded his arms. "You stick to your homing pigeons and horses and don't worry about anyone else."

Sam subsided into muttering. I leaned over. "I don't know if I'm more pleased about not having to do animals in war or not having to work with him. Thanks for rescuing me."

Gilly looked surprised for a second, then shrugged. She'd pulled her jumper down over her hands, hiding the bandages. She was doodling, her pen tracing triangles and cubes down the side of her page. Every page in her notebook was decorated the same way, the edges curling up, heavy with ink. Patterns, not pictures. Geometrical. Ordered. As I watched, she dug the tip of her pen in so hard the paper ripped.

I looked up to see that Mr. Lowell was watching us. He had bright blue eyes which he opened very wide, so he had a tendency to look startled even when he wasn't. He was leaning against his desk, arms folded, legs crossed at the ankle. Relaxed, you'd have said. But he wasn't. He never made that particular mistake.

He clapped his hands. "OK, everyone. I want you to fix up a time to work together on the project. You can use the school library or the main library in town for research. Don't do it all on Wikipedia, please. I will know if you just rehash whatever you can find on the Internet. I will also know if one of you leaves all the work to the other person. Don't think you can slack off because you have someone else to share the workload. You need to get cracking on this one—projects are due in the second week of January so must get the reading done and start writing when we come back in the new year. If you're a day late with this, you automatically drop a grade. Two days, two grades. And so forth."

There was a rumble of conversation as soon as Mr. Lowell stopped talking. Some of it was probably to do with the project.

"So when do you want to work on it?" I asked Gilly. "Tonight? Tomorrow?"

She shook her head. "I can't."

"What about Friday, if you have time after school?" A thought struck me. "You're not going away for Christmas, are you?"

"I'm not sure."

How can you not be sure? I didn't say it out loud, but she must have assumed that was what I was thinking.

"I just don't know yet." She was blushing again but her face was composed. "I might be going to see my father. I haven't decided. But I should be around on Friday after school."

"You could come to my house for an hour or two. There's plenty of space. I mean, it's noisy. I live with my cousins and they're insane. There are seven of us in the house but it sounds like seven hundred most of the time."

"It's just me at home."

Something we had in common at last. "I'm an only child too," I said, and saw her flinch as if I'd said something wrong. I plowed on, "I've lived with my cousins for five months, but

I'm not really used to the noise level yet. Though my room is at the top of the house, and no one will disturb us if we hide up there."

"I don't think I can."

"Why not? Is it too far? It's only about ten minutes' walk from the center of Port Sentinel. I mean, it is uphill. But still. Downhill on the way back."

"I can't." Something in Gilly's voice told me that she wasn't in the mood for a debate about it. She'd said no and that was that. *Why* she'd said it I didn't know.

"What about your house?"

"It's too small."

I looked down at myself. "There's only two of us and neither of us is exactly huge. How small can it be?"

She didn't laugh. "It's on Pollock Lane."

"Oh, one of the cute cottages?" They were small, brightly painted, older than my family's Victorian villa by a century or more. They had been fishermen's cottages, once upon a time. Now they were featured on postcards that captured Port Sentinel's "unique character," when actually they were the last vestiges of the old town. These days Port Sentinel was all about modern sea-facing homes, stacked up the sides of the hill like very expensive shoeboxes.

"I live in number fourteen," Gilly told me, then added, "I don't think they're cute, particularly."

"I'd love to live there."

"That's what everyone thinks." *And everyone is very wrong* was strongly implied.

"Right," I said. "Not your house, not my house. What about the library?"

21

"In school?"

"No, the main library in town."

"All right." She bit her lip. "I mean, I'll have to check with my mum. But it should be OK."

"Great. After school?"

"Not straight after. Maybe at five?"

"OK."

"Just for an hour."

"That's fine," I said, thinking that I had better things to do after the end of term than hang out in the library and an hour would be more than enough.

Gilly looked as if she was regretting it. "You'd better give me your mobile number in case I need to change the arrangements."

I wrote it down for her. "And what's yours?"

"I don't have one."

"What?"

"I used to, but I— I lost it."

"It's a nightmare, isn't it? Losing all the contacts, all the pictures and stuff."

"Yeah," she said quietly. "A total nightmare."

The bell rang and there was general upheaval as everyone rushed back to their places to grab their stuff.

"Remember, this is an important part of your work this year," Mr. Lowell yelled over the noise. "Make sure you take it seriously, because *I* will."

I shoved my books into my bag and headed for the door. Gilly was in front of me with a couple of people between us. Suddenly she stopped, muttered something, and fought her way back into the classroom.

"Sir, can I have a word?"

Mr. Lowell turned from cleaning the whiteboard, surprised. "Of course, Gilly."

She stood waiting for everyone else to leave, twisting her hands together inside the sleeves of her school jumper. I walked past her, baffled about what had made her double back, until I reached the corridor. Max Thurston was waiting there, his face dark with anger. His arms were folded and he had one foot braced behind him against the wall. He looked as if he was prepared to stay there indefinitely.

"Sorry for taking your place," I said.

"Not your fault." His eyebrows were a straight, heavy line across his face and his jaw was still clenched tight.

"No," I agreed. "I don't really understand what the problem was."

I was hoping that Max would tell me what he thought about it, but he returned to staring at the closed classroom door, as if he could X-ray it if he just concentrated hard enough. It was very clear that he had no interest in talking to me. It wasn't that he didn't like me; it was just that I was irrelevant. Whatever he cared about, it was taking up all the space in his brain and he didn't have enough room left for me.

There was no reason for me to hang around and wait for Gilly to emerge, even if I was desperately curious to see what happened. I walked away, wondering. Wondering whether Gilly had objected to working with a boy, as Mr. Lowell had said, or whether it was Max she specifically wanted to avoid. Wondering if Max had been at Claudia's party, and if he had been in the crowd behind me when Gilly cut herself.

Wondering if he could have been the person whose voice

23

had prompted her to break the glass, or if there was something else going on—something I couldn't understand yet and maybe never would.

I told myself to forget about it and get on with going home, but it bothered me, like a stone in my shoe. And I knew that it would keep bothering me unless—OK, *until*—I found out the truth.

3

It would be an exaggeration to say that I was delighted to be spending the first hours of my holidays in Port Sentinel's drafty library. I walked down through town, past shop windows full of Christmas decorations and fake snow, wishing I had other plans. I'd have been happy to stay at home, where I could have curled up by the Aga and read my book in peace. I'd have been even happier to go out. In front of the library, Port Sentinel's Christmas market was in full swing, little chalets lining the railings, and fairy lights strung through the bare trees, and a small ice rink right in the center of Percival Square. Voices rose on the clear night air, laughing and talking. Most of my friends would be there, taking turns to spin around the ice with varying degrees of skill and grace. When you were inside the square, it was close to magical, with music tinkling and mulled wine scenting the air and shoppers browsing the stalls.

As I trudged the long way round the outside, I could only

hear the hum of the generators that powered the market, and smell the gasoline fumes that competed with the grease from the various food vans. The market was just an illusion, another way of making money from the tourists who wandered through Port Sentinel's winding streets all year.

I would have preferred to believe in the magic, but it wasn't how I was made. My mother was artistic, creative, gentle, and imaginative, while my father was hard-edged and cynical, realistic to a fault. His genes had won that particular battle, though I tried very hard to keep the curious side of my personality under control. I'd interfered before, to good effect and bad, and as a result I'd learned a few lessons about involving myself in other people's lives.

I felt a little happier as I pushed open the glass door that led into the central atrium of the library, inhaling the distinctive leather-and-old-book smell I loved. The building was old, and no expense had been spared in furnishing it, although now it was looking somewhat frayed around the edges. There were occasional murmurs about refitting it with more computers and modern seating, but so far they had come to nothing and I was glad. It was dark and cold but atmospheric, and I'd spent many hours doing homework there.

I walked through the seating area in front of the door, where there were armchairs in little groups, and where I'd expected to find Gilly waiting for me. No one at all sat there, let alone anyone I knew. I checked the different areas of the atrium, hoping I might find her at one of the long tables in the history section. Or biography. Or (getting slightly desperate) the children's section. They were all deserted, the cream-shaded lamps shedding pools of light on the scuffed mahogany tables. There were two people reading in the fiction section, and I saw a librarian shelving books in travel, but otherwise I was alone.

I came back to the front door and checked the time. Ten past five. I'd been a few minutes late so there was a chance that Gilly had already left. But even if she'd gone at one minute past five precisely, I would have seen her as I walked toward the library. It was more likely that she just hadn't arrived yet. I sat down on one of the armchairs and unwound my scarf, staring at the door like a dog waiting for its owner to show up. The sun had set an hour earlier, so it was properly dark outside and the wind was picking up. A handful of rain scattered against the glass, which was just perfect as I'd left my umbrella at home.

I peeled off my coat and gave myself a good talking to. There was absolutely no reason to think it was strange that Gilly had turned up. She wasn't outrageously late. She didn't have a mobile phone, so there was no point in checking mine every two seconds for a message that wasn't coming. I took my book out of my bag and started to read, glancing up every now and then.

A quarter past five.

Twenty past five.

Twenty-three minutes past five.

At twenty-five minutes past five I put the book down, not having taken in a word of it. I went over to the main desk where the librarian was now sitting, working at her computer. She was young, her hair swinging in a ponytail, her nails dark purple.

"Excuse me, can you tell me what time the library closes?"

"Six." She smiled at me. "You still have half an hour."

I retreated to my chair. Half an hour wasn't going to be long enough to talk about the project, even if Gilly turned up now. And there was still no sign of her. I played back our conversation in my head. We had definitely agreed to meet there, at five, on Friday. I'd seen her in the corridor at school earlier and she'd nodded when I said I'd see her later. So she hadn't forgotten about it.

After we'd agreed on when to meet, we'd talked about her house and where she lived. I chewed the edge of my thumbnail. Was it possible that she'd got confused? Had she thought we were going to meet at her house rather than the library? Or maybe something else had come up; something that had delayed her at home. I could go there and see if she was in.

But I knew she would *hate* that. She'd given me the very definite impression that she didn't want me anywhere near her house.

I stood up, knowing that it was pointless to spend the extra—I checked—twenty-four minutes waiting for the librarian to kick me out. Gilly wasn't coming, and whether I went to try to find her or not, I wasn't staying where I was. I slid my arm into my coat and turned to find the sleeve with the other hand, and as I did so, I saw a movement behind one of the bookshelves at the end of the room. It was a furtive movement, as if someone had quickly stepped out of sight, surprised that I'd turned in their direction. Not Gilly; too tall.

And maybe it was nothing to do with me, and I was being paranoid. I turned my head away, bending to get my bag, and then suddenly looked back, in time to see Max Thurston leaning out from behind the bookshelves. He was staring straight at me, his long face pale against the dark background of paneling and books. He ducked out of sight again, and I felt my heart thudding with surprise and irritation and—just a little— fear. He didn't have to lurk like that. I knew him and he knew me, so he could have walked over and spoken to me. And I didn't like being watched.

I strode across the library, my boots thudding on the floor, so he knew very well that I was coming. I walked round the side of the bookshelves to find him leaning against them. His head was tilted back and his eyes were closed. Rain flecked his jacket and he was breathing hard, as if he'd been running.

"What the hell are you doing?" I whispered, trying to get as much outrage into my voice as possible, even though I couldn't shout at him in the quiet library.

Max looked down at me, and again I had the impression that I was completely insignificant to him, an irritating distraction from his thoughts. "What do you mean?"

"Don't give me that," I snapped. "You were watching me, and now you're hiding."

He shook his head, but weakly. "I wasn't watching you."

"Why are you here?"

"It's a public library. I don't have to explain myself to you."

"You do if you're here to spy on me." I thought back to our history class. "Or Gilly."

Max shivered at the sound of her name, an involuntary movement that made the hair stand up on the back of my neck. His voice was sharp as he said, "Is she here?"

"No. She didn't show up." I frowned. "What do you know about it? How did you even know she was supposed to be here?"

"Is there some problem here?" The librarian was standing at the other end of the bookshelves, her expression saying very clearly, *Not in my library, thank you very much.*

"No," Max said. "Sorry." He stepped away from the shelves and pushed past me. He was too big for me to be able to block his way, but I hurried after him, grabbing my things as I passed my chair. I got to the door just as he let it swing back behind him, and I had to stop sharply to avoid getting a slab of solid glass in the face. I pushed it open and followed him out, but the second or two had been enough to enable him to get a head start. I saw him running through the gate of Percival Square, and watched from the top of the steps as he shoved his way through the crowds of shoppers, dashing away from me. He was too tall to hide, but there was precisely no chance of me catching up with him, even if I ran round to the other side of the square. I frowned. Something was going on here, something I didn't understand. Max was literally running away from me, and Gilly hadn't turned up to meet me.

Max might have known that I was meeting Gilly at the library. We hadn't been quiet when we discussed it. Or at least, *I* hadn't been quiet. I hadn't known I needed to be.

Max had been upset when Gilly refused to work with him. He had taken it personally.

Max, who had waited outside Mr. Lowell's classroom so that he could talk to Gilly. I didn't know if he'd succeeded.

What I *did* know was that he must have come in while I was talking to the librarian about when the library was closing, because he hadn't been there when I searched for Gilly and I'd been watching the door pretty much the entire time after that. There was no other entrance to the building in regular use—the emergency exits had alarms on them and the windows were barred. So he had slipped in behind my back.

And maybe—just maybe—Gilly hadn't come to the library because she'd known Max was going to be there. Maybe she'd seen him outside, and hadn't dared come in.

30

And maybe it was a good idea after all to go to her house in Pollock Lane, to see if she was there. To warn her that Max was looking for her. To see if she wanted to talk about it. To see if she was all right. That wasn't interfering, I told myself. That wasn't poking my nose in where it wasn't wanted. That was just being friendly.

I shouldered my book bag and started walking, cutting down side streets to avoid the crowds and get to Pollock Lane more quickly. The rain was light now, more like sea mist than proper drops of water, and I folded my arms, tucking my chin down into the collar of my coat, pretending I didn't mind. It was strange: I knew Port Sentinel very well by now and was generally quite happy to walk around it at night, but I still felt uneasy. I was unsettled by Max's behavior, and worried about Gilly: I saw the blood sliding between her fingers at the party, and the blank look in her eyes. The desperation on her face in history class. Her friend Nessa saying she was sorry in that low, hoarse, hurried way. Abigail's face twisting in disgust as she looked at Gilly. Whispers and rumors and people hiding in shadows added up to a mystery, and mysteries weren't fun. They were secrets that had to remain hidden. They were thoughts that couldn't be spoken. They were sacrifices and struggles and actions that didn't make sense in the cold light of day. They were a narrowing set of choices that could lead to disaster. And I'd blundered into the middle of this particular mystery by chance. I didn't know where it had started, or how. I didn't even know what it was. But I knew that there was something to know.

The streets in this part of Port Sentinel were narrow, the buildings leaning out over the pavements at crazy, drunken angles. The lanes were too narrow for proper streetlights, so there was just the occasional lantern mounted on a wall, shedding not quite enough light. I walked quickly, checking behind me now and then to see if anyone was following me—if Max had doubled back, or if there was someone else to fear. I'd been a little too successful in getting away from the crowds. There was no one around at all. My footsteps echoed as I ran down a flight of steps that brought me to the seafront, where the wind was stronger and the waves were breaking close to the shore. I tasted salt on my lips, and I still wasn't used to it, even after five months. This was the way Gilly would have walked to meet me, if she'd started at her house, and I couldn't help peering into the shadows and side streets I passed, just in case she was there.

As I got closer to Pollock Lane, I started to feel more nervous, not less. I didn't know what I was going to say to Gilly apart from, *Where the hell were you?* It was hard to know how to start a conversation with someone about the fact that they possibly—no, definitely—had a stalker. Pollock Lane ran parallel to the seafront, but it was a little way back up the hill and I trudged up the road that led to it, my bag thumping on my hip with every step. There was no pavement at that point, which wasn't all that unusual in Port Sentinel; there was barely enough room for a car to drive down some of the streets. I was a few meters away from Pollock Lane when a car drove out of it and turned toward me, much too fast, the headlights pinning my shadow to the wall behind me as I jumped back out of the way. The light slid over me as the car passed by, and I didn't have time to see who was inside or what kind of car it was or even what color it might have been. At the time, it didn't occur to me that it was anything more than someone driving badly.

That happened. Locals were arrogant and tourists were ignorant, and everyone was in a hurry all the time. My heart was thudding again, my knees trembling, and I strode on, eager to get to Gilly's house now. Whatever was waiting for me there, it surely couldn't be more intimidating than the shadows that were pressing on my heels.

But as it turned out, I was wrong about that.

4

Pulling myself together, I headed up Pollock Lane. It was cobbled and steep, and more or less like stepping back in time, if you ignored the cars. They were parked with two wheels up on the pavement, on one side of the road only, and just barely fitted. The cottages looked pretty even in the dark, with Christmas wreaths on the front doors and sparkling Christmas trees in the front windows. The cottages were tiny, now that I looked at them properly—two windows at the top, a door and a window on the ground floor. I tried and failed to imagine my adopted family, the sprawling collection of Leonards who filled my life, managing to fit themselves and their personalities into a Pollock Lane cottage. Gilly's silent withdrawal seemed more appropriate. *It's just me at home*, she'd said, and *I might be going to see my father*. So I'd assumed it was just her and her mother living in Pollock Lane. Looking back on it, she hadn't said that. She hadn't said much at all.

Number fourteen was about halfway along, and in contrast

to the others, there was no wreath on the door. The shutters were firmly closed, with just a little light leaking through to make me think that someone was at home. The cottage was painted a drab shade of gray with a black front door, and the overall impression it made was grim. I stood there for a second, apprehensive, then reached out and knocked on the door. It was a good loud knock, as if to make up for my lack of confidence. For all that, no one came to answer it for a long time—more than a minute. I could hear movement inside the cottage—a strange shuffling sound that made me uneasy all over again. Something being dragged. No, someone walking—but slowly. Someone old? Scuffling from within, and a bumping sound that made me wince without knowing why. I looked up and down the street, seeing no one, squares of light falling on the cobbles from the ordinary, normal houses on either side of number fourteen. How I wished I was knocking on one of the other doors.

A scrabbling sound came from behind the black door, and I fought the urge to run away as the latch turned and it opened, very slowly. A woman stood there, clinging to the door for support. She was tall and very slender. She had a long, angular face with a square chin, and bony hands. I saw the resemblance to Gilly in the color and texture of her hair, and in the pale blue of her eyes. This woman's eyes were cloudy, though, and she frowned as she tried to focus on me.

"What is it? What do you want?" The words came out slowly, so slurred that I hesitated before replying, not sure I'd understood her.

"Mrs. Poynter? I'm Jess Tennant. I'm looking for Gilly."

"Gilly?" She said the name as if it belonged to a stranger. "Oh, Gilly."

"I was supposed to work on a history project with her." Something told me not to mention the fact that Gilly hadn't turned up at the library. "Is she here? Could I see her?"

Mrs. Poynter stood in the doorway, not moving, considering what I'd said. I didn't know if she'd been drinking or if she'd taken something, but there was no way she was sober. Her face was slack and she swayed where she stood. She put a hand to her head and I saw blood on her knuckles, a graze right across them.

"Gilly," she said eventually.

"Yes."

"What did you say your name was?"

"Jess." I waited another few seconds. "May I come in, Mrs. Poynter?"

Her gaze fell on my very old, very battered boots and she frowned, slowly, with effort. "You'll have to take them off."

"Of course. No problem."

She hadn't moved from the doorway. I stood outside on the doormat and yanked off my boots, shivering as the cold seeped up through the soles of my feet. It was enough, apparently, to pass muster with Mrs. Poynter, who stood back and motioned for me to come in. She collided with the wall behind her, which seemed to come as a surprise to her. I sidled in past her, not wanting to get too close. There was something witchlike about her, something off, even allowing for the effects of whatever she'd taken. I was starting to see why Gilly hadn't been all that keen to meet at her house.

I went straight into the living room because there was nowhere else to go—there wasn't a proper hallway. I put my boots down side by side on the floor by the wall. The room was cold and unwelcoming, with no fire in the grate. There was a single lamp on in the corner, beside a battered armchair. Paperbacks filled shelves on either side of the empty fireplace, but that was it as far as entertainment was concerned. No television that I could see. No music system. No pictures on the walls. Definitely no Christmas decorations.

Behind me, Mrs. Poynter swore quite comprehensively as she overbalanced. She managed to cling onto the door latch so she didn't actually fall, but she was by no means steady on her feet. I went to help her and she allowed me to take her by the arm. I guided her slowly across the living room to the armchair in the corner, where she collapsed. There was no glass near the chair, no sign that she had been drinking, and I couldn't smell alcohol on her breath.

"Mrs. Poynter, are you all right?"

She had her eyes closed. Her face was pale, and slightly sweaty. "Fine," she said on a gasp, looking and sounding anything but.

"Can I get you some water?"

She shook her head, then seemed to change her mind. "Yes. All right. Water."

I went through the door at the back of the living room, past the dark stairs that cut the cottage in two, and found myself in a kitchen that was marginally more cheerful than the living room. It was warmer, anyway, thanks to the cast-iron range that filled the fireplace. An old worn table with three chairs stood against one wall. One door stood open, revealing a tiny bathroom, and there was another door that gave onto the small yard behind the cottage. I looked in the sink and found a single plate covered in crumbs, and a badly chipped mug. There was

37

a half-inch of brownish liquid in the bottom, and when I tilted it to tip the liquid out, a gritty residue coated the inside. I abandoned the thought of washing it out and went looking for a clean glass. I filled it at the tap and went back to Mrs. Poynter, who had slumped sideways. Her eyes were closed again and her breathing was heavy. I put the glass down beside her dangling hand and felt the inside of her wrist for her pulse, not really knowing what it should be like. It was slow but regular, and when I shook Mrs. Poynter's shoulder, she woke up easily enough.

"What is it? I'm sorry." She said it all in a rush, then put one hand over her eyes. "What's happening?"

"I'm looking for Gilly," I said clearly, crouching down in front of her to make it easier for her to see me.

"She's upstairs." Mrs. Poynter's eyes closed again.

"Are you sure?" *She'd have come down if she'd heard voices*, I thought. I was almost sure that the house was empty apart from the two of us.

"Leave me alone." She snuggled down in the armchair, her head leaning against the back of it. I stood up, wondering what to do. It couldn't hurt to look upstairs, although I was worried that Gilly might come back and find her mother passed out in a chair, and me snooping around upstairs, and be mortified and angry in equal measure.

But it wasn't snooping exactly. It was making sure she was all right.

I went back to the living room door and looked up the dark, narrow stairs. I didn't want to climb them. They were steep and forbidding, and there was no landing at the top— just a door on either side. One would be Gilly's bedroom. The other would belong to her mother, and probably wouldn't have a chalk pentagram on the floor. Probably.

I passionately didn't want to pick the wrong one.

In the end I decided that Mrs. Poynter would have the room at the front of the house, overlooking the street, and Gilly would be in the back room, so there was no danger and I should just open the door on the left. I ran up, noticing how steep the steps were and how narrow the treads. I tripped halfway up and put a hand out to save myself from sprawling. The carpet burned my palm and I winced. I had to use my left hand to open the door I'd decided was Gilly's, and I fumbled for the light switch. I found it eventually. A weak yellow light filled the room from the bulb in the middle of the ceiling, and really, it needn't have bothered. Bleak was the only word for what it revealed. Before I did anything else, I turned and softly closed the door behind me, feeling better with something solid between me and Mrs. Poynter's pale gaze. I didn't actually think she was capable of climbing the stairs in her current condition, but I wasn't in the mood for surprises. The latch clicked into place and I moved away from it on tiptoe, trying not to make too much noise on the bare floorboards.

It was Gilly's room, but only the school books on the desk confirmed it. There was nothing personal to be seen at all—no photographs or posters. A framed picture of a rabbit hung above the bed, but it was yellowing and dusty. I guessed a previous tenant had forgotten it because it was far more suitable for a nursery than a teenager's room. The walls were a depressing shade of beige. A small bookcase stood against one wall, but it was half empty and all the books in it were secondhand classics or school textbooks, nothing like the ones I read for pleasure. The single bed was an old wooden one, scuffed and secondhand like the desk and the bookcase. I glanced at the bedside table, expecting to see a novel or a magazine, but there was only a lamp. The bed was rumpled, as if someone had been lying on it earlier. That wasn't actually surprising: there was nowhere else to sit in Gilly's room, unless you counted the up-right chair at her desk. I thought of the warmth and chaos of life in Sandhayes, the big Victorian villa I lived in, and of the huge room at the top of the house, the one I'd inherited from poor Freya, full of posters and books and art that meant some-thing to me. The contrast with Gilly's life was painful.

I went over to the bed and put a hand on it, half expecting it to be warm, but the blanket was cool to the touch. The pillow was hollowed by Gilly's head. My toe hit something solid under the bed and I bent down to see her school shoes, kicked off. Her uniform was thrown over the back of the chair. She'd come home, changed, and flung herself down on her bed. On the other side, a small wastepaper basket contained balled-up tissues, as if Gilly had lain down and wept. Or worse. I tilted the basket, and saw that a few were spotted and streaked with red. Cutting . . . I knew plenty of girls who did it, slashing their skin to ribbons in neat lines down arms or thighs, because physical pain was better than the emotional kind. Cuts healed, if you let them. Scars soothed.

The room hummed with recent occupancy: I could feel Gilly's presence even though she was gone. She was there and not there.

I edged over to the desk and looked at the books, hoping for something like a note or a diary or the receipt for a train ticket to somewhere better than Pollock Lane. Failing that, something that told me what was going on between Gilly and Max Thurston would have done. All I found was a space in the dust, a rectangle where something had rested. I bent and looked under the desk, seeing a twin socket with an adaptor in one side for the desk lamp and the small light on the bedside table. The other socket was empty. So it was a fair guess that whatever was missing had been plugged in. A computer, I thought, and wondered how Gilly had been able to afford one—wondered why she'd been allowed to have one—when everything else in her house was so basic, so pared back and old-fashioned.

A creak from downstairs made me jump—were those footsteps coming up the stairs? There was a shuffle and a sliding sound that ended in a thud. Definitely someone coming up the stairs. I grabbed a notebook from my bag and pulled a page out of it, then, on a whim, put the notebook on Gilly's desk, on top of a stack of other books. I scribbled a brief note, folded it over, and tucked the corner of it under the desk lamp to stop it from blowing off the table. Then I crossed to the door and reached out to open it just as someone turned the door handle. The door burst open and I jumped back, stifling a scream. Mrs. Poynter stood there, leaning at a dangerous angle. She looked at me blankly.

"Gilly?"

"She's not here," I said. "I was just leaving her a note."

"Are you finished?" The last word fought its way out of her mouth, suffering serious injuries as it went.

"Definitely." I nodded emphatically. "I should really go."

She looked at me blearily. "Go. Now."

"That's just what I was thinking." *But you're standing in my way. And if you try to make me walk past you, I'm just not going to be able to do that.* I was scared of her, I realized, and even though I rationalized it immediately—of course I was afraid she might fall against me because we would both definitely fall down the stairs—I knew that wasn't it.

She turned away from me and opened the other door, half falling up the step that led into her own dark bedroom. The only light came from the street, and heavy net curtains blocked out most of it. The room was too dim for me to be sure, but I thought I saw a streak of something on the wall before Mrs. Poynter shut the door; something dark. Something that could have been blood.

That was just my imagination, I told myself, shivering as I snapped off the light in Gilly's room. Breakneck speed on those stairs wasn't very fast at all, but I hurried, reckless now, worried that the cold air of her bedroom would revive Mrs. Poynter, and revive her interest in what I was doing in her house. The light was off in the living room, and in the darkness I stumbled over something on the floor, something solid and unyielding that proved to be one of my boots. I searched the floor on my hands and knees, my fingers snagging on knotholes and old nails that stuck up from the floorboards. I covered ever-wider circles, hunting, increasingly desperately, in vain. I couldn't find the switch for the lamp either. In the end I opened the front door and let the light from the street guide me to the far corner where the second boot lay, miles away from where I'd left it. I shoved my feet into my boots and didn't take the time to lace them up properly.

42

Nothing and no one could have made me spend a minute longer in Gilly Poynter's house, even if it unlocked the answer to every question I had. I pulled the front door shut after me with a clatter. It was only when I was sure I was free that I let out the breath I hadn't even known I was holding.

5

It was so much more than the cold evening air that made me shiver as I ran away down Pollock Lane. I folded my arms and hugged myself to stay warm, but it was no good. The chill was deep inside me.

At the end of the road I stopped for a moment, looking up and down the deserted street to see if Gilly was walking home. There was no sign of her.

I started to hurry up the hill toward town and heard a noise from behind me: a double click that made my heart jump. It was a car door opening, the rational part of my mind informed me, while a more basic bit of my brain told me to run. I compromised on spinning round, ready to run or fight or scream, and it was both reassuring and terrifying to see who was standing behind me, leaning on the open door of his Range Rover. Dan Henderson. Inspector Dan Henderson, to give him his full title. The most senior police officer in Port Sentinel. My mother's childhood sweetheart.

My boyfriend's dad.

Obviously it was a complicated situation. But then, Dan Henderson was a complicated man. And at the moment he was smiling at me—a smile that meant nothing since I wasn't prepared to trust it. I did my usual mental checklist for Dan. Still tall, dark, exceptionally threatening, disturbingly like his son. Oh, and possibly angry.

In other words, just the same as usual.

"What are you doing down here, Jess?"

"Visiting someone." I started to walk back toward him. I didn't know which role he was playing at that precise moment, but I knew which one I wanted. The policeman. "Actually, you're just the person I wanted to see."

His eyebrows drew together, and all right, it was unusual for me to be enthusiastic about running into him. He was far too interested in rekindling his relationship with my mum for my liking. Even if you overlooked the fact that he was married, or that his wife was dying a slow, horrible death (and I wasn't prepared to overlook either detail), Dan Henderson had been bad news eighteen years before, and he was still bad news. He'd broken Mum's heart and driven her into my father's arms, and I owed him my life twice over, and I didn't like him one bit.

"What do you want with me?"

"I'm worried about a friend of mine. Gilly Poynter. She lives back there." I jerked my thumb in the direction of Pollock Lane. "She was supposed to meet me and she didn't turn up."

"When was this?"

"We were supposed to meet at the library at five."

"Five o'clock this afternoon? An hour ago?" Dan started to laugh. "Come off it, Jess. She's a teenager, I presume?"

I nodded. "She's the same age as me. But—"

"But nothing. She didn't come to the library on a Friday night. Can't say I blame her."

"It's out of character."

He raised one eyebrow, sardonic as the devil. "Is that right?"

"Yes, it is." I was refusing to be flustered. "And there's no sign of her at home."

"Is that where you've been?"

I nodded.

"Looking for another mystery, Jess?"

"Not looking." I sounded defensive, even to myself. "I just wondered. Her mum was weird too. Kind of out of it. You know, there was some stuff in a mug in the kitchen that looked like powder. Maybe she was drugged. Or maybe she took something herself."

Dan shook his head. "I'm not going to go and arrest Mrs. . . ."

"Poynter," I supplied.

". . . for being out of it on a Friday night. She'd probably been having a well-earned glass of wine before you turned up to terrify her about her daughter's whereabouts. It's Friday night. She's probably at a party."

"Gilly had taken her laptop with her."

"All right, then she's probably using it somewhere. Why don't you send her an e-mail and see?"

"I don't have her address."

Dan shrugged. "Not my problem. And neither is the fact that she stood you up at the library."

I thought about arguing with him—telling him about Gilly cutting her hands, about the blood-stained tissues in the bin, about Max Thurston lurking in the library—but he would have laughed at that too. It didn't add up to a reason to call in the cops, and if I hadn't run into him, I wouldn't have done anything so dramatic. But it annoyed me that Dan was so dismissive. I didn't know Gilly well, but he didn't know Gilly at all.

And I'd been right before, about Freya and about Seb Dawson, which Dan might have remembered.

"Well, if she turns up dead in a ditch, at least I warned you." I turned on my heel and started to walk away.

"Wait a second, young lady. Where are you going?"

"Home," I said over my shoulder.

"I'll give you a lift."

"I don't need one."

"Come on, Jess. Let me drive you home. I've finished work for the day, so I'm heading that way anyway."

Dan lived in the house directly behind mine. It did make sense to go with him if he was driving up through the hilly streets to our neighborhood.

That didn't mean I wanted to do it.

"That's very kind of you, but I'd rather walk. It's a nice night."

"Your teeth are chattering."

"Yeah, I said it was nice, I didn't say it was warm out." His face darkened and I hurriedly added, "I just meant that it's not raining now. I'd better go. Thanks again."

"Jess."

I'd already turned to go, but I turned back. There was something in Dan's voice that made me quite sure he'd find a reason to arrest me if I didn't cooperate.

"Get into the car."

"But—"

"Now."

There was no way round it. I'd already used up all my polite and not-so-polite ways of saying no. I trudged back to the passenger door. There was a part of me that was very glad not to be hauling my bag up the hill. There was another part that was replaying the last time Dan had given me a lift, when he'd been terrifying and unsettling.

I got into the car and shut the door, feeling as if I'd have been much safer wandering the streets alone. Dan had already put his seat belt on.

"Buckle up."

It was surprisingly hard to do that when you were perched on the extreme edge of the seat. I yanked the seat belt across and leaned over to click it into place.

"Need any help?"

"Nope." Seat belt on, I wedged my bag between me and Dan and tried not to look at his profile as he started the engine. Straight nose, long eyelashes, square chin—Will, exactly. And it was beyond strange to see someone I cordially disliked wearing the features I adored more than anything in the world. It was like something from a nightmare.

"It's a bit late for you to be out on your own, isn't it?"

I checked my watch. "It's twenty past six."

"It's dark. You're on foot. You're alone. You're vulnerable."

Because I was a girl, I knew he was thinking, and my feminist heart was outraged. I wanted to make him say it so I could argue the point with him. "Vulnerable to what, exactly?"

"You could get mugged. Pickpocketed. You could have that bag stolen."

"Because there's so much street crime around here." I didn't have to look around to know that there wasn't so much as a

48

piece of litter or a spray-painted tag on a wall to hint at criminal behavior. I had grown up in a mildly edgy bit of North London where you could buy pretty much any drug you wanted just outside the train station (not that I had been in the market for that kind of thing). Muggings weren't even reported in the local paper. I couldn't quite take Dan's concern seriously.

He glowered. "You think you're safe because you're not in London any more, but there's plenty of people out there who wouldn't think twice about taking everything you have. Especially at this time of year. Criminals want a bit of cash to spend on their kids, and it's in your pocket."

"Thanks for the advice," I said, and tacked on an innocent smile when he whipped round to glare at me. I might possibly have taken his point on board if he'd been a bit less patronizing about it, but being patronizing came naturally to him.

Dan had fallen silent, listening to the radio traffic on the set he had in the car. The beeping and static would have bothered me, but he seemed to tune it out. I listened to something that turned out to be a report of a stolen moped that might have been in the area. Once I'd got used to the stuttering transmissions and radio jargon, I found I was fascinated. Dan was frowning. He dug in the door pocket beside him and threw a notebook into my lap.

"Write down the license plate for me."

"Pen?"

He fumbled in his pocket, swearing under his breath, and found a Biro with a broken end.

"Is this standard police issue?" I asked, inspecting it.

"No, but it works. And since you don't even have a pen, you don't get to criticize it."

"I do have one." I peered into my bag. "Unless I left it at Gilly's house."

Dan tapped the notebook without looking at me. "Write. Now."

I did as I was told.

"Read it back to me," he demanded.

"HX53 HPJ."

"Did you get a description of the vehicle?"

"It's a moped. Silver with a white carrier on the back. No front number plate."

His eyebrows went up. "You got it right."

"You sound surprised."

"I didn't think you were listening."

But you thought you'd test me anyway. "I was. It's interesting."

That got me a look. "Most people don't think it's interesting. Most people would ask if I could turn it off."

I shrugged. "It's your job. Driving me around isn't. I mean, I know this isn't a taxi." *Although you are behaving as if it is and I wish I knew why.*

"No, it isn't." Dan drove in silence for a minute. The car was warm, the seat comfortable, even if I was hunched up on one side of it. I felt myself start to relax.

Which was, of course, a mistake.

"So how are you and Will getting on?"

I sat up straight. "Um. He's not back from school."

"Aren't you in constant contact with one another? I thought teenagers spent their lives on their phones."

"I didn't say we weren't in touch." I was blushing. "I just didn't want to talk to you about him."

"Oh, come on," Dan said. "I was just asking if it had turned out to be true love after all. I don't want the details."

I tried to keep all the emotion out of my voice. He'd never know I was embarrassed. "Things are going fine."

"Fine," he repeated. "You know, Jess, you seem like a sensible girl. But I know teenagers, and I know you have no sense at all when you're with someone you care about. It's too easy to get carried away. Let things go too far. Take risks."

I felt my stomach lurch as if we'd just driven over a bump in the road. He couldn't be talking about what I thought he was talking about. Especially since it wasn't even relevant, currently. We hadn't. We hadn't even talked about it. I wasn't going to say that to Dan. "Um. OK."

He glanced at me, frowning. "You know what I'm trying to say. Make sure you're taking the appropriate precautions. You only have to be careless once to ruin your whole life."

I swallowed a couple of times before I could trust myself to speak. "I did know that, actually."

"Yes, because you're sensible. I said as much to Will."

I was stuck between thinking how unappealing it was to be described as "sensible"—and cold horror. "You talked about this with Will?"

"Of course. It's his responsibility too."

"Did you say about the life-ruining bit?"

Dan considered it. "Yeah. Pretty much."

Will had been an accident, the product of a rebound relationship that had limped on into marriage. A relationship that had started when Dan and my mother had broken up, eighteen years before. "So you basically just told him he ruined your life."

In the light of the dashboard, Dan looked amused. "I'm always honest with him. No point in pretending."

Only so you don't make your child aware you wish he didn't exist.

I hadn't said anything but Dan glanced at me again. "You disapprove."

"I don't think it was right to say that to him. It wasn't his fault."

"No." A muscle flickered in Dan's jaw. "It was his mother's."

"It takes two people to make babies, as I understand it."

"Yeah, but only one of them gets to decide whether they go ahead and have the baby."

"Her body, her choice."

"That's exactly what she said."

"And if you'd got your way, there would have been no Will." Just thinking about it made me shiver. It felt like walking out of bright sunshine into cold, dark shadows.

"I suppose not. So it's a good thing Karen was determined to have him, isn't it?" Dan gave me a tight-lipped smile that I didn't return.

The truth was, I felt sorry for Dan, when he wasn't tormenting Will. He was trapped with Will's mother, Karen. She was a grade-A cow who hated me, my mother, and anything that might threaten her marriage or her son. She was also dying, slowly, of motor neuron disease.

It made it really hard to feel good about hating her.

"How is Karen?"

"The same." Dan rubbed a hand over his jaw, testing the stubble. "She just stays in her room, popping pills and waiting for the end. If this was a decent society there'd be some arrangement for putting people like her out of their misery."

"She's not that ill at the moment." I couldn't hide the shock in my voice.

"Maybe not, but she will be. She'll be trapped. No trips to Switzerland for a quick, dignified end if she leaves it too late."

"Does she want to . . . ?" I trailed off. I couldn't say it. Dan, of course, could.

"Kill herself? I haven't asked. But I would if I was in her shoes."

I could imagine that. Dan was such a physical presence, strong and forceful. Being incapacitated would be worse than death for him.

We were heading along the main road. Just as we reached the end of Will's road, a car slid out of the junction in front of us and fishtailed slightly before the driver got it under control. Dan swore as he hit the brakes, then looked sideways at me.

"Sorry."

"I've actually heard those words before," I said.

"Stupid . . ." He cast about for a suitable word and settled on: "Idiot. He could have caused an accident."

"Well, it wouldn't be the first time he made trouble."

"What do you mean?"

It was my turn to look sideways at Dan. "Didn't you recognize the car? That was my dad."

We had just turned the corner into my road. Instead of driving along it as far as Sandhayes, Dan pulled in to the curb and put the hazard lights on. "Say that again."

"It was my dad."

"What was he doing up here?"

I shook my head. "You're asking the wrong person. I see as little of him as possible."

"He doesn't live near here."

"No. His apartment is by the marina."

Dan nodded, thoughtful. "I knew that. So why was he here? Seeing your mum?"

"Wrong road—and ugh, I hope not."

Dan's expression darkened. "Is he still bothering her?"

"Not as much. He wants her to work for him."

"He wants her back."

"Probably," I admitted.

"She's not going back."

"I hope not."

Dan narrowed his eyes. "Why would she?"

"Look, I don't know why she married him in the first place." *Except that she wanted to escape this place, and you.* "I'm glad she did because otherwise I wouldn't exist, but it was a total disaster for her. She'd have to be out of her mind to consider going back to him."

Dan ran his hand round the steering wheel, obviously concentrating on something else. "She fell for him before."

"That was a long time ago. And she was running away. People do stupid things when they're desperate."

"I know all about that." Dan gave me one of his very rare real smiles. It faded as he stared out through the windscreen. Almost to himself, he said, "I wonder . . ."

What I was mainly wondering was whether we were going to sit in the car all night. I put my hand on the door handle. "Thanks for the lift. I can walk from here."

It made him snap back to reality from wherever he'd been

54

drifting. He started the car again. "Don't be silly. I said I'd take you home."

He meant what he said. When he got to the big stone gateposts that marked Sandhayes out from its more modern neighbors, he drove the car in, wheels crunching on the loose gravel. The headlights swept across the front of the house, catching the yellow of Hugo's battered Fiat, and my uncle's pick-up truck, and Mum's tiny Nissan Micra.

"I see Molly's at home." Dan sounded relieved.

"Well, her car is." I saw it hit home. *Here's some payback for making me paranoid about Will. How does it feel, Dan?*

"Is she out?"

"I don't know," I said, undoing my seat belt. "But it's possible."

Dan tapped his fingers on the steering wheel. "Give her my best."

I popped open the door and jumped out. I turned back to throw the notebook and pen onto the passenger seat. "Thanks again."

He didn't answer. He didn't even wait for me to close the door before he began to turn; the handle was pulled out of my hand and the door slammed shut all by itself.

And somehow I wasn't surprised when I heard the car accelerate away, heading down the hill into town, rather than up to where his dying wife was waiting for him to come home.

6

I let myself into the house, and was halfway across the hall when I stopped. It was the sharp, sweet scent of pine that got my attention; that and a certain tension in the atmosphere. Oh, and the tree trunk that was sticking out of the living room door.

"Um. Hello?" I said.

"Jess, is that you?" My aunt Tilly peered out from behind the tree, batting branches away from her face. She and my mother were identical twins, but I never confused them with one another; to me they looked totally different. "We're all completely trapped in here, isn't it ridiculous? Jack and Hugo managed to get the Christmas tree this far and no further, and now it's stuck in the doorway. I don't suppose you have any bright ideas?"

Standing on tiptoe, I could see that most of the family was in the living room. My youngest cousin, Tom, was balancing on the arm of the sofa, licking the jam off a piece of bread. Next in age was Petra, who was sitting on the floor, her dark, untidy head bent over a grubby tapestry she'd been working on for months. It was entirely like her to be getting on with her own task while chaos unfolded around her. Hugo, my older cousin, was sprawling in an armchair, looking tormented in a languid way, as if the entire situation was too much for him. Jack, my uncle, stood behind Tilly with his hands on his hips, looking as if he'd like to disown us all and use the tools on his work belt to reduce the tree to sawdust.

"Whose idea was this?" It seemed like a safe question to ask.

"I chose it." Tilly bit her thumb, as close to shamefaced as she ever got. "It looked smaller when it was with all the others."

"There was a label on it saying it was a ten-foot tree," Jack said.

"I know, I saw it. So?"

"So you clearly don't understand that a ten-foot tree is unlikely to fit through the doors. Just like last year." Jack put his arms around Tilly and squeezed her, taking the sting out of his criticism. "I knew it was trouble when I went to collect it. And just like last year, we got it through the front door but came a cropper when we reached this point."

"What did you do last year?" I asked.

"Jack hacked it to bits," Tilly said.

He clutched his head, outraged. "I trimmed a bit off the sides. It was the only thing to do."

"It looked terrible. Completely the wrong shape." Tilly frowned at the tree. "I don't want that to happen this year."

"Then you should have bought a smaller tree." Hugo sat up in his armchair. "Really, this is so boring. It won't fit through the door as it is, Mum. You are going to have to cut it back to get it into the room."

"Or you could set it up out here," I suggested. "The hall is big enough. It could go by the stairs."

Petra looked up from the tapestry, pushing her heavy fringe back. "It always goes in here."

"Maybe it's time for a change," I said.

"Yes." Jack grinned at me. "Finally, someone who understands logical thinking."

Tilly sighed. "I was sure it would fit."

"But it doesn't." Hugo unfolded himself and stretched, taking up an unfeasible amount of space as he did so. He had the wingspan of an albatross. "Let's move it back."

"You'll damage it." Tilly crouched down and put her arms over the tree protectively. "You can't just shove it. All the little branches will snap off and I'll have nowhere to hang the decorations. I know you, Hugo. You'll pretend to be careful and then you'll ruin it."

"I won't," he protested.

"You don't care about how the tree looks."

"I do, but I also want to leave this room at some point in my life." Hugo ran his hands through his hair, making it stand on end. "Please let's just move it and decorate it and have done with it. I've got things to do and Tom is hungry."

Tilly looked perplexed. "How do you know?"

"He's always hungry."

Tom launched himself off the arm of the sofa and landed on the floor with a thud that shook the glass in the dusty old chandelier. "I am hungry, Mum."

"Eat your bread and jam."

"I did."

Tilly closed her eyes for a moment. "All right. You can put

58

the tree in the hall. But you're not climbing out over it. You'll have to go out the living room window."

"Yay!" Tom scampered over and started undoing the locks with practiced ease.

"I thought that was banned," Petra said. "Because of Tom falling out and breaking his arm."

"This once, it's all right."

"But if there's a rule—"

"Petra!" We all said it together.

"Sorry for asking." Petra went back to her tapestry.

"So, why do we have to have such a big tree?" I asked.

"Because we have to fit those on it." Tilly pointed at the stack of battered cardboard boxes that was occupying one corner of the big drafty hall.

"There are a million Christmas decorations in those boxes, and they all have to be on the tree or someone will complain," Petra said.

"Who would even notice?"

"Everyone. We all have our favorites. You'll see."

What I mainly saw was that my Leonard cousins had a way of turning everything into a ritual that had to be observed in minute detail: you could have the yellow jug at breakfast but never at tea, and family birthdays had to be celebrated for a full week, and whoever got up last on Saturday morning got stuck with doing the dishes for the rest of the week. Every day there were new rules and traditions to learn, new family words to adopt, new in-jokes and favorites and grievances. I hadn't grown up with siblings and I sometimes felt like a castaway learning how to live with a strange tribe on a distant island where I'd washed ashore. There were times when I felt uncomfortably aware that I was a Tennant, not a Leonard. My dad's side—logical, cynical, practical, stubborn—ruled my head, even though I longed with all my heart to belong to my mother's family.

Tom and Hugo sauntered into the hall behind me, followed by Jack and Petra, who had abandoned her tapestry for the time being. Mum came out of the kitchen, looking tired, but she smiled when she saw me. I felt a huge surge or relief that she was at home after all, safe from my father's attentions, and Dan's.

I put my arms around her. "Good day?"

She'd been working at the Christmas market, running a stall for the gallery that was her main source of income. "It was busy. And cold. Are you helping on the stall tomorrow?"

I'd promised to, I remembered. "Yeah. Of course."

"Wear thermals," Mum whispered, and gave me another hug.

Hugo tripped and swore. "If you're going to bring half the garden into the house, Mum, the least you could do is put it somewhere well-lit."

"Sorry," Tilly said. "I wanted to cut the holly and ivy before it got dark."

Hugo was crouching down beside the heap of greenery. He looked up, his cheekbones so sharp you could cut yourself on them. "All this holly and ivy, and no mistletoe."

"We didn't have any in the garden."

"It's the most important thing. Isn't it, Jess?" He grinned slyly. "Especially since I hear Will is back in town."

"Don't be a creep, Hugo," I said. He was always trying to get a reaction from me, which I took as a sign of affection. He'd added me to his list of legitimate targets as soon as he'd decided I was family.

He widened his eyes, all innocence. "It's not for my benefit."

"I should hope not, since Ella's in London." Ella was my best friend and Hugo's girlfriend, a fact that made my head spin slightly. Hugo had been edgier than usual since she left Port Sentinel. Since Hugo was edgy at the best of times, that didn't make life easy for the rest of us.

"I'd never cheat on Ella," he said flatly. "I'm thinking of you and Will."

"Well, stop," I snapped. The wind blew the front door back against the wall, catching loose holly leaves and sending them skittering across the tiles like mice, and a voice came from behind them.

"Yes, stop."

I turned, along with everyone else in the hall, and looked at the tall figure standing in the doorway. Broad shoulders. Dark hair. Clear gray eyes that were currently narrow with amusement.

"Will . . ." I said it on a breath and it was barely audible.

"You're back! That's so . . . nice!" Petra was rather unsuccessfully trying to hide her crush on Will, a crush that predated my arrival in Port Sentinel by many years.

"You get more grown up every time I see you." Tilly beamed at him with maternal pride.

"Oh, good. You can help with the tree." Jack, pure practicality, as usual.

"Now that Will's here, is it time for dinner?" Tom, inevitably.

"Speak of the devil." The last contribution was from Hugo,

who crossed the hall and pulled him into a hug. Partners in crime, inseparables, friends above all, through everything—it made me jealous to see how close Will and Hugo were. "It's good to see you."

"And you." Will worked his way round the hall, doling out hugs and kisses on cheeks and a brief ruffle of Tom's hair. I saw Mum's face when he bent to kiss her cheek; there was something sad in her eyes. Of course, Will reminded her of his father at the same age. I just hoped we weren't doomed to repeat our parents' ill-starred relationship. He went past me without even glancing in my direction. I stepped up onto the bottom tread of the stairs and leaned my head against the newel post. This was his first visit to Sandhayes since he'd got back and he'd known the Leonards for a very long time. He was closer to them than to his own parents. In a very real sense, they were his family. So of course he had to concentrate on them, and not on me. But it made the doubt prickle under my skin again.

And then he turned away from Jack and came straight toward me, the compass needle to true North. Because I was on the step, my face was almost at the same level as his.

"Hi," I said.

"Hi, yourself."

"I didn't think you were coming back for ages."

He grinned. "I wanted to surprise you." Then his mouth was on mine. I slid my arms around his neck, ignoring a sigh from Petra and a snort of derision from Hugo and retching sounds from Tom as his father cuffed him round the head.

Obviously I wasn't able to ignore them completely. But I gave it my best shot.

"Break it up. Come on." Hugo sounded bored. "Do I have to get the hose out?"

"You were the one worrying about the mistletoe," I broke off to point out.

"I'm glad there was no need." You could have etched a picture with the acid in Hugo's voice.

"Hugo, come and help me. Now." Even Hugo couldn't ignore his father when he spoke that firmly. He did as he was told.

"Right," Jack said, looking around. "We're going to move this tree now. We're all going to work together."

"I'm in charge," Tilly said.

"No, I'm in charge." Jack grinned. "You got it stuck in the doorway, darling, remember?"

Tilly stuck her tongue out at him.

"We're going to lift it, draw it backward until the top is clear of the doorframe, tilt it and land it there." He pointed at the stand that was now in position beside the stairs. "Simple."

For the next few minutes we heaved and staggered and struggled with the tree. Hugo swore cheerfully the whole time, much to Tom's delight and Jack's annoyance. I narrowly avoided getting blinded in one eye. The tree was a monster, a bristling, heavy heap of prickles and whippy branches that slid through your hands to cause maximum damage.

"God almighty, I've got pine needles in my mouth." Hugo turned his head and tried to spit them out.

"It might be an idea if you kept your mouth closed, Hugo," his father snapped.

"*Mmmph. Blech.*" Hugo was making retching noises as we lifted the tree into the stand.

"That's it! Don't move . . . don't move . . . All right, now lower it. Just keep it straight. Straight, Hugo." Jack threw himself down on the floor to tighten the screws that held the tree in place. "Don't let go, anyone, or it will just fall over."

My arms were aching and my hair was in my eyes. Will leaned out and pulled a face at me and I felt reassured, suddenly. Everything was going to be all right. Why wouldn't it be?

From under the tree, Jack called, "Right. Done. Let go and move back, everyone."

"What if it falls on you?" Mum asked.

"It won't."

Tilly scampered to the other side of the hall. "It's not straight."

"I don't care," her husband said pleasantly.

"It needs to move two feet that way."

Jack was still invisible under the tree. "Which way is 'that way?'"

"Left," Tilly said, pointing to the right.

"Does she mean right?"

"Yes," we chorused.

Will and Hugo helped Jack to shift the enormous tree into the perfect position as Tilly stood with her head on one side, considering it.

"I can't think why we've never had the tree in the hall before."

"Because it's not how you do things in Sandhayes," I said. "And that's what matters."

"You're learning." Jack wriggled backward to get out from under the tree. "It took me a good five years to work that out when I married Tilly."

64

"You've always been a slow learner." Tilly tapped her fingers on her cheek, distracted. "What did I do with the lights last year?"

"Put them in the box marked 'lights?'" I suggested.

"No, that's glass trinkets." Petra was already grinning.

"Well, what's in the box marked 'glass trinkets?'"

"Angels."

"Angels," I repeated. "So obviously the box marked 'angels' is . . ."

"I can't remember . . ." Tilly's face cleared. "I know. Decorated pinecones. Hugo and Freya made them when they were five or six."

"This is going to drive me insane, isn't it?"

"It's best not to worry too much about the details." Will had moved to stand behind me, his hands on my waist, holding me close to him. I leaned against him, my stomach turning somersaults just because he was holding me. It was hard to think about anything else—even the question of Gilly's whereabouts had faded to a distant niggle in the back of my mind. All around us the Leonards were squabbling, searching through boxes or fiddling with the tree. No one was paying any attention to us. No one would notice if we slipped away.

As if he was able to hear what I was thinking, Will whispered one word in my ear: "Upstairs?"

I nodded, and the two of us melted away into the shadows, running up the stairs on silent feet, and if everyone knew we'd gone, no one said anything. I opened the door to my bedroom and turned to say something to him, and he caught hold of me, laughing under his breath as he did so, and I felt it vibrate through my bones and shiver in the ends of my hair and tingle across my skin as he kissed me. Every atom in my body was floating, spinning, like countless tiny stars of happiness.

We broke apart eventually, because humans need to do things like breathe and blink and stare at one another's faces to learn them all over again. I was recalculating the precise angle of Will's left eyebrow when he tucked a lock of my hair behind my ear.

"What were you saying?"

"I have no idea." I shut my eyes again for a second, trying to reset my brain. "Right, it's coming back to me now. When did you get back?"

"Just now."

"But your dad said—"

"Dad?" Will frowned, looking exactly like his father. "When did you see him?"

"He drove me home from town."

"Why?"

"Who knows why your dad does anything?"

"To make trouble," Will said grimly. "You know he hates us being together."

"I do." I shrugged. "Usually parents like me. I don't really understand what his problem is."

"It's not about you. It's me. He can't stand to see me succeed where he failed."

"But I'm not my mum."

"And I'm not my dad." A muscle flickered in Will's jaw. "If he didn't think he owned me, he might realize that."

I leaned back, safe in the circle of his arms. "Anyway, you're back now."

His face cleared. "Until the new year."

"You realize that will be the longest we've ever spent together? As a couple, I mean?"

"Yes." He ran his thumb down my cheek and across my lower lip. "I can't wait."

We really didn't miss the mistletoe at all.

7

I hadn't worked at the Christmas market before, but Mum was right about one thing: it was cold. I was wearing plenty of layers and a huge scarf and fingerless gloves, but it was still deeply cold in the little hut where the gallery had a pop-up shop, selling decorations and prints. I hopped from foot to foot, breathing warm air into my clasped hands, trying to get some feeling back into them.

"I warned you." Mum set a box of decorations down beside me. "Can you put these out?"

I started to hang them up, my fingers trembling. "This is ridiculous. It's far too cold." Even the shoppers looked miserable, trudging past in clouds of their own breath, clutching steaming cups of mulled wine. "How is this a good idea, exactly?"

"The tourists like it. It's seasonal." Mum looked up at the clear blue sky, her eyes narrowed against the brightness. She picked up the camera she had stashed down under the counter and took a couple of pictures. I looked in the same direction and saw bare branches threaded with lights, and I could have looked at it for a million years without thinking it would make a good picture, but that was why Mum was the photographer and I wasn't. "It's *supposed* to be cold at Christmas," she murmured.

"Nick should be paying you extra for working in these conditions."

Mum blushed at the very mention of her gorgeous, wealthy boss. "He's getting us some coffee."

"Oh." I was disarmed. "Well. That's nice of him."

"Yes, it is." Mum's blush had deepened, I noticed, though her voice was casual and her expression carefully neutral. From one moment to the next, it changed to dismay. "Oh no. What's *he* doing here?"

I looked to see who she meant and spotted him straight away: my father, Christopher Tennant. His fair hair—the same color as mine—stood out. He was focused on Mum, walking toward the hut with the kind of determination I associated with supervillains.

"Molly."

"Christopher." To give her credit, Mum sounded calm, but her knees were trembling, and I was fairly sure that it wasn't just the cold. "What can I do for you?"

"I wanted a word." He looked at me. "Alone."

"We're working," I said firmly. "We can't leave the stall. Either of us."

"It won't take long."

"I'm not going anywhere." I wasn't going to leave him on his own with Mum if I could help it. Dad spent his life undermining her confidence in any way he could. If he hadn't left

69

her, she'd never have had the courage to ask for a divorce. It was the best thing that had ever happened to her, and I had made it my business to prevent them getting back together, ever. Other teenagers might wish their parents would remarry, but not me. Anything would be better than that.

"It's important." I could tell that Dad was irritated, but he was trying to be civil. "I think you really need to hear what I've got to say, Molly."

She leaned on the counter. "What's it about?"

Dad looked at me again, then back at her. "It's personal."

"Then absolutely not." Mum turned and started reorganizing a shelf that didn't need to be reorganized.

"Molly." Dad had that glint in his eye that I recognized all too well. "Talk to me."

"Not now," she said through gritted teeth.

Not ever, I thought.

A noise at the back of the hut proved to be Nick Trabbet, Mum's boss, opening the door. He ducked his head under the lintel and straightened up warily, having banged his head a few too many times on the low ceiling. He was carrying a tray of coffees. He looked from Mum to me, his face quizzical. Mum gave him a look that was a pure appeal for help, and I did my best to match it. When Nick's gaze fell on Dad standing outside the hut, his eyes narrowed.

"Buying something?"

"I want to talk to Molly."

"Sorry." Nick's voice was so cold, the temperature in the hut plunged to at least ten degrees below zero. "She's busy."

Dad smiled, and it wasn't a pleasant smile. "I wouldn't have

70

thought you needed so many people working on this stall. The customers aren't exactly queuing up."

Nick was unmoved. "Maybe you're putting them off."

My father laughed with absolutely no warmth. "Maybe that's it. When are you going to give up on this little ego trip of yours? The gallery can't be making you any money." Dad was a financial advisor, which apparently made him think he had the right to make rude remarks about other people's businesses.

"Making money is boring," Nick said. "I've done enough of that."

I could see Dad struggling to understand someone choosing not to make money if they had the ability—and Nick certainly did: he was a millionaire many times over, even if he didn't act like one. Dad settled for glowering at him. Then he turned to Mum.

"What time is your break?"

"I—I'm not sure."

"Molly." His voice cracked like a whip and she flinched.

"Eleven," she admitted. "Some time around then. But not if we're busy."

Dad snorted. "What are the chances of that? I'll see you then." He turned and walked away, and the three of us watched him go.

"Molly," Nick said, "I don't think I need you today. Feel free to go somewhere else if you don't want to hang around."

"Thanks, but I don't want to let you down just because my ex-husband is hanging around causing trouble."

"Just don't talk to him, Mum. He'll upset you. Whatever he has to say, it's not worth hearing."

"Jess is right," Nick said. "Probably. I mean, I've never heard him say anything useful. I can't see why he would change now."

"Thanks, both of you." Mum turned away. "Let's just forget about him now. Which coffee is mine?"

Nick and I went along with her, talking enthusiastically about the market and the cold and the coffee, even though Dad was far from forgotten. And then the customers started to come, buying decorations and handmade cards and prints, and we were actually, genuinely, too busy to think about Dad and what he had wanted to say. I found I was enjoying selling things again, persuading people that they really needed five porcelain tea-light holders, not three. The shop where I usually worked at weekends was closed, the owner having decided to go to Fiji for Christmas, and I'd been missing the buzz. Nick seemed pleased, and Mum was delighted to leave the hard sell to me, spending her time wrapping things beautifully and chatting to the customers. She really was a useless sales assistant, but Nick didn't seem to mind.

I was unpacking some Christmas cards at the back of the hut during a rare lull when Mum called me. "I think this customer is for you, Jess."

I could hear the smile in her voice, and when I straightened up I understood why. Will was there, tall and broad-shouldered in his long, dark coat and a gray scarf that matched his eyes. His nose was red from the cold, and I was still completely dumbstruck by how utterly beautiful he was.

He grinned. "Hey. I thought I'd come and see how things were going."

"Really well."

"We're going to run out of stock at this rate," Mum said, nudging me. "Are you shopping, Will?"

"I thought I'd have a look around." He raised his eyebrows at me. "Want to come?"

More than anything. I checked the time. Ten to eleven. My shoulders slumped. "I can't."

Nick elbowed in between me and Mum, and turned his back on her. He dropped his voice to a murmur. "Why don't you go for your break now?"

"But isn't it Mum's break first?"

"Not if you're missing. I couldn't possibly do without both of you."

"Which means that Mum couldn't possibly go and talk to Dad," I said slowly.

"Exactly."

"I don't like leaving Mum on her own. Will you make sure she doesn't let Dad boss her around?"

Nick sighed. "This is absolutely none of my business, you know."

"I know."

"Or yours, probably."

"That's debatable."

"If Molly wants to talk to him, I can't stop her."

"I don't think she does want to talk to him. She just can't stop him from bullying her. Could you just make him go away?"

"Not permanently, I regret to say. But I'll do my best." Nick drew his eyebrows down into a glower that made me take a step back. "Do I look scary?"

"Very," I said.

"Good. Now get going."

I went to the back of the hut to let myself out. I really, really hoped Nick would be able to terrify Dad into the middle of next week, but I'd only ever seen one person scare Dad, and things were not so bad that I was prepared to ask Dan Henderson to intervene.

Not yet, anyway.

I walked round the side of the hut and bumped straight into Will, who caught and held me. "What's wrong?"

"How do you know there's something wrong?"

"You get this cute little wrinkle when you're worried about something." He bent and kissed my forehead. "Just there. So what's wrong?"

"Parent trouble." I tried to smile at him. "Nothing important, I think. I hope."

"Is my father involved in any way?" He asked it lightly, but it was a serious question and I answered it seriously.

"Not as far as I know."

"Then it can't be that bad."

He was trying to make me smile, but I actually felt like crying. "Maybe not. I kind of wish your dad was involved too, though. I'm all on my own with this one."

"Why?"

"My mother. My father. My problem."

"*Their* problem." Will put his hands on my shoulders and shook me gently. "Don't let them make you unhappy."

"That's not how it works."

"You need to think about yourself. Not them. Forget about them."

74

"I wish I could. I can't trust them. At least, I can't trust Dad. And Mum isn't equipped to cope with him. He almost broke her when they were married. Then he left, and she fell apart. And then we came down here so she could put her life back together—and he followed us." I still couldn't believe the casual arrogance he'd demonstrated. "I have to keep him away from her."

"When are you going to realize that not everything is your responsibility?"

I stared up at him. "You just don't get it. She needs help. She needs me."

"You're putting yourself in the middle of something that's none of your business." *As usual.* Will didn't say it, but he didn't have to; it was easy to read that into his tone.

"Well, apparently no one else is going to lift a finger to help, so it's up to me," I said.

"Only because you're the self-appointed guardian of what's right." Will gave me a lopsided smile. "You can't fix the world."

"That's not going to stop me trying."

"I can't think of anything that would stop you once you decide to do something." He let go of me, stepping back. "Let's go and get a drink."

I walked along beside him, my hands jammed in my coat pockets. It was all very well for Will to tell me to forget about everyone else and just concentrate on myself, I thought, glancing at him. He'd been known to ride to the rescue too, once or twice, and he never put himself first. Everything he'd said to me applied to him just as much as to me.

Anyway, I didn't want to argue with him, but he was wrong. I didn't want to fix the world.

Just my bit of it.

We queued for two mugs of mulled wine (the nonalcoholic version, naturally) and find an empty bench where we could sit to drink them. I held the mug so the scented steam could warm my face, and took a tiny sip.

"Oh, that's better."

"Good." Something in Will's voice made me look up.

"What?"

"I'm just glad you're looking happier. It kills me when you're miserable, and there's nothing I can do to help."

"It helps just to have you here," I said. I slid my hand into the pocket of his coat where one of his hands was buried. I took hold of it and held on tightly. He put his mug down and turned to pull me toward him. His mouth tasted of cinnamon and his hand was warm on my neck. His thumb stroked the skin just under my ear and I shut my eyes, lost in him. When we broke apart I looked at him for a long moment, no longer aware of being cold or upset or anything except his thigh against mine and the silvery gray of his eyes.

Will looked past me then, and straightened up a little. He raised a hand in a wave, and I twisted round to see who he was greeting.

Ryan Denton, inevitably, who was leaning against the mulled wine stand, watching us.

"Didn't you tell me he was completely over you?" Will murmured in my ear.

"He is. That girl beside him is his girlfriend." Yolanda looked distinctly underdressed in a short fluffy jacket and spray-on jeans, but if she was cold she wasn't admitting it.

"So why is he looking at you and not her?" Will asked.

"Don't," I said softly. "You won. He's moved on. That's the end of the story."

The corner of Will's mouth curled up in a way I found particularly distracting. "If you say so."

I looked back to see that Ryan had stopped looking in our direction, for the very good reason that he was talking to Max Thurston. Max threw him a car key and clapped his hand against Ryan's arm.

"Thanks, man."

"No problem." Ryan slipped the key into his pocket. "Glad I could help."

Max turned away from him and started to walk off. I happened to be watching when a small figure in black burst out of the crowd and collided with him. I heard the air whoosh out of his lungs. He bent over, clutching his stomach and wincing.

"God, watch where you're going."

Instead, the other person shoved him again, and it was obvious this time that it was deliberate. Max slid on a patch of ice and went down on one knee, looking up at his attacker. She was wearing a hat pulled down over her eyes, hiding her hair, but I recognized her at the same time as he did. The ring piercing her septum helped. She was pale, zipped into a leather jacket that was as tight and unyielding as armor.

"Nessa?"

"What have you done?" Her voice was tight with fury. "I know it was you. What have you done with her?"

"I don't know what you're talking about." Max moved to stand up, and Nessa grabbed him by the throat. She was about half his size but strong as steel, and I found I'd got to my feet

77

without realizing it, as if I was about to hurry to Max's assistance. Will grabbed my arm and held on to stop me from interfering. Instead of rushing to intervene, the crowd had formed a kind of ring around the two of them. No one wanted to get involved but everyone wanted to see what was going to happen.

"What's going on?" Will asked me.

"I don't know."

Max was choking, his face red, and Nessa let go. She jabbed a finger in his face. "I'm warning you—if you don't bring her back, I'm going to tell everyone the truth about you."

Max laughed, but he sounded uneasy. "You don't know anything about me."

"I know enough."

"Obviously not, or you'd know I haven't even seen her." He started to get to his feet again just as Nessa stepped forward. I actually couldn't tell if it was planned or not, but her knee collided with his nose. He jerked his head back, and a spray of blood splattered the fake snow that decorated the mulled-wine stand. There was a collective gasp from the crowd, and then a disturbance as someone made a path through it.

"What's going on here?" Dan Henderson, very much in police mode. Also very much in a towering rage.

"Nothing," Max said, holding his face. He stood up successfully this time, even if he was wobbling. "An accident."

Nessa looked at him, her face pale, then nodded. "Just an accident."

"Then get out of here, you two. I have more important things to worry about than accidents." Dan watched them go in opposite directions, then stared at the crowd until they too found they had better things to be doing with their time and melted away. There was no sign of the nasty little scene we'd witnessed except for the splash of blood, as red as holly berries, on the side of the mulled-wine stand.

Dan looked at it for a moment, frowning, then turned and saw us on our bench. His expression didn't change as he came toward us.

"Brace yourself," Will muttered. I could feel him tensing beside me, and I didn't blame him. When Dan wanted to speak to his son, it was rarely because he had something nice to say.

But it wasn't Will Dan wanted. It was me. When he reached us, he spoke without any preamble.

"That girl you were talking about. Gilly Poynter. She didn't come home last night, and no one knows where she is."

I'd known it. I'd been expecting it. But I still felt my heart plummet into my boots.

Gilly was gone.

8

Dan was standing over me, waiting for a response.

"How do you know she didn't come home?"

"Her mother reported her missing this morning."

"How did she seem?"

Dan twitched, irritated. "How do you think she seemed? She was worried about her daughter. She was upset."

"I told you," I said, probably unwisely. "I said Gilly was gone."

"And that's why I wanted to talk to you. How did you know?"

"It just wasn't like her to disappear."

Dan gave me a long, dubious look. "What else do you know?"

"Nothing." *Nothing that you would consider useful, anyway.*

"We're looking for her," he said. "I have my men out searching. If you see her or hear anything useful, I expect you to let me know."

"I will."

"And I'm going to want to speak to you again if she doesn't show up in the next twelve hours."

"When did her mother see her last?"

"At home, yesterday afternoon. She said she was going to meet you."

"And she never got there."

"Obviously not."

"Did Mrs. Poynter remember her leaving the house?"

"She said she didn't hear her leave. She couldn't say exactly what time it was. Before five, she thought."

My eyebrows shot up. "How is that even possible? The house is tiny. You could hear a mouse cough in the kitchen from the front bedroom."

"You said she was out of it."

"And you told me I was overreacting."

"What do you want me to say? You were right and I was wrong?"

I shook my head.

"If you think of anything I should know," Dan said heavily, "call me." He glared at his son, but turned away without speaking to him.

Will put his arm round my shoulders as his dad disappeared into the crowd. "Who was he talking about?"

"A girl called Gilly Poynter."

"Do you know her?"

"A bit. She's in my history class. She was supposed to meet me at the library yesterday and she didn't turn up."

"And you told Dad."

"He told me not to worry about it." I had thought I was

cold before, but now the chill was inside me, around my heart. "Will, what if something's happened to her? She could have been kidnapped on her way to the library. Or she might have run away and got into trouble. It was so cold last night. If she's outside somewhere—if she fell into a ditch on the moors, or even got lost—"

"They'll find her." Will sounded infinitely reassuring. "They're good at finding people."

"What if they don't? What if she harmed herself? Deliberately, I mean?"

He frowned. "Why would she do that?"

"I don't know." I told him about the party, and how she had cut herself.

He winced. "Sounds nasty."

"It was."

"And public. She wasn't trying to hide it, was she? Do you think it was a cry for help?"

"I don't know." I hugged myself. "What if it was, and no one heard her?"

"You mean, what if *you* didn't hear her?" Will's arm tightened around my shoulders. "Why was it your responsibility to rescue her?"

I turned to look at him. "Why shouldn't I take on that responsibility?"

"Because it makes you miserable."

"It makes me miserable that I failed." I shook my head. "I should have asked her about what happened. I should have insisted—"

"Jess, it's not your job." Will shook me gently. "You did what you could. You told Dad she was missing. If he'd started to

82

look for her earlier, he might have found her last night. That's his problem, not yours. You can't make him do anything he doesn't want to do—you know that. And now he *is* looking for her, he has the resources to find her. He'll have the search dogs out, the helicopter up—he's on the case. So please, stop worrying."

"You want me to forget about her."

"I want—" He broke off and sighed. "I want to spend two weeks with my girlfriend without having a shadow hanging over us. I don't know what's happened to this girl, but you're right, the chances are she is in some sort of trouble. I don't want you to get caught up in it for no other reason than that you feel obliged to, just because you happened to be near her when she went mental at a party."

"That's not who I am," I said. "I can't be like that."

Will's eyes had gone very dark. "You think I'm selfish."

"Not exactly. But . . ." I was struggling to put it into words. "I have a life here. When you're at school, I mean. I'm more than your girlfriend. And I can't drop everything else just because you happen to be here."

His mouth thinned. "I see."

"Don't be angry about it. You should be glad I don't spend the weeks simply waiting for you to come back."

"I don't have many reasons to look forward to coming home, Jess." Will took his arm away from me and bent over, bracing his elbows on his thighs. He dropped his head into his hands. "I have to have something."

"I'm a person," I said quietly. "Not a consolation prize."

"Right." His voice was as dark as midnight, and my heart twisted in my chest.

83

"I care about you, Will." I put my hand on his back. "But I'm not going to turn my back on Gilly, either. She's a person too. If I can help her—"

"*If* you can."

"If I can help her," I repeated, "I *should.*"

I felt him take a deep breath and let it out slowly.

"Then I hope you find her." He looked sideways at me and smiled wryly. "And I hope it's not selfish to hope you find her sooner rather than later."

Later, after my shift at the market had ended, I headed down to the seafront. It was dark and cold, but I wasn't planning a walk. I shouldered open the door of Mario's and walked into the warm, slightly stuffy café I loved. It was busy, as usual, and at a glance I knew about half the customers. Darcy was there, as she generally was, perched on the back of a booth with her legs swinging. Today she was all in black, her hair in ringlets, her eye makeup a very punchy dark blue.

"Hey, babe. How was work?"

"Fine." I had overheated the minute I walked into the café, and now I was stripping off layers of clothes. "Freezing."

"Did you see Will? He was looking for you earlier."

"Oh, I saw him." I couldn't stop myself from sounding very slightly grim, and Darcy raised her eyebrows.

"Trouble in paradise? Don't break my heart. You're my OTP."

"Not this again," I said.

"My One True Pairing," she said dreamily. "Because you've mated for life."

84

"What do I have to do to get you to not ship us, please?"

"Stop being perfect for one another." She grinned. "Just kidding. Never stop. What are you doing?"

I was scanning the café, looking for someone in particular. I spotted a familiar sleek blonde head right at the back, in a booth. "Is that Abigail Norris?"

"The one and only." Darcy rolled her eyes. "Is it too much to hope she gets a curling iron for Christmas? Or heated rollers? Should I drop a hint that someone needs a new look?"

"No." I took her arm and pulled her off the back of the booth to stand beside me. "You should find a way of persuading her to talk to me."

Darcy fluffed her ringlets thoughtfully. Her nails were the same color as her eye shadow, and scattered with tiny silver stars like the night sky. "Um, do I look like a miracle worker?"

"I know you're capable of magic."

"Three words," Darcy said. She held up her hand and counted them off on her fingers. The silver stars twinkled at me. "Not. A. Hope."

I gave her a little shove in Abigail's direction. "Do what you have to do."

I watched her go, then turned to greet Lily Mancini, one of the waitresses, who was a friend of mine.

"Something to warm you up?"

"Tea?" I suggested.

"Good choice." She led me to a table in the window. "It's just you and Darcy, isn't it?"

"Me and someone, anyway. I think Darcy is too busy working the room to sit down with me."

Darcy was standing at the end of Abigail's table. She hadn't been invited to sit down yet, I noticed, which was both bad and good. Good because I didn't want her sitting down and getting stuck into a big gossip session. Bad because even Darcy couldn't always persuade people to do what she wanted.

On this occasion, however, she was coming up roses for me. She threw me a significant look as Abigail began to extract herself from her booth. She said something to Darcy that I couldn't catch, smoothed her hair, then sashayed toward me, looking around the room as she went to see who was watching her. She sat down in the seat opposite mine and made eye contact for a brief, wary moment.

"Darcy said you wanted to talk to me."

"What else did she say?"

"That it was important." Another glance from narrow blue eyes. "That I needed to hear it."

Good enough. I could have kissed Darcy for being vague. It gave me more to work with.

I leaned forward, lowering my voice. "Did she tell you that the police are looking for you?"

"What?" Abigail was genuinely shocked. "Why?"

"Gilly Poynter has disappeared."

"What do you mean, *disappeared*?"

"She went out last night and she hasn't been seen since."

She frowned. "So? What's that got to do with me?"

"The party the other night, Abigail. Everyone saw you. You made her hurt herself."

"That wasn't me," she said quickly. "She did that to herself."

"Why would she harm herself like that?"

"Why are you asking me?"

"Because you were talking to her right before she hurt herself."

"It was just an ordinary conversation." Abigail pressed her hand against her chest, outraged—or pretending to be. "I swear, I didn't do anything wrong."

"What were you talking about? You said it was love and life, if I recall correctly."

"That's right." She sounded sulky now, and scared. "It was friendly."

"So friendly you didn't want an audience? So friendly you wanted me and Darcy to leave?"

"I didn't want you gossiping about it. We were having a private talk."

"About what?" I leaned closer. "You know I know Inspector Henderson, don't you? He's my boyfriend's dad. He's looking for you. He wants to know what was going on in Gilly's life before she disappeared. Someone told him you knew more than anyone else."

"You did, you mean."

"I haven't said a word," I said truthfully. "Come on, Abigail. Everyone at the party was talking about it. It only takes one person to mention your name and you're in real trouble. I mean, do you even have a solicitor?"

"No." She bit her lip.

"I'm trying to help you. I didn't have to warn you." I looked at my phone as if I was considering making a call. "Maybe I should tell him where to find you so you can clear all this up with him."

"No, please don't." She was almost crying. "My parents will kill me if I get arrested."

"I think he just wants to interview you." I waited a beat. "At the moment, anyway. And obviously he'd have to get your parents' permission. They'd probably want to sit in on the interview. Along with your lawyer, I mean."

Tears were standing in Abigail's eyes now. "If I tell you what happened, can you tell him? Pass it on, I mean? So he doesn't have to speak to me?"

I pretended to think about it. "That could work. Initially, anyway. I mean, if you're saying there was nothing strange about your conversation, there's no point in him wasting his time on you, is there?"

She seized on it gratefully. "No. Exactly what I was thinking."

"So what were you talking about?"

Abigail smoothed her hair, recovering her composure as far as possible. "We were just asking for her advice."

"About what?"

A dimple appeared in one of Abigail's cheeks, unbelievably. "The best places to have sex at school."

I blinked. "Why would Gilly know about that?"

"Didn't you hear about her?" It was Abigail's turn to lean forward. "She lost her diary in the locker room at school. I don't know who found it, but they read a bit before they gave it back to her—I mean, who wouldn't?"

"Absolutely," I murmured. "What did she say in the diary?"

"That she'd screwed someone in the disabled toilet near the staff room."

"*Gilly* did?"

Abigail nodded. "The diary didn't say who and she wouldn't tell. But, you know, rumors were flying."

88

Sent on their way by Abigail and her friends, I had no doubt. I certainly hadn't heard about it, but then they didn't really talk to me. "So who was it? Not Max Thurston?"

"No, not him." Abigail grinned triumphantly. "That was the whole point. They were going out—which no one knew, by the way. When he heard about it, he broke up with her. I mean, he went completely crazy. He told her she'd humiliated him. She tried to apologize, but he wouldn't even speak to her. She had a black eye and everything."

"Did he *hit* her?"

"Yep." But then she added, "At least, that's what I heard. She was off school for a few days until it healed so I didn't actually see it."

And neither had I.

"What else did you hear?"

"Well, you know she and Nessa Mullen were best, best friends? Nessa wasn't talking to her, either."

"Why was that?"

Abigail shook her head. "Neither of them would say. I asked. Gilly just told me to get lost."

Good for her. "Was this at the party?"

"Yeah. It seemed like a good opportunity to find out what was going on." Abigail smoothed her hair again, a giveaway that she felt guilty about the next bit. I was willing to bet the next thing out of her mouth was going to be a lie. "So we asked her about it. It was totally her choice to tell us. We didn't make her talk or anything."

I could imagine how they'd done it—friendly at first, then more insistent. *What did you do? Why aren't you talking? Did you really do it at school? Who was it? Why did you cheat on Max?*

89

Do you love him? Why not? Do you love the guy you screwed at school? Why not? Are you just a slut? Tell us the truth, Gilly. Tell us everything. We're your friends. Trust us, because if you don't, we can break you . . .

She'd talked, of course. Not much, but she'd had to give them something. She had no way out. And then I'd blundered in, along with everyone else in the world. Gilly had been trapped, and it had tipped her over the edge.

"What did she tell you?" I asked Abigail. "Before I came in?"

"Just that she had done something at school but we'd never guess who it was with." Abigail looked bored. "We tried, obviously. But she said we were way off."

"Who did you suggest?"

"Um, everyone? Every single guy in our year, the year above and the year below." Abigail began listing names, counting them off on her fingers, and it was true: she had been thorough. I was dazed by the sheer number she could remember. It was a feat of memory that would probably have surprised her teachers too. Abigail was known to be impervious to knowledge of all kinds, which was another way of saying she was spectacularly dense. Eventually she wound down. "Unless she was cradle-snatching and it was someone further down the school, I think we covered everyone."

I nodded. "Well, I'll be sure to pass on what you've told me to Inspector Henderson. He might still want to talk to you himself."

She opened her mouth to complain, but I hurried to reassure her that it was unlikely. "He'll probably be able to leave you alone because you've been so forthcoming and honest."

"Thanks so much for this." Abigail reached across the table

and patted my hand. "I'll never forget it. I completely owe you one."

I twisted my face into something like a smile and watched her wiggle away. Darcy skidded across the café and plumped down in the seat she'd vacated.

"Well, that looked like fun. What did she tell you?"

"More than she realized."

"What do you mean?"

I shook my head at Darcy, and laughed when she sulked, but my mind was racing. Because while Abigail was listing all the people she'd suggested as Gilly's possible partner in crime, I'd thought of quite a large group she'd left out.

The girls.

9

I wasn't stupid enough to go straight round to Nessa Mullen's house and accuse her of anything. I'd seen what she'd done to Max Thurston. Although if he had hit Gilly—*could he have hit her?*—I wasn't hugely upset he'd had a chance to see what that was like. But Nessa was a tough prospect. I needed to be better informed before I took her on. I knew where I had to start, even if that was with the one person I really never wanted to see again.

I left the café and made the short journey to Pollock Lane, choosing the quieter streets and checking both ways before I attempted to cross any of the roads. It was dark by now, and a late-afternoon mist had come in from the sea, filling the streets with a lung-searing chill. Every sound was muffled or distorted by it, and I jerked round once to see who was walking behind me before I realized that it was the sound of my own footsteps. The air was bittersweet with wood-smoke that the mist had trapped. These days you were no one in Port Sentinel if you didn't have a wood-burning stove. And if ever there was a night for a fire, it was this one. I pulled my sleeves down over my hands and drew my scarf up around my face, hiding from the cold. If Gilly was out of doors . . . if she wasn't capable of calling for help . . . I tried not to think about it.

I made it to Pollock Lane unharmed, and found it looking much the same as it had before, with the exception of Gilly's house. Every light seemed to be on, shining through thin curtains. This time when I knocked, firm footsteps came toward the door within seconds, and Mrs. Poynter wrenched it open before I had time to think.

"Yes?" This version of Mrs. Poynter was pin-sharp, with neat hair and an intense, hawkish stare. I found myself cringing, almost preferring the zombified Mrs. Poynter of the previous night.

"I'm sorry to bother you again, Mrs. Poynter. I just needed to get something I left here."

She frowned. "Who are you?"

"My name's Jess Tennant, Mrs. Poynter. I'm Gilly's friend from school. I was here yesterday, looking for Gilly."

She obviously had no recollection whatsoever of having seen me before. "Do you know where she is?" she asked abruptly.

"No. That's why I came here yesterday. She was supposed to meet me at the library and she never turned up."

"That's what the police officer said." Mrs. Poynter muttered it. I could see she was thinking. "What did you say you wanted?"

"I left something here. In Gilly's room. My notebook."

"Oh. That's where that came from." Very reluctantly, she stepped back. "You can come in and get it, but be quick about it."

I pulled off my boots without being asked and padded in. I'd been expecting her to be with a friend, or family, or even a police family-liaison officer, considering her daughter was missing. But the sitting room was deserted. The armchair was surrounded by books that lay open, splayed and bent. They ringed the chair like the petals of a daisy. I imagined Mrs. Poynter sitting there, hour after hour, reading a line or two from a book and letting it fall from her hands. There was a smell in the air, and not a pleasant one: bleach. Because of course, that was your first thought when your child went missing: domestic tasks.

"I'll be really quick, I promise." I shot through the living room. Mrs. Poynter was right behind me. I wondered if she was going to follow me all the way up the stairs, but she stopped at the bottom with her arms folded and watched me walk up, as if to make sure I went only where I was supposed to go.

In Gilly's room there was no time for subtlety in case Mrs. Poynter decided to check up on me, or in case Dan arrived to search it. He would kill me stone dead if he knew where I was and what I was doing. I ignored the little voice that told me I was out of my depth, and put on the overhead light. The room looked just as bare as it had before, though the bed was neatly made now, and the wastepaper basket was empty. Someone had searched through the books and papers on the desk. Mrs. Poynter? The police? Maybe I was too late. I found my notebook quickly, and my note to Gilly, and started to search, looking for something I didn't know if I'd find. If I had a diary, where would I keep it?

On my computer was the answer, and maybe Gilly had taken the same approach after her diary went missing at school. But she had liked pen and paper. I remembered the doodles down the side of her school notebook. There were people who thought best with a pen in their hand, and I hoped Gilly was one of them.

I went and stood by the bedside table, trying to think. Under the pillow. Nothing, and of course if she had kept it there, her mother would have found it when she made the bed. The mattress. There was nothing but the bare bed frame underneath. I peeled back the rug on the floor and saw floorboards, but there was no loose board to lift. I checked the bedside table, knowing that it was too obvious. It would have taken hours to search through the clutter and mess of my bedroom, but Gilly's was so bare I could see at a glance there was nothing to find. I went over and flicked through the books on the shelf, finding nothing. Frustrated, I stared around the room again. The little rabbit picture looked back at me. It was aiming for whimsical but landing on creepy because of the pale brown spots that had almost obliterated its face. The frame had left a mark on the wall like a shadow, it had hung there for so long.

And I shouldn't have been able to see the mark, I thought, frowning. The picture was hanging slightly crooked. I went over and lifted the frame off the wall, very carefully, and turned it over. It was the kind with two loops of wire across opposite corners to hold the picture in place, and tucked under the wire, wedged tightly against the cardboard backing, was a small blue notebook. I pulled it out of the frame and hung the picture back on the wall. Then I opened the notebook and flicked through, seeing Gilly's writing, seeing dates and names I knew. Bingo! I slid it inside my notebook and headed for the door. Mrs. Poynter wasn't waiting at the bottom of the stairs, I was relieved to see. I paused on the top step. The door to her bedroom was very slightly ajar. Gently, tentatively, I pushed it open and peered inside, curious about the mark I'd seen on the wall.

Curious was how I would have to stay. Where the mark had been there was a patch of missing wallpaper, about thirty centimeters by twenty. Someone had peeled off the old cream wallpaper with its pattern of roses, just in that place and no other. And while the wallpaper had definitely had its day, there were other places on the wall to start peeling, like where there was a giant damp patch the shape of Italy.

I'd spent more than long enough upstairs. I padded down, holding my notebook tightly so the other one didn't fall out of it.

"Did you get it?" Mrs. Poynter asked, her voice harsh.

"Yep." I held it up. "I couldn't find it straight away."

"I tidied Gilly's room." Her mouth tightened. "She was supposed to keep it clean, but that didn't always happen."

It had been more or less immaculate both times I'd been in it. The first time there had been a sense that someone lived there. This time, the space was dead.

Like Gilly? I pushed the thought to the back of my mind. Gilly couldn't be dead. Gone, yes, but not dead.

"Are you and Gilly . . . close?" Mrs. Poynter ground out the words as if it pained her to say them.

"We're in the same history class. We were supposed to do a project together."

Mrs. Poynter's face lightened a fraction. "Gilly's good at history. She's going to study it at university."

"Oh," I said. "Great." I couldn't remember Gilly ever demonstrating a particular gift for history, but it was the first warmth I'd seen from her mother, so I was going to go with it.

"I just don't know who helped her," Mrs. Poynter said, and

96

it took me a minute to realize she meant when Gilly disappeared, rather than anything to do with history. Before I had to answer, I heard a knock on the front door and Mrs. Poynter clicked her tongue, annoyed.

"What is it now?"

She strode across to answer it, and I heard Dan Henderson's voice. I stayed where I was, biting my lip. Mrs. Poynter left the door open and walked back to her chair, leaving Dan and two uniformed police officers to come in by themselves. I should have been grateful she'd held the door for me, it seemed.

Dan's expression was serious as he walked in. He glanced across and saw me, and surprise briefly flickered across his face. "Jess."

"Hi," I said, and felt compelled to add, "I was just getting my notebook."

The corner of Dan's mouth tilted upward, and it reminded me so sharply of Will that I bit my lip, tasting blood.

He turned back to Mrs. Poynter. "It would really help us, Mrs. Poynter, if we could take the investigation forward. At this stage Gilly's been missing for twenty-four hours. I don't want to make you think there's a reason to be concerned, but I would like to have a look in her room, just to see if there's anything there that might give us a clue to her whereabouts."

"I don't want you in my house." Her voice was quiet but determined.

I blinked, surprised, but Dan looked weary, as if this conversation was all too familiar. He took a deep breath and went on, "It's routine, Mrs. Poynter."

"No. I don't want you here." Her hands were folded in her lap, her eyes fixed on the floor.

97

Dan's expression was murderous, even though his voice was soft. "We're trying to help you and Gilly."

"You don't need to poke around in our business to find her. She's not here. You should be looking for her out there. That's why I called you, so you could look for her. I've looked in her room. There's nothing there."

Not any more, anyway. My hands tightened on the notebook.

"We're trained to see things that other people might miss," Dan said.

"I know what should be there and I know what isn't there. How could you begin to guess what clothes she's taken with her? What bag?"

"So she did take things with her?" Dan checked.

"There are some clothes missing. And a shoulder bag."

"What color is it?"

"Blue."

"I'm going to need a description of the clothes too," Dan said, and I could see that he was struggling to keep his temper.

"Two pairs of jeans, a gray jumper, underwear. That's all I noticed."

Dan's voice was pleasant, conversational even. "When did you find this out?"

"Earlier today? Around lunchtime, I think."

"Do you see," he said carefully, "that it's important for the police to know this kind of thing? If she was planning to leave, that makes a difference to how we look for her. It suggests that she wasn't taken off the street, Mrs. Poynter. It suggests that she was a willing participant in what happened. It makes it more worthwhile to do an appeal for her to contact you."

Mrs. Poynter's eyes were hooded, her expression remote. "Is that all?"

"I still want to search Gilly's room."

"No."

"If you make it necessary for me to get a search warrant, I will do that. But it would be a lot easier if you'd let me and my officers have a look upstairs now. I promise we won't do any damage or interfere with your property."

"No."

Dan's voice was cold. "If I have to get a warrant, it will be for the whole house and garden, and we will tear it apart. We'll be back later on, probably late tonight, when it's far less convenient for you to let us into your home."

Mrs. Poynter's face hadn't changed. "There's nothing for you to find here."

"I'll be the judge of that," Dan said. He turned to the uniformed officers. "Off you go, lads." They went out. Dan looked around. "Are you finished here?"

I nodded. "Thanks, Mrs. Poynter."

She ignored me. I picked up my boots and hurried out, aware of Dan behind me. He slammed the door as hard as he could, relieving his feelings just a little bit. I stood on one leg, my feet freezing as I tried to get my boots on quickly. It was all so much more complicated because I didn't want to put the notebook down. Dan watched grimly. When I was finished, he jerked his head toward his car and I went to sit in the passenger seat again. He clambered in the other side and sat for a moment, not looking at me. I braced myself to face the music. And I needed to brace myself, because the look on Dan's face when he turned round told me exactly how much trouble I was in.

"Talk," he said. "Now. And this time, tell me everything. What were you doing there?"

"I had to get this book for homework." I held it up. "Mrs. Poynter let me go up to Gilly's room."

"Did she?"

"Yes." I blinked up at Dan, all innocence.

"Find anything?"

I shook my head, mute. I was going to tell him about the diary at some stage, but not until I'd looked through it myself. An hour or two couldn't delay the investigation too much. If I gave it to him now, I'd never see it again.

"What did you make of her?"

"Anyone would think she didn't want the police to find her daughter."

"You thought that too." Dan rubbed his jawline with a pensive thumb. "You said she was out of it last night."

"Yeah. She was slurring her words, stumbling around. She seemed totally different today."

"Maybe that's why she doesn't want me to search the house. She's afraid I'll find her stash."

"Maybe," I said slowly. "Or it could be that she has something else to hide."

"Like what?"

I told him about the mark I'd seen on the wall, and how carefully the wallpaper had been excised, and the bloody tissues in the bin.

As he listened his frown deepened. "How much blood was on the tissues?"

"Not a huge amount," I said. "I mean, I didn't go through the whole thing, but it was splotches."

"And you're not sure it was blood on the wallpaper."

"No, I told you. I just saw it as she went into her room and the lights were off."

"We might still get something if I send in the forensic officers." Dan started the car. "Thanks, Jess. Very helpful."

"Where are we going?" I asked, alarmed.

"I'm driving you home."

"I wasn't going home."

"You are now. I'm going to keep looking for Gilly. Don't even think about going out to do the same. If I find you wandering the streets I'm going to lock you up for the rest of the night."

"Is that even legal?" I couldn't help asking.

"It is if I say it is. And don't think your mother would stop me if I told her why I was doing it. She's had enough of you getting yourself into trouble, and so have I. I'm too busy to waste time making sure you're safe."

"I've just helped you," I pointed out.

"You've done your bit." Dan looked sideways at me. "No arguments, Jess."

There was no point in trying. The journey back was quick and yet it seemed endless. I sat in silence, glowering. My only consolation was the diary I'd lifted. There was no way I was handing it over now, and I didn't even feel bad about it.

When we pulled up at Sandhayes, Dan said, "In there. Until tomorrow morning at the earliest."

"OK."

"I mean it, Jess."

"I know," I snapped. "I heard you."

I got out of the car. Before I shut the door, Dan leaned across. "You did well."

"Thanks," I said, disarmed.

"But that's enough now. Stay out of it. Promise me."

I slammed his car door instead, with about as much force as he'd used on the cottage's front door. He grinned at me through the windscreen before driving off. Something told me he'd noticed I hadn't promised anything, and despite himself, he approved.

And despite myself, I was glad.

Gilly Poynter's Diary

3 SEPTEMBER

I have no idea how I'm going to manage this year at school. M is on my case all the time. I have literally no freedom. I'm not allowed to talk to anyone—especially a boy. That is COM-PLETELY out of the question. I see everyone else just being happy—going out, meeting up with friends, getting drunk, having fun—and I don't understand why I can't have that.

I don't understand why I can't be normal too.

23 SEPTEMBER

So tired today. All that extra work for history is a giant pain in the ass. I know I should be grateful to Mr. L for taking an interest—I wouldn't even have a computer if he hadn't said I needed one—but I just can't deal with all the reading and the extra essays. I don't see the point. But I suppose it's a reason to go out. And I can keep in touch with people more easily. And that's the big news: I had a really sweet message from someone, and

I'm not going to say who here because I haven't really convinced myself to believe it's real yet. I keep reading it and reading it. It says I'm beautiful. I never knew anyone had noticed me. I never knew anyone even knew I existed.

3 OCTOBER
Imagine, though, what it would be like if the person you liked . . . liked you back.

10 OCTOBER
SO HAPPY.
   I wish I could scream. I'll just scream here.
   AAAAAAAAAAAAAAGH.*
   (*BRB, hyperventilating.)

15 OCTOBER
I saw R after school for a few minutes—that was all we could manage. Oh my God. It was incredible, just being alone. Imagining is one thing—and we have both been doing a lot of that. But actually touching. Kissing. I wanted more and so did R.
   I don't know if I'm more frustrated or excited. I've never felt this way before. EVER.
   OMFG. R has my heart completely. It scares me, almost. I wish I knew if R felt the same about me.

4 NOVEMBER
Something very strange has happened. SO strange. And I feel really weird about it.
   But also kind of amazed and happy and scared. Very scared.

Because before, it was all just normal and easy, even if my stupid life made it complicated and difficult.

This is different.

This is real.

No more playing around.

[UNDATED]

Why do people have to let you down? Always. Just when you think you can trust them—God, I'm just sitting here shaking my head. I can't even write about this.

I just can't.

But it F*****G hurts.

11 NOVEMBER

I don't even know who I am anymore. I can't really believe I'm doing the things I'm doing, but I LOVE IT. I feel as if I've grown up overnight. Or—let's be honest—in about twenty minutes. I HAD SEX!!! In the toilet by the staff room of all places! Not the most romantic place, or comfortable. We ended up on the floor and I was trying not to think about whether it was clean or not. Y-U-C-K. This is what I mean—when would I have done something like that before? With anyone? What can I say, though—we got carried away. I mean, I did. I was the one who wanted it. I insisted. And it felt amazing (and strange, to be fair, because it is a strange thing to do when you take a step back and look at it—I keep having flashbacks). But the main thing is that it felt RIGHT. That's why it's so sad that I can't tell anyone, and I do mean ANYONE. They wouldn't understand. They'd say it was wrong. How can it be when it feels so natural? It's just love, isn't it? Proper love. It doesn't matter who the person is or whether it's what people expect you to do. It just IS. And I'm really kind of proud of myself. I made it happen.

I feel like this is the person I was always meant to be.

18 NOVEMBER

I thought I was in love before, but this is on a whole new level. I can't eat. I can't sleep. I just wait for the times we can be together, alone.

It's not enough.

I can't get enough.

I just look back on the person I was two months ago and I feel so sorry for her. She had no idea what was waiting for her.

Life has begun!

28 NOVEMBER

When I'm eighteen, I'm going to leave this horrible dump of a town and go somewhere else. And I'm going to have a little house with a little garden. And X is going to be there too. And all day, every day, we're going to love each other. And no one is going to care. We'll just be a couple. Ordinary. Just like everyone else.

And nothing will have to be a secret any more.

4 DECEMBER

I've just been reading through this and crying. THANK GOD I didn't use any names. At least no one knows what's really been going on.

Why did I bring my diary into school? Because X wanted to read it as soon as I mentioned it. I shouldn't have shared it anyway. These are just my thoughts, for me. No one else. And now everything is unravelling and it's all. My. Fault.

106

What an idiot.

What a stupid, stupid jerk.

8 DECEMBER

I never thought this would get so complicated. I never thought I would have so many secrets.

No one knows the truth. No one knows everything—except for me. That's how I wanted it. But I'm starting to wish there was someone I could talk to. Someone who would listen to everything I've done and not hate me for the mistakes I've made.

Someone I could trust.

I don't know anyone like that, though. And even if I did, I don't think they would understand. How could they? I mean, I can't understand how I've ended up in this situation. I don't know when I started down this road. I don't know when I chose this life. I don't know if there was a point when I could have made it all stop.

I didn't, anyway. I missed my chance. And now I'm trapped.

That's the thing about secrets—they're like walls. When I started hiding things, I thought the walls were keeping me safe.

Then I realized I'd built my own prison.

And now there's no way out.

12 DECEMBER

I wish so much I hadn't gone to the party.

I thought it would be fun.

Excuse me while I try to laugh.

(I don't think I have any laughter left. I just have this horrible pain inside me, blocking everything else. I can't even cry. I feel as if I'm at the bottom of a hole, looking up at a tiny

pinprick of light in the distance, and that's the sky, and it's so far above me I'm never going to reach it ever, ever again.)

I thought I could forget about everything that's been going on, just for a few hours. I thought I could dance and be normal.

But then I got cornered by Abigail and her friends. I could have told them everything. I wanted to, even though I knew it was a bad idea.

Then again, it wouldn't have helped. What could they do? Tell me I've got problems? I know that already. Tell me I need help? I worked that out a while ago.

But if I ask for help, who is going to believe me?

Who would ever think I could be in this mess?

I always wanted someone to love me. I thought it would make everything better.

Now I understand that you should be careful what you wish for.

16 DECEMBER

I can't stop cringing. I hate myself. I knew what X wanted me to do and say, so I did it.

I'm such a coward.

I keep telling myself I couldn't have done anything different, but I know the truth. Hurt people I love or get hurt myself. That's not much of a choice. But I shouldn't choose me all the time. It's not as if it's helping.

I was scared before, but now I'm terrified something bad is going to happen. I feel like a fly caught in a web. The more I fight, the more tangled up I get.

I think I've made a terrible mistake.

10

I was so tired I didn't even take off my boots when I lay down on my bed, disturbing Aristotle, the fatter of the two house cats, who had been fast asleep. He looked up and gave a small, silent meow of disapproval. I curled myself into a ball around him, breathing in the sweet warm smell of his fur. He rubbed his head against my leg, a low, rusty purr vibrating in his broad chest, then slowly sank back to sleep, the purr disintegrating into a snore. I lay beside him and read Gilly's notebook over and over again, trying to work out what had been going on in her life. Nothing good, it seemed. It was a shame that she'd been writing the diary for her own benefit, not mine, and that she had been so vague at times I struggled to understand what she meant. And she'd only written in it now and then, when something big had happened, to let out her feelings. So I was stuck with a lot of feelings and not enough facts. I tried my best to work out who she meant by M, R, and X. It was like the worst sort of algebra problem. If X is around more than M, R equals who? M was clearly her mum. I spent ages writing out all the male names beginning with R I could remember, trying to match them up with boys from school or from around Port Sentinel. Ryan was on the list, inevitably, but I knew he wasn't involved; he would have been bewildered at the suggestion. Gilly was not his type. He was much more straightforward than that.

In fact, he was straightforward in every way, I thought, and liked him for it. I was still struggling with Will's hissy fit about me spending time away from him. I didn't like him being so possessive. It reminded me too much of his father.

I read through the diary entries again, puzzling over the identity of X, looking for anything that might give me a clue. It was like panning for gold in a particularly muddy river. I got to the end, went back to the start, skimmed through again.

Now there's no way out . . .
X is going to punish me for this . . .
I always wanted someone to love me . . .
No more playing around . .

She'd fallen in love twice over, and someone had let her down. The first person she loved? The mysterious R? Or someone else? I couldn't guess who X was any more than Abigail and her friends had been able to.

I hate myself. I knew what X wanted me to do and say, so
I did it . . .

I stopped. *There* was something specific. She was referring to something that had happened that day. The sixteenth of De-

110

cember. I got off the bed, leaving Aristotle to resettle irritably. I lifted up a flyer so I could see the calendar above my desk. It was a Tuesday.

It was the day I'd had to swap partners so she didn't have to work with Max. Because X wouldn't have liked it?

What if X was in our history class?

I sat back in my chair, swinging from left to right, thinking about the boys in the class, working from the back row to the front. Not Max. Sam Milner, so laidback he was practically vertical, seemed unlikely. In fact, they all did. Phil Nolan, with his pale eyelashes and rounded shoulders and silence in the presence of girls. Zayn Khan, madly in love with a girl named Lorna and unlikely to notice anyone else. Rich and Ben and Charlie—none of them seemed the kind of boys who would be threatening, let alone violent.

I did know of one person who'd been violent.

Who'd apologized to Gilly—begged her for forgiveness, really.

What had Mr. Lowell said? Gilly couldn't work with a boy. Because X wouldn't like it.

I feel like this is the person I was always meant to be, Gilly had written. *This is different.*

It's just love . . . it doesn't matter who the person is.

I sat and thought about love and rejection and broken promises, and just what you might do—just how desperate you might be—if the person you cared about more than anyone in the world cut you off.

And I thought about Nessa Mullen. I didn't know where she lived, but I knew who would. I dug out my phone.

"Why do you want to know that?" Darcy sounded intrigued.

111

"Because she's Gilly's best friend and I thought she might know something about where she is."

"I heard Gilly ran away to London."

"Who told you that?"

"I can't remember. I mean, everyone's talking about it. I heard . . ." Her voice went faint for a minute, and when she came back she was saying, ". . . completely impossible, obviously, because how could she have run away and also been kidnapped and also be hiding somewhere just to see who really cares about her once she's gone—"

"Is that what people are saying?"

"That and a few other things." She broke off again, leaving me listening to silence, followed by a sniff. "I still don't know why you want to speak to—" A sneeze.

"Darcy, what are you doing?"

"Plucking my eyebrows." She sniffed. "Sorry. It always makes me sneeze. And cry." Another sniff. "They say your eyebrows are sisters, not twins—did you ever hear that?"

"Of course not."

"It means they should look similar but not identical." A pause. A sniff. "I think my eyebrows had different fathers."

"Darcy."

"They definitely don't get on. They're not even on speaking terms."

"Are you still talking about your eyebrows?"

"Gilly and Nessa." She said it as if it should have been obvious. "They haven't been talking since . . . I don't even know when."

"Try and remember."

"November?" Her voice was muffled again. "Why does this hurt so much?"

"Because you're pulling your hair out of your skin."

"Well, obviously. Oh, that looks better."

"Good. Are you sure it was November?"

"Wait . . ."

"Put the tweezers down, Darcy, and help me."

"I *am* helping you." She sounded defensive. "It was around then because I have a free hour before lunch on a Tuesday and they were always in the school library together when I went."

"Why were you in the library?"

"Trying to have a little nap—not that I could with all the chatter from the two of them. Then it was just Nessa, on her own, and vast, awkward silence." Darcy sighed. "I still couldn't sleep."

"Stop, I'm welling up."

"I'll remember this the next time you want me to help you with something."

"You know I appreciate it."

"I do."

"So do you know Nessa's address?"

"Yeah. Well, not in detail. She lives on Bayview Drive."

I whistled. "Swanky."

"I can't remember what number it is, but the house has pineapples on the gateposts." The shrug traveled across the air. "Do not ask me why pineapples."

"I won't," I promised.

"Jess, don't get yourself in any trouble."

"As if I would."

Darcy snorted. "That's all you do. I mean, you should be OK. She doesn't look dangerous, unless bad haircuts are contagious."

"I'll keep my distance, just in case."

The next day I went looking for Nessa. The house with the pineapples, Darcy had said, and there it was, halfway along Bayview Drive. The road was a terrace of Georgian houses, tall and white, overlooking the sea. It was remarkable that they had survived the local passion for refurbishing old properties by obliterating them. It was a conservation area, so the council could impose strict rules about how the houses should look, and that had saved them, more or less, except where the gates were concerned. Nessa's house wasn't all that bad—the gateposts were round columns, and the pineapples were at least traditional. The house next door had black granite gateposts topped with silver unicorns. Stay classy, Port Sentinel.

I trotted up the steps and used the big lion's-head brass doorknocker, hearing the sound echo through the house. I looked out to sea while I waited for someone to come. The bay was full of white horses, the wind ripping spray off the top of the dark gray water. The clouds were low and heavy with rain that hadn't yet fallen. I wished I'd remembered to bring an umbrella.

"Hi." Nessa was standing in the doorway behind me, wearing a big sweatshirt, skinny jeans, and high-top trainers. She'd pulled back her hair so the undercut was visible, the hair so short I could see her scalp underneath it. Out of school, she filled the piercings in her ears with silver hoops that ran all the way up into the cartilage at the top as well as the ring in her septum. Her eyeliner was smudged. "What do you want?"

"It's about Gilly," I said. "Can I come in?"

She held onto the edge of the door, as if she needed it for support. "I don't think that's a good idea."

"I'm trying to help her," I said simply. "I don't suppose she's been in touch with you."

"No."

The wind gusted, and I took a step forward without meaning to, blown off balance. "Look, you don't have to talk to me. I'm not the police. But the police are looking for her. They're taking it seriously. I found a diary she was keeping, and—"

"You found her diary?" Nessa's voice was sharp.

"Yeah. And I read it." *And I understood one word in ten, to be honest . . .*

Nessa drummed her fingers on the edge of the door. "OK. Come in. But you can't stay long."

She led me into the room beside the front door, a formal drawing room full of antique furniture, a huge oriental rug, and elaborate curtains. Nothing could have looked more incongruous than the two of us in our jeans perching on brocade-covered chairs. The blinds were pulled down so the light was dim.

"No one comes in here," Nessa said, seeing me looking around. "They only use it for parties. Just keep your voice down and they won't even know you're here."

"Your parents?"

"Yeah." She seemed to realize that she might have sounded rude. "It's not that I don't want you to meet them. It's just that they'd get so overexcited. 'Oh, Nessa's made a friend. Let's take

115

you out for dinner. Why don't you stay over?"' She rolled her eyes. "I like my own company."

"And Gilly's."

"Yes." She squeezed her palms between her knees. "It's not what you think."

"What isn't?"

"The reason we stopped being friends."

"Why do you think I think you stopped being friends?" I asked carefully.

"Because of what people were saying about Gilly at school."

"After someone read her diary?"

Nessa nodded. "People were calling her all kinds of things. I knew none of it was true."

I was about to get thrown out of Nessa's house, I thought, and braced myself. "Were you the one with her? In school?"

"Me?" Her eyes went wide and then narrowed. "That's a pretty big assumption you're making there. Actually, two. That I'm interested in girls and that I was interested in Gilly."

"I could be wrong," I said.

"People assume I'm a lesbian because of the way I dress." Her eyes were fixed on me and there was a challenge in them.

"You might be. You might not. What does it matter?"

A little of the defiance went out of her face. "My parents are sure I am. They keep trying to get me to come out."

"Why don't you?"

"Because I should be able to sleep with whoever I like without explaining myself to anyone—as long as it's legal and safe. I bet you don't talk to your parents about who you're sleeping with."

"Definitely not."

Nessa sat back. "They'd just boast about it to all their friends. About how cool they are about it and how much they've donated to LGBT causes and this really important campaign they're supporting."

"That sounds really annoying."

"Doesn't it?" She almost smiled for a moment, then went back to looking pained. "Anyway. I like to keep them guessing. I like to keep everyone guessing."

"As long as you know what you like, that's the important thing."

She wriggled. "I kind of haven't made up my mind yet."

"Fair enough," I said. "So if it wasn't you, who was it?"

"I don't know." Nessa's shoulders slumped. "She never told me. I just assumed it was a mistake and she wanted to forget about it."

"That's not the impression I get from her diary."

"Can I read it?"

I hesitated. "I don't think it's a good idea."

"Why not?"

"It might upset you," I said, thinking of the entry where Gilly wrote about being let down. Was it Nessa who'd hurt her? "What happened with you and Gilly? You were such good friends."

"She cut me off." Nessa looked bleak. "She was hiding something from me. She wouldn't tell me what was going on or who she was with at school. She was keeping all kinds of things secret. And I couldn't leave her alone, even though I knew I was pushing too hard." Tears glittered in her eyes. "I just wanted her to talk to me."

"What happened?"

117

"She cut me off and then we argued, not the other way round. I racked my brains to work out what it was I'd done wrong, and I still don't know. I mean, we didn't fight. We never fought. But I'd started to think she was avoiding me."

"Why?"

"Twice in the same day she saw me and turned round and walked away. She still had her phone then, and I texted her a few times, trying to get a response." Nessa bit her lip. "I got angry. I was frustrated. I started saying mean things just to provoke her into replying. It was the silence I couldn't stand."

"Did she reply?"

"No. She came and found me. She told me to stop texting her. She told me she was getting rid of her phone so I was just wasting my time. She said we couldn't be friends anymore and she couldn't say why."

"Couldn't? Or wouldn't?"

"I'm sure she said 'couldn't.'" Nessa looked perplexed. "I hadn't thought about that."

"Did she seem angry? Upset? Worried? Scared?"

"Um, all of the above." Nessa shook her head. "I handled it superbadly. I started shouting at her about how she was letting me down, and she just looked at me and said, 'Sorry,' and walked off. And that's the last time I spoke to her."

"Did she try to talk to you again?"

"No. She avoided everywhere I went, as a rule. I wouldn't stop going to the places we used to go together, but she did. I saw her at school, but we never spoke."

"It sounds as if she picked a fight with you deliberately. She pushed you away."

"That was how it felt. I told her I wasn't going to be her

friend anymore." Nessa's voice was husky. "I told her we couldn't be friends if she didn't trust me. I told her I didn't trust her since she'd been lying to me for months."

"Why wouldn't she talk to you?"

"Because she was scared. And I let her be scared. I abandoned her to sort things out for herself when I knew she was struggling."

"But if she wouldn't talk to you—"

"I shouldn't have gone off in a huff."

"When did it start?"

It was as if Nessa had been waiting to say it. "When she started seeing Max Thurston." Her upper lip curled in disgust. "He wanted to own her. He didn't like me and he didn't like the fact that I was close to Gilly."

"So you two never got on."

"Never." She frowned. "He wasn't good enough for Gilly. I let him know I felt that way. He treated her like dirt until he found out there was someone else, and suddenly Gilly was the love of his life. Sorry if I didn't believe a word of it."

"Did Gilly like him?"

"Ye-es," she admitted. "But he was her first-ever boyfriend. Her mum didn't want her to see anyone while she was at school. She had nothing to compare him to. And he knew she was going to wake up one day and realize he wasn't Mr. Right, so he did his best to control her."

I thought about the way he'd hung around, trying to force her to talk to him. "Someone told me he gave her a black eye."

Nessa nodded. "That's what I assumed. She did have a black eye, but she wouldn't talk to me about it."

"Do you think she was scared of him?"

119

The reply was immediate. "I'm sure of it. He was obsessed with her. And she wanted to stay away from him."

Something occurred to me. "Was he at the party the night Gilly cut herself?"

"He was standing right behind you," Nessa said simply. "I went past him to help her."

"Did she tell you why she cut herself?"

"She just said it was all too much." Nessa's face twisted as if she was about to cry. "I thought it was going to be different from then on. I thought she'd forgiven me. But she was just the same afterward. She didn't talk to me or look at me."

"Why did you hit Max at the market yesterday?"

"Because he knows where Gilly is."

"Are you sure?"

There was total conviction in her eyes and voice. "I don't know if he made her leave or if he just helped her, but he knows, believe me. If you want to know where Gilly is, make Max Thurston tell you."

11

Max Thurston lived on Ogilvy Close, a small cul-de-sac of five houses that were about average by Port Sentinel's standards but practically mansions anywhere else. They were white-painted with big bow windows on either side of a vivid front door. The Thurstons' door was blood red. I rang the bell, even though the blinds were still down at the front of the house. I wondered, as the seconds passed and no one came, if they were away, or asleep, or refusing on principle to come to the door.

But when he opened the door, Max was dressed, and he looked as if he'd been awake for a while. His clothes were rumpled and there were violet shadows under his eyes. His nose looked bruised and a little swollen from the previous day's altercation with Nessa. He seemed on edge and he barely met my eye—a quick glance, a look of surprise that immediately became sullen.

"What do you want?"

"To talk to you." I thought he'd say no—he looked as if he wanted to say no—but he stood back and let me walk in. I stopped in the hall, wondering where to go. The rooms on the left and right were dark, shaded by the blinds.

"I was in the kitchen. Down here." Max shouldered his way past me and led the way to a sunny room with a white kitchen and yellow blinds. The sink was full of dirty dishes, though, and the room was untidy. A mug of coffee stood on the table, steam spooling out of it.

"Where are your parents?"

"In Edinburgh for the weekend." He opened the back door and shook a cigarette out of a crumpled packet. He lit it and blew a plume of smoke into the garden. "Next question."

"Have you been up all night?"

"Most of it." He rubbed his eyes, then shook his head like a dog coming out of a pond. "I couldn't sleep."

"What's wrong?"

"Nothing."

"Good answer," I said, sliding into a chair at the table. "Do you want me to tell you what I think is the matter?"

Max looked at me warily.

"Gilly Poynter," I said.

"What about her?" His voice was so low I could barely hear him.

"She's disappeared. And I think you know more about it than you've been letting on."

A swallow made his Adam's apple bob up and down. "What do you mean?"

"You were following her around. Watching her. I saw you." I leaned on the table. "If anyone knows where Gilly is, it's you."

"You're out of your mind."

"I don't think so," I said. "I saw you at the library on Friday night."

"Which was when Gilly went missing." Max took another drag on his cigarette and blew three smoke rings that shivered and disappeared in the cold air. "So how could I have been involved?"

"I don't know. Why don't you tell me?"

"Obviously I wasn't." A glance up to see how I reacted to that.

I was underwhelmed, and looked it. "That's not what I've heard. I know you were obsessed with Gilly. Especially after she broke up with you."

"Piss off." He looked at me with total disgust. "You don't know anything about me."

"I know what I've seen, and I know what other people have told me."

"What people?" Max demanded, flicking the cigarette butt into the garden in a shower of sparks and slamming the back door. He dragged out the chair opposite mine and sat down. "Who said that?"

"Nessa."

He nodded. "Why am I not surprised you said that?"

"She's not your biggest fan."

"No, she's not."

"How do you feel about her?"

"I can't stand her," he said frankly. "She tried to get Gilly to dump me."

"Why was that?"

"Because she wanted to keep her for herself. She's a twisted little dyke. She couldn't accept that Gilly was straight and she thought she could convert her."

My eyebrows shot up. "Wow. That's absolutely not what Nessa said."

"Yeah, of course Nessa denies it. But Gilly told me Nessa was freaking her out."

"In what way?"

"She told her she had feelings for her that went further than friendship. She tried to kiss her." Max snorted. "Gilly wasn't having any of it, obviously, because she wasn't like that. She felt completely betrayed. She just kept saying how much it hurt to be let down by someone she'd trusted."

I flashed back to the diary entry, written in pencil that dug into the paper.

Why do people have to let you down?

I shouldn't have been surprised that Nessa had lied to me. I shoved it to the back of my mind to think about later, and frowned at Max.

"Didn't Gilly feel as if *you'd* let her down?"

Max looked down at his hands. "Probably. I was a bit of a jerk when we were going out, if I'm honest. But it was such hard work. She didn't want her mum to know about us, so I couldn't go round to her house and she couldn't meet me. We'd get together after school for a few minutes. Sometimes at weekends we'd both go to the library and pretend to work. It was hard to find places to be together in private. She came here a couple of times when Mum and Dad were away, but that was it."

I thought about the few snatched moments I'd managed with Will, and felt the first hint of sympathy for Max. It wasn't easy to have a decent relationship when you never saw one another.

But then he went on, "I mean, I liked her a lot, but I got fed up with her not being at parties and not hanging out. It was like I was single but I couldn't pull anyone else."

"Poor, poor you." I'd cranked the sarcasm up to eleven, and he winced. "It was worse for Gilly, wasn't it, if you were out having fun and she was stuck at home."

"Yeah, that wasn't great," Max acknowledged. "Her mum is crazy strict with her. That's why—" He broke off.

"Why what?"

"Why I wasn't surprised when I heard that Gilly had done a runner."

My interest sharpened. "Why's that?"

"Because I was supposed to help her get away." He paused to let that sink in. "She wanted to go and live with her dad, so she was planning to run away. That was always her plan."

"Where's her dad?"

"Bristol. Her little sister lives with him."

I rocked back on my chair, thinking about how Gilly had reacted when I said I was an only child. "So you think she ran away to be with him? Have you tried to find out?"

"I don't know where he lives. I don't have his number." Max ran his hand through his hair. "I'd have called if I did."

"Presumably the police will have been in touch with him. They'd know if she was there. They wouldn't be looking for her any more."

Max shrugged. "I just know that she talked about leaving Port Sentinel all the time. She hated living with her mum."

"Because she was so strict."

125

"And because she was crazy." He shook his head. "I only met her once, but I thought she was going to knife me then and there. We bumped into her on Fore Street and Gilly was terrified. I was holding her hand and she snatched it away, like even holding hands was enough to get in trouble. Her mum made her come home with her straight away."

"What happened to her when she went home?"

Max looked shifty. "She never said."

"You never asked."

"Look, I said I was a terrible boyfriend, all right? I made mistakes. Everyone makes mistakes. But I really did care about Gilly, and I was worried about her. She was behaving so weirdly. That thing at Claudia's party . . ." He ran his hand over his face. "That freaked me out. I knew she didn't want to get back together with me, but I really thought she needed a friend."

"Oh, right. So your interest was purely friendly."

"Yeah. It was." Max stared at me, daring me to argue the point. "You say I was obsessed with her, but I wasn't. I just wanted to talk to her, that's all. I missed her."

"She tried to talk to you, though, didn't she? To explain what was in the diary. But you wouldn't speak to her about it."

"Not at first. I was so angry with her. I'm not going to pretend I was OK with it. We were supposed to be together and she was seeing someone behind my back. That was bad. But it was a hundred times worse that she wouldn't tell me who she was with." He stood up, shoving his chair back so hard it tipped and fell over. He walked around the kitchen in a tight little circle. "Imagine what that was like for me—looking at all my friends, wondering who it was who had gone behind my back with Gilly."

126

"It must have been hard to know who to trust."

"Yeah." Max braced his hands on the kitchen counter and dropped his head down. "And it was hard to know that she'd done it too. That she'd let someone do that to her. That she had so little self-respect."

"Is that what you said to her?"

"At first." He looked sideways at me. "Not the best reaction."

"Not really." I frowned, thinking. "Did she ever give you any hints about who she was seeing?"

"No."

"Did you have any suspicions?"

Max blew out a lungful of air. "Everyone? No one admitted it to me. And whoever was lying, they made a great job of it. Usually that sort of thing gets out, but no one seemed to hear. Or if they did, they didn't tell me."

"I read her diary. She wrote about it, but she didn't use any names or anything that would help me identify the person. She just called them X."

Max nodded. "She liked nicknames."

"What did she call you?"

He ducked his head, embarrassed. "Um. Not sure."

I thought about the chronology. "R?"

His ears were flaming. "Yeah, probably. It stands for . . ." He trailed off.

"Tell me. I promise I won't laugh."

"Romeo. It was her idea," he added quickly as I tried not to smirk. Max was not my idea of a Romeo, but that didn't matter; Gilly had loved him

"It makes sense," I said. "Star-crossed lovers. Did you call her Juliet?"

"I called her Gilly," he said, his voice level.

"In the diary—she seemed scared, Max. Was she scared of you?"

"I hope not," he said, but he didn't say it was impossible. And I remembered the look on his face when he stood outside Mr. Lowell's classroom waiting for Gilly—that brooding determination—and I wondered.

"She wouldn't work with you on the history project."

"Yeah, that was a kick in the teeth." He looked bitter. "I thought we were getting on better, you know? I'd been trying hard to tell her I'd forgiven her, and I thought I'd been making some progress. And then she embarrassed me in front of the whole class, like I was the one who'd cheated on her instead of the other way around. It hurt."

"So you thought she would do the project with you."

Max shrugged. "Why not? I mean, it was a bit awkward, but we'd have got over that. I still liked her. A lot. I'd have been respectful. We could have worked together."

"Did you ever hurt her?"

"I hurt her feelings. I never laid a finger on her otherwise."

"Nessa said she had a black eye after she tried to talk to you about the rumors."

He looked outraged. "Yeah, but not from me. Did Nessa say it was from me?"

"That was her impression."

Max leaned back against the sink. "No way. No, no, no. Not me. I would never hit a girl. I didn't even hit Nessa yesterday when she kneed me in the face, and she barely qualifies as a girl."

That was it. I snapped. "Why do you care if Nessa likes girls anyway? Why does it threaten you? Why can't you just leave her alone and let her get on with her life while you get on with yours?"

He looked startled. "I just don't like her."

"She doesn't like you either, and she's a lot tougher than you are, but that has nothing to do with her sexual preferences."

"She's been telling you all kinds of lies about me. Can't I defend myself?"

"You don't have to call her names to defend yourself."

Max folded his arms. "OK, well, you saw her yesterday. She hit me. It was an unprovoked attack too. So who do you think was more likely to hit Gilly, her or me?"

"I don't know," I said, being honest. "But I can see why you both want to put the blame on each other. And it doesn't get us much further with finding Gilly."

"I've told you what I can." That sounded like the truth, for once, and I couldn't think of anything else to ask Max, apart from why he wasn't a nicer person.

I stood up and wrote my phone number on a piece of junk mail that was lying by the cooker. "Let me know if you hear from Gilly."

"I will."

"I think you should talk to Inspector Henderson too. Tell him everything you know about Gilly. Tell him about her mother."

"Can't you do it?" Max shoved his hands in his pockets, obviously uneasy.

"I think it would be better coming from you," I said. "It might be better if you didn't mention me, by the way. I'm not really supposed to be here."

"OK." He still didn't look happy.

"Assuming you really want to help Gilly."

"Of course I do."

"Then do the right thing," I said simply.

"I don't want to get in trouble."

"Why would you get in trouble?"

"I watch TV," he said. "When a girl goes missing, they always look at the boyfriend."

"Ex-boyfriend in this case."

"That's even worse." Max hugged himself. "I don't want to get mixed up with all this when it's nothing to do with me. But I do want Gilly to come home."

"Then you'd better make the right choice," I said. "And I hope it works out."

As I left the house, I was thinking about Gilly's diary.

I was scared before, but now I'm terrified something bad is going to happen.

She wasn't the only one.

12

My route home took me past Will's house.

All right, I planned my route home to take me past Will's house. I hadn't seen him all day and it nagged at me that he was so close. I wanted to fall into his arms, to lose myself in his touch.

Or, you know, say hi.

But I forgot all about that when I got close enough to see the car that was parked outside, at an angle to the curb that suggested the driver had left it there in a hurry. A blue BMW, past its prime, with a dent in the passenger door. My dad's car.

I stopped where I was, then stepped back into the shelter of a bush so I couldn't be seen so easily. I was trying to get my head around the implications of my father being parked outside the Hendersons' small, shabby house.

As I watched, the front door opened and Dad stepped out. For a moment I saw him as others did: fair and handsome in an arrogant way. He turned and said something, and another figure came into view, a dark-haired woman. It took me a second to recognize Karen Henderson, Will's mother. I'd met her once, but I'd never seen her standing up before. In fact, I'd assumed she was bedridden. I knew she used a wheelchair usually. I hadn't known it was optional. If I'd cared more, I might have found out about her disease, I thought guiltily. I might have known that walking was a possibility, now and then. But I'd met her, and I hadn't liked her one little bit. I hadn't wanted to know about how ill she was, in case it made me sympathetic to her against my will. She didn't look exactly healthy, standing there. She was painfully thin, and her skin was bleached white from a life spent largely indoors.

The big question, of course, was what she was doing with my father. I hadn't even realized they knew one another. She looked up at him and made a comment I couldn't catch. Her expression was sour. He shook his head, then leaned down to kiss the air near her pale, thin cheeks. There was nothing romantic about the gesture, I thought, grateful for small mercies. It was politeness, nothing more.

Karen shut the door, and Dad stood there for a moment, putting on his sunglasses. Then he strode down the path toward the car, digging in his pocket for his keys as he went. Before I had even decided what to do, he had unlocked the car and disappeared into it. I was going to have to be fast.

I shot across the road to the passenger door, getting it open just as the engine hummed into life.

"What the— Jessica?" Dad sounded completely baffled.

I climbed into the passenger seat and shut the door, then pulled on my seat belt. "Let's go," I said briskly.

"What—why are you—?"

"I don't think now is the best time to start on the whats and whys," I said. "Not when we're sitting outside Dan Henderson's house."

Perhaps remembering that Dan was taller, stronger, and more frightening than him, Dad took the hint. He drove away at speed, complete with a screech from his tires.

"Subtle getaway. I like it."

Instead of answering me, he clenched his jaw. He was looking wary and quite flustered, as if he couldn't work out what to say to me to explain what he'd been doing. Up close he didn't look so good, with stubble on his jaw and bags under his eyes.

I let him sit for a minute, then said, brightly, "Where shall we go?"

"You usually don't want to go anywhere with me."

"And you're usually keen to persuade me to spend time with you." I smiled. "Father–daughter time, remember?"

"What do you want, Jessica?"

I want to find out what you're up to.

"I want to find out how you are. I haven't spoken to you properly for weeks. The last time I saw you was at the Christmas market when you were trying to talk to Mum." I paused for a beat. "Why were you talking to Mum?"

"Never mind." Dad drove down the hill toward the marina. With every meter he put between himself and Dan Henderson's house, his mood seemed to improve. "Why don't you come and see the apartment? You haven't even been in it since I unpacked."

Generally I wasn't looking for reasons to extend our conversations, but this time I was interested. "I'd love to."

The enthusiasm in my voice was so obviously fake I cringed,

but he didn't seem to pick up on it. He looked pleased, even if he was still slightly confused.

The apartment building where he lived was square, about six stories high, and it completely dominated Port Sentinel's little marina. In the summer the marina was full of pleasure boats and small yachts riding the swell as the wind rang music from the ropes tapping their masts, but it was winter now. Most of the boats were ashore, raised on blocks in boatyards up and down the coast, waiting for the warm weather. The marina looked bleak, even in the morning sunshine, and the apartment building had a dingy air. Dad swung into the car park and slotted the car into a space.

"Come on," he said, switching off the engine. "Come and see the place and then I'll take you out for lunch."

"You don't have to." I felt a squirm of alarm. Finding out what Dad had been up to was one thing; spending the day with him was another.

"It's no trouble. Anyway, I don't have any food in the flat. I think the milk's gone sour so I can't even make you a cup of tea."

"You need to look after yourself better."

He sighed. "It's hard when you live alone, Jess. There's no one to see. No one to care."

Spare me. I tried to think of something nice to say. "I hadn't thought about that. It must be hard."

"Sometimes." Dad flashed me a grin, looking just handsome enough to make it slightly more believable that Mum had fallen for his dubious charms once upon a time. "Grab your things and come on."

It took me a moment to get my bag, which had slid under

134

the seat. I was also playing for time. I wanted to work out what I was going to say to him about Karen before I got out of the car. When I emerged, Dad was leaning on the top of it, looking bored.

"Finally. You're so slow. I thought it was just your mother, but maybe it's all women."

"Yes, that's right, Dad. All women take ages to do everything. We can't help it. It's our ovaries slowing us down."

He laughed. "Don't tell me you've turned into a feminist."

"No, I haven't turned into one." *Because I was one already, as you might have noticed if you ever spoke to me.*

I followed him into the building and up the stairs to the second floor, allowing myself the luxury of wondering, not for the first time, how it was that I got half my genes from him and yet disliked pretty much everything about him.

"Here we are. Home sweet home." Dad opened the door of his apartment and stood back to let me go in. I hesitated on the threshold, looking around. The front door opened directly into the open-plan living room and kitchen. Beyond that there were two bedrooms—a small one that was intended for me, though I'd never slept there, and a larger one that Dad used. The living room had a big window that framed the marina, with Port Sentinel behind it, like a postcard. There wasn't much furniture—a huge leather sofa, a weird modern armchair that looked like a grasshopper and had cost a fortune, a coffee table, and a high-end TV that was on the wall where Mum would have put a painting or a photograph. I recognized most of it from our old house.

"What do you think?" Dad was watching me.

"I think it's weird to see all our London furniture here."

135

"Not all of it." He patted the back of the sofa. "Just the stuff I got in the divorce."

"You got all the good stuff in the divorce." Leaving us sitting on lumpy third-hand armchairs Mum got from the British Heart Foundation shop. I didn't miss those armchairs.

"I got all the good stuff because I paid for it in the first place."

"Mum couldn't afford to pay for things."

"No one expected her to. But then you couldn't expect me to leave everything behind when she kicked me out."

"Some men would." *Fathers who cared about their children, for instance.*

"I'm not one of those men," Dad said, blissfully unaware of what I'd been thinking.

"No, you're not," I agreed.

"So what do you think?" he said again, and this time he sounded a little anxious and unsure of himself. My opinion really mattered to him, I realized, and I felt horrible.

"It's great. Really nice. You've done a good job."

"Your mother liked it too. I think it surprised her that I was able to make it look nice by myself. She always thought she was the only one with good taste."

"Mum was here? When was Mum here?"

"She's been here a few times, Jess." Dad sat down on his enormous sofa, stretching his arms across the back and propping one foot on the opposite knee. He still looked tense, even if he was pretending to be relaxed.

"Why? I didn't think she was spending any time with you." *And I didn't want her spending any time with you, either.*

"You thought wrong."

I sat down too, on the end of the grasshopper chair, more because I couldn't stand up than because I wanted to. Alarm bells were ringing so loudly in my head I was surprised he couldn't hear them. "What's going on, Dad? What's happening with you and Mum?"

"We're talking."

"Talking?"

"About the future. You know I want her to come back to work for me."

It would be the worst thing for her. "She'd have to give up her job in the gallery."

"Yes, well, she'll never make a salesgirl, as I said to her." Dad gave me a look that was supposed to be mischievous. "You're far better at that than she is, aren't you? I think you get it from me."

"Probably," I said, my voice faint. "Is she considering it?"

"Working for me? Yes. And I probably shouldn't say this, but I think it might lead to more."

"More?" I croaked. My vocal cords had dried out from sheer terror. "You mean you might get back together?"

"It's possible. What do you think about that? Do you want us to get back together?"

"A world of no," I said, so appalled I forgot to pretend I was on his side. "That would be the worst thing ever."

"Thanks. Thanks for telling me how you feel." Dad looked out of the window, tapping his fingers on his knee irritably.

"Seriously, Dad. You and Mum were disastrous together."

"That's not true, Jessica. Things fell apart in the end, but we could put them back together."

"Things fell apart because *you* were putting *your* things

together with a twentysomething dental hygienist. Among others." I leaned my chin on my hand. "I think that's how it happened. I'm pretty sure I remember it accurately."

"We both made mistakes, Jess."

"Uh-huh." *And Mum's was marrying you in the first place.*

Dad pinched the bridge of his nose, closing his eyes, as if he had a headache. "Anyway, you might change your mind about all that when you consider the alternative."

"The alternative?"

"Your mother and her old boyfriend getting back together. Your boyfriend's father. That would be a complicated little set-up, wouldn't it?"

"She's not getting back together with Dan," I said flatly.

"That's what you think."

"Look." I refused to be anything other than calm. "Dan is never going to leave Karen. Not when she's so sick."

"Ah. Yes. You've got me there." There was a glint in Dad's eye that I didn't trust, though. He knew something that I didn't.

"What were you doing with Karen, anyway? I didn't think you even knew her."

"Slightly. We've met a couple of times."

"So it was just a social call?" I snorted. "You must be joking, Dad. You're up to something."

He held up his hands. "Really, I'm not. The absolute opposite. I want to help your mother. I just can't decide the best way to do it."

"I don't understand," I said.

"Karen wanted me to help her make sure Molly and Dan don't get back together. I would say she feels even more strongly

138

about it than I do, and I care very much about your mother's happiness."

I frowned. "But Mum says there's nothing going on between them."

"And you believe her?"

"Of course," I said stiffly. "They were together a long time ago—when they were *my* age. If I had any suspicions that they were sneaking around with one another, I'd tell you. But I don't."

He shook his head slowly, which was irritating.

"Anyway, why does Karen care? Does she want you to persuade Mum to come back to you so Dan doesn't get to have her even after Karen—" I checked myself, then said it anyway: "After she's gone?"

Dad's foot was waggling, a sign that he was stressed about something. "There was a little more to it than that, but you get the idea."

"She's got to let that go. She can't control what happens once she's dead. And you've got to let Mum go."

"Jessica, if you would just stop being bitter and immature for a moment and think about what's best for *you*, maybe you'd choose the correct side," Dad snapped.

"What do you mean?"

"Do you want Dan as a stepfather? Then Will would be your stepbrother. Can you imagine playing happy families forever, even if you break up? Or worse, if you don't?" He started to laugh. "I can't see you going for a double wedding, but stranger things have happened, I suppose."

I stared at him, thinking fast. I wanted to know what was going on. I wanted him to think I'd picked him over Mum. I

139

wanted him to trust me. And I really didn't want Dan as a step-father. So I took a deep breath.

"Oh my God, that would be horrendous."

"Exactly." Dad leaned back. I could *see* him thinking how good he was at this. Talking me round—easy. Getting Mum back—straightforward. Living happily ever after—a certainty.

"But I don't understand what you want me to do."

"I want you to back me up." Dad's foot was still waggling. "I've found out something important. Something that your mother needs to know. But I'm worried it will make her think she and Dan should get back together. I want you to make her feel as if she'd be letting you down if she chose him over me."

I laughed. "You must be out of your mind. I've spent years telling her to stay away from you."

"That's why it will mean so much more if you change your mind now." Dad looked pained. "I'm trying to do the right thing, Jessica. I want to help your mother."

"I don't understand," I said flatly. "What could you possibly have found out that would affect Mum?"

"Nothing I'm prepared to share with you now." Dad tapped his fingers on his mouth. "I haven't even decided what to do. Maybe I shouldn't say anything at all."

Ordinarily I would have thought it was a good idea for Dad to stay out of Mum's business. But it worried me that *he* was worried. Even if what he was mainly worried about was Mum and Dan rediscovering their long lost love for one another.

"I suppose you have to do the right thing," I said. "For once."

He looked pained. "Jessica, I'm not the bad guy in this situation. I know that's hard for you to believe."

140

"Just a bit."

"Well, it's true." Dad sighed. "I don't like Dan. And I don't trust him. And I want to do what's best for everyone."

"Then I suppose it's true what they say," I said faintly. "There really *is* a first time for everything."

13

Sandhayes was quiet when I let myself in, and only Hugo's car was outside. I stopped in the hall beside the ridiculous, glorious Christmas tree, and fiddled with an angel carved out of a piece of driftwood, obviously homemade. Hugo was the one who was good at working with wood, but he didn't do it much anymore. I couldn't imagine being able to make something like the angel, turning a bit of rubbish into something beautiful, something to be treasured. And Hugo took it for granted. I wished I had a talent like that, that I could make something beautiful and perfect, like my mother, like all the Leonards. But Dad's blunt practicality was what I had, in spades, and there was no point in wishing to be different any more than there was in wishing I was two inches taller.

A low rumble of voices came from the kitchen, along with the unfamiliar sound of Hugo laughing. I wandered down and pushed open the door to the warm, chaotic room where the Leonards spent most of their time. Hugo was sitting on the kitchen counter with his hair all over the place, wearing the ancient T-shirt and shorts that were his version of pajamas. Will was sitting on a chair by the table, tilting it back, his long legs propped up on the corner of the Aga. He was still laughing when I went in, and it killed me—it just *killed* me—to see the smile fade from his eyes. He looked wary instead, and watchful.

"Hey."

"Hi," I said, a tight feeling in my chest making it hard to breathe. *What do we do to each other?* The thought filled my head, crowding out everything else. I covered it with a smile.

"Oh God, you're dressed." Hugo ran his hands through his hair, making it even more untidy. "I bet you've been up for hours. Don't you ever relax?"

"I'm not lazy, if that's what you mean." I twisted to look at the clock. "It's ten to two, Hugo."

"I'm aware of that."

"So what time did you get up?"

"When Will came round. An hour ago, maybe?" He yawned, stretching, and the kitchen wasn't a small room but he seemed to fill it. "I need to have a shower."

"I was going to say." Will waved a hand in front of his nose.

"I don't smell," Hugo said with tremendous dignity. "But I need a shower to wake up properly. Or a bath."

Hugo's baths were legendary, hours-long affairs that involved hogging the bathroom, using all the hot water, and ignoring anyone banging on the door in favor of reading whatever book absorbed him.

"That should sort out what you're doing with the rest of your day, then," I said.

143

"Jessica," Hugo growled. It was just one word, but it gave me chills.

"Ugh. Do you mind? I really don't need you doing an impression of my dad." I went over to fill the kettle. "Who wants tea?"

"Me," Hugo said instantly.

"And me." Will swung his legs down from the Aga and stood up to give me his mug. He leaned across the table to give it to me, instead of coming round as I'd sort of hoped he might. And then he went back and sat down again. I felt cold air where his body should have been behind me, a chill where the ghost of his arms wrapped around me. This wasn't how it was supposed to be.

I didn't say much while I made the tea, listening to Hugo and Will bickering affectionately. I sneaked an occasional look at Will, who wasn't paying the slightest attention to me. There was something wholly pleasing about the way he moved and spoke, the way his expressions changed, the way he listened when Hugo was talking and the way he laughed.

I loved him so much, I ached.

Make it right, I thought.

Easier said than done.

I waited for a gap in the conversation to ask, "Where is everyone?"

Hugo listed everyone briskly. "Mum and Tom are shopping. Dad is working in the garden. Petra is upstairs somewhere. Your mum is . . ."

I knew this one. "At the market, working."

"And we're here," Hugo finished.

"Have you any plans today, Will?" I asked, trying to sound casual.

"No, Jess, I do not," he said, very serious as Hugo laughed into his mug. "Have you?"

"I'm sure I'll think of something."

Hugo slid off the counter. "All this dynamism makes me think I should get a move on."

"You can do it, man. I believe in you." Will grinned at him as he shuffled to the kitchen door, where he stopped and turned to give us both a warning look.

"Play nicely, you two. I don't want to hear any squabbling."

"Hugo," I said pleasantly, "get out."

He cackled all the way down the hall. As the sound died away, I looked at Will and found he was watching me. The tick of the kitchen clock sounded extra loud in the silence.

"Hi," I said eventually.

"We did that bit already."

I looked down at my mug, turning it round and round. "OK, don't help."

"Is it that difficult to talk to me?"

"Apparently so."

"Well, that's no good."

I dragged my eyes back up to him and found I couldn't quite look straight at him, at his face, at what I might see he was thinking. "Will, I'm scared."

He'd gone very still. "Of what?"

"Saying the wrong thing? Again?"

"I think," he said carefully, "I was the one who got it wrong the last time."

I shrugged. "It was half you, half me."

"That's too generous. I was the one whining because you have a life. I was the one who wanted you to abandon your principles." His eyes shone. "You're right. You're not my consolation prize."

I felt my lower lip tremble. I shut my eyes and two tears slid down my cheeks. I heard Will's chair scrape on the floor as he stood up.

"But you are everything that matters to me."

He started to move toward me—and at exactly, precisely the wrong moment, the back door burst open.

"Out of the way, Jess." My uncle elbowed the door shut behind him, then barged past me, holding his hands up. They were liberally coated in mud. "Can you turn the tap on, love?"

I did as I was told, then stared at Will mutely. The sound of rushing water meant I didn't have to say anything, which was lucky. I was all out of words. Jack was lathering up a storm, humming under his breath as he scrubbed his nails. He wasn't going to be finished quickly, that was clear. And then he would probably want a cup of tea, and a chat. I loved Jack, but he was impervious to hints about being left alone. Every second would be a second wasted from my precious time with Will.

Who was thinking along the same lines. He put down his tea and nodded to my mug. "Ready?"

I nodded, finishing it in one gulp.

"See you later, Jack," Will called over the sound of the water drumming in the sink, and got a grunt of acknowledgment. He held the kitchen door open and I shot through it. "Your room?" he said, following me, his voice slightly rough.

Not as calm as he was pretending to be. Not by a long way, I found, when I turned to say yes and found myself pinned against the wall. He kissed me, hard, and my heart took off, fluttering in my chest like a hummingbird. "Not here," I managed to say when I could get enough air into my lungs, and he backed off, nodding, as aware as I was that Jack was on the other side of the kitchen door and might appear at any moment.

"Upstairs, then."

"Yep." I led the way, at speed, floating up the endless stairs to the top of the house as if my feet weren't even touching the ground. Will and I would be safely alone in a few seconds, and—

I opened my bedroom door to find Petra standing in front of the mirror, eyeliner in hand. My desk was completely covered in what looked like an entire cosmetics counter, a jumble of brushes, used tissues, and balled-up bits of cotton wool.

"Oh, Petra, you're here." I kept my voice super-calm, even though I was screaming inside. I didn't want to provoke a teenage tantrum for two reasons: it wouldn't make her leave any quicker, and I liked her too much. Since I'd moved into Freya's room, I'd taken on the mantle of big sister in her place, and I'd promised myself to live up to my dead cousin's example.

And OK, maybe Freya would have been livid and would have thrown her out, but I just couldn't do that. I'd been welcomed into the family with open arms. Playing my part meant being a better person that I was used to being. It meant sharing and compromising. I'd grown up an only child, but I'd longed for siblings. Fundamentally, I was glad to have the problems that came with being in a big family.

Only, not so much at that precise moment, with Will standing behind me.

So maybe there was the tiniest edge to my voice when I asked, "What are you doing here?"

"Practicing my evening look. Darcy was teaching me how to do a winged eye." Petra turned her head from side to side. "I don't think I've got the hang of it."

"It's next-level makeup." I was twisting the door handle to relieve my feelings. "You'll get there eventually."

"Looks great to me," Will said from the doorway. "You look beautiful, Petra."

She blushed, probably all the way down to her toes. "The left eye is a bit wonky."

"No one would notice." He smiled at her.

"I'm just going to try it again." Petra leaned in to stare at her reflection. "You don't mind me being up here, Jess, do you? It's much easier here than in my room. My mirror is rubbish and I don't have anywhere to put my stuff."

I went over and picked up the bottle of liquid foundation that was oozing brown goo onto a magazine, standing it upright. "Just be careful, OK? I don't want makeup all over everything."

Petra bit her lip. "Sorry, Jess."

"Don't worry." I put my arm around her shoulders and gave her a squeeze. "Did Darcy show you the dot trick for the eyeliner?"

"Yep. She's a genius," Petra said reverently.

I was mildly nettled. Petra hero-worshipping Darcy was a step too far. "She got it from YouTube."

"She's still a genius."

"An evil one, maybe." I headed for the door.

"You can stay here. Just ignore me," Petra said. "I won't get in the way."

"That's OK," I said hastily, pulling the door closed after me. "You just do your thing. It's fine."

"I can go somewhere else."

"No need. Really." I shut the door and looked up at Will. "What now?" I whispered. There was another bedroom on the top floor, but it was small and bleak and, most importantly, freezing. The mattress on the bed was bare and there was nowhere else to sit.

He looked up and down the hall for inspiration. "Stairs?"

"Stairs," I agreed. I followed him to the steps, glad that the Victorians had built their staircases with broad, shallow treads. Will braced his back against the wall, stretching his legs out. He pulled me down to sit opposite him, my legs tangled up in his. His right hand was on my left thigh; his right held onto my knee. We were face to face, and alone at last.

"So," he said.

"So."

"Where were we?"

I cleared my throat. "I'm everything that matters to you, if I recall correctly."

"That was it." He grinned at me. "Your turn."

"I love you," I said. "That's all I have."

Will took a second to reply, as if he had to get his breath back before he could speak. It was the longest second in the world. His voice was gruff and much lower than usual when he said, "I think that's enough."

I slid across from my side of the stairs into his arms. I felt him tense and shiver as I touched him, as I kissed him, and I knew he felt the same way.

And yes, the stairs were just the worst possible place to kiss someone, but we coped.

The sound of my bedroom door opening drove us apart. I shot back to my side of the stairs, my head spinning, my eyes fixed on Will's, both of us laughing shakily.

"Jess?" Petra padded down the landing, a frown on her face under the metric tonne of make-up. "What's this?"

She was holding a blue notebook.

Gilly's diary.

The warm feelings disappeared, and fast.

"Give me that." I stood up and reached out for it. Long training as a younger sibling made her hold it back, too far away for me to be able to grab it. "That's not yours, Petra. Give it to me or put it back where you found it. You shouldn't have been poking through my stuff anyway. That's the deal if you use my room. You don't go through my things."

"I wasn't. I was cleaning it." She showed me the edge, smudged with black. "It's liquid eyeliner."

"Petra! For God's sake, I warned you."

Her face crumpled. "I'm sorry. I was being careful. The brush just rolled."

"Oh, did it?" I managed to reach the notebook and yanked it out of her hand. I flicked through it, checking the damage. One page was badly smudged where she'd tried to wipe the make-up off, but the words were still just about legible. "Petra!"

"Are you cross with me?" she sobbed.

"Just a bit." I couldn't pretend it didn't matter. It did. The diary wasn't mine and, much more importantly, it was evidence. I could just imagine Dan's face when he saw it.

"Let's see." Will had got up. He reached over my shoulder for the diary.

I held onto it. "No, it's OK."

"What is it?"

"It's someone's diary," Petra said helpfully. "But that's not your writing, Jess. I couldn't work out who it belonged to." She shivered. "It gave me the creeps. She sounds really upset about something."

Will hadn't let go of the diary and he was a lot stronger than me. I gave in to the inevitable and let go of it. He flicked through it. "Who wrote this? Jess? Who does it belong to?"

"It's Gilly Poynter's," I said reluctantly.

"The missing girl? How do you have this?" He looked down at me, doubt in his eyes. "*Should* you have this?"

"Technically, no," I said, "but I can explain."

He was a policeman's son, when all was said and done, and he knew more than I did about handling evidence. There was nothing exaggerated about his horror when he said, "Jess, what have you done?"

"I'd left something in her house that I needed. And while I was there, I had a look around her room."

"And you just *took* this?"

"I wanted to read it." It sounded bad when I said it out loud. I tried to think of a better way, and couldn't. "I found it. It was really well hidden, behind a picture."

He frowned. "Did Dad miss it?"

"He hadn't actually searched the room yet." I quailed at the

151

look on his face. "Mrs. Poynter wouldn't let him. So if I hadn't taken it, we wouldn't know what was in it."

"But Dad doesn't know you have this."

"No," I admitted.

"So he doesn't know what's in it anyway."

"No. But—"

"He doesn't even know it exists."

"Possibly not. Well, probably."

"When did you find it?"

"Yesterday," I said. "Yesterday evening."

"Yesterday? When were you going to tell him?"

"Today. I was going to give it to him today."

Will shook his head, and it wasn't in an admiring way. "Jess. God. You know better than this, don't you? He's going to kill you, and I think he'd be justified."

"Thanks for your support," I snapped.

"I'm not going to support you if you do something criminally stupid, Jess."

Petra was looking from me to Will and back again. She was still crying. "Are you going to get in trouble, Jess?"

"So it seems."

"What else did you think was going to happen?" Will demanded.

The truth was, I hadn't thought about that. I hadn't considered the consequences. I had just wanted to read the diary and hadn't thought about what was going to happen next.

But I wasn't going to admit that.

"I was going to explain it to him."

"Oh, right. That usually works well." Will turned away and

started to walk down the stairs, muttering under his breath. He still had the diary. I ran down a few steps.

"Where are you going? What are you going to do?"

"I'm going to give this to Dad right now. No more delays. He needs to see it straight away."

I swallowed the lump in my throat that was a ball of pure fear. "What are you going to tell him?"

"I don't know." Will paused to look up at me and his eyes were as cold as the December sea. "I'll think of something."

14

The next morning I went down to the Christmas market. I hadn't planned to go there, but I drifted in that direction. The streets in the old town were deserted. Fore Street was usually thronged, but the market had drawn the tourists away. As for the locals, the great migration had begun, the wealthy residents fleeing for warmer climates. There was something bleak about the Christmas lights swinging over empty pavements, the decorations sagging in the windows. It was almost Christmas Eve, but the holiday spirit was thin on the ground.

Or maybe that was just my mood. I'd spent the previous afternoon and evening in Sandhayes, staring into space, waiting for the knock on the door that would be Dan Henderson breathing fire—justifiably for once. Or for Will to shoulder open the back door and look for my face amid the assembled Leonards, to seek me out and put his arms around me and tell me I'd been stupid but that he forgave me for it. I imagined it a hundred times, a hundred different ways, and it didn't happen. Petra had sat near me the whole time, not talking, all elbows and knees and hunched misery. She reminded me of a cat, wanting to give comfort but not being doglike and direct about it. Instead she sat beside me at dinner, and curled up on the floor near my feet while we were watching a film later. (I hadn't heard a word of the dialogue or followed the plot in any meaningful way.)

And I'd told her not to worry. I'd told her it was my fault. I'd promised her I didn't blame her for Will storming out. I'd begged her not to feel bad.

Because it wasn't her fault.

It was entirely, completely mine.

I hadn't been walking with any particular destination in mind. All I knew was that I didn't want to go home. I'd stayed in bed for a long time after I woke up, not wanting to face the day, but in the end my thoughts drove me out. Now the sound of the piping Christmas music drew me down to the Christmas market. The weather wasn't helping the traders much: it was cold again, and the shoppers had mainly congregated around the hot food stands. I waved to Mum, who was leaning on the counter of the gallery's hut, her chin in her hand. She waved back, but I didn't go over. I knew she would know—with her magical maternal intuition—that something was wrong. I didn't want to talk about it with her, or anyone else.

"Rudolph the Red-nosed Reindeer" floated out across the park from the rink, sounding haunting rather than cheery. The rink wasn't too busy, I saw—only a few people skating. I leaned on the barrier at the edge and watched a couple slipping and sliding, half hysterical with laughter as they tried to hold each other up.

155

"Waiting for me?" Ryan dropped an arm around my shoulders. "Wait no more. Your skating partner is here."

"I was just watching." I slid out from under his arm and turned to face him. It was easier to persuade him to keep his distance that way. He looked very tall and very handsome, his hair perfectly ruffled, his eyes that pure blue that made me think of summer.

"You wanted to skate, I can tell." He gave me the full benefit of his wide, charming smile. "Come on, Jess. What's the worst that can happen?"

"What do you think Yolanda would do if she heard we'd been skating together?"

"She wouldn't mind."

"Um, I think she would."

"Why? There's nothing romantic about it." Ryan's expression was a challenge. "Unless you think there is."

"No, of course not."

"Because we're just friends."

"Yes."

"No attraction here."

I felt the color rise in my cheeks and looked away first, annoyed with myself. He put a hand on my shoulder and ran it down my arm slowly.

"Come on, Jess. What are you afraid of? Will? Is it because he'd mind too much?"

"Stop." I held up my hand. "Right now. We've done this before. You and Will are supposed to be friends now."

"Friends." Ryan nodded. "You're right. So I shouldn't be trying to steal his girl."

"I'm not a *thing* to be stolen. I hope I'd get some say in it."

156

I frowned at him. "Why do you behave like such a Neanderthal all the time?"

He leaned down. "Because it's fun. And girls love it."

"Not this girl."

He stayed where he was, his face close to mine. "I'm going to persuade you to like me one day, Jess Tennant."

"I like you already. As a friend." A really disturbingly attractive friend.

Ryan smiled. "I remember the exact moment I first saw you. It was on the seafront."

"You were balancing on the railings."

"Trying to get your attention."

"It worked."

"Not well enough." He said it lightly. But then, "Every time I see you with Will, I wish I'd got there first."

I looked down. "I'm sorry."

"I know." Then, "How is Will, anyway?"

"Fine." I smiled, though my lips felt stiff and it sat awkwardly on my face. I couldn't help thinking back to the last time Ryan had seen us together, sitting on the bench by the mulled-wine stand the previous Saturday. The scene replayed in my mind: arguing, kissing, Will noticing Ryan and reacting like a wolf, with watchful but controlled aggression, while Ryan smiled and probably thought about the ifs and the maybes.

And then Max had interrupted the staring competition.

A thought occurred to me. "Why did Max have your keys?"

The change of subject threw Ryan. "Huh?"

"Max Thurston. Your car key. He had it on Saturday, didn't he? I saw him give it back to you."

"Oh, yeah. He borrowed the car."

"When?"

"Um . . ." He thought about it. "Friday evening. After school."

"When did he ask you for it?"

"He texted me." Ryan dug in his pocket and checked his phone. "Ten past four. But I didn't get it straight away. I texted him back at a quarter to five to tell him where I was."

"Did he tell you why he wanted it?"

He looked away, across the rink, trying to remember. "I don't know. I mean, I wasn't exactly keeping track of where Max went and what he did with the car, as long as he didn't use too much gas or wreck it. I wasn't using it, so he was welcome to have it."

And that was like Ryan—being open-handed and generous. That was one reason why he had such a massive cohort of friends, unlike my lone-wolf boyfriend.

"So he had it all night on Friday?"

"Yeah. You saw him give me the keys back on Saturday morning, hawk-eye. You don't miss much, do you?"

"I try not to." I thought for a minute. "Did you notice anything strange about the car?"

Ryan shrugged. "Not really. It was filthy when he got it. Still filthy when he gave it back. I tried to get him to wash it for me, but no go."

"Did you notice how far he'd gone?"

A shake of the head. "But I know he filled it up for me because it was full when I got it back and I only had a quarter of a tank."

"OK," I said. "Thanks." I turned away, trying to work out if it mattered that Max had had a car on Friday night, or if it was just a coincidence. Ten past four: before Gilly disappeared. And then I'd seen him in the library, out of breath, hanging around in a look-at-me-don't-look-at-me way. He hadn't been all that subtle.

It was almost as if I'd been supposed to notice him.

"Where are you going?" Ryan asked.

"Just for a walk. And to think," I added.

"So you're not looking for company." He shoved his hands in his jeans pockets and sighed, resigned. "Fine."

"Sorry." I stood on the edge of one foot, feeling awkward. I hated to see him look so disappointed. It wasn't as if I had anything better to do.

And there was a tiny part of me that wanted to prove I was my own person—that Will didn't own me. It was the part that knew I was in the wrong about the diary—and I hated to be wrong.

"Or . . . we could skate?"

"Seriously?" His face lit up. "You will?"

I nodded. "But I warn you, I'm terrible. I've only ever skated on indoor rinks with thousands of other people, in London. This is a bit different."

"Don't worry about that," Ryan said. "It's easy. At least, it's easy if you have someone to skate with who knows what they're doing."

"And you do."

"You have to ask?" He grinned. "It's all about balance."

"That's not traditionally one of the things I'm best at."

159

"No, but I am." He wasn't boasting. It was probably true. He was one of the most naturally gifted athletes I'd ever seen, good at everything he tried.

I smiled at him. "I believe you."

"OK." He caught the change in my mood as if it was the trailing string of a kite. Ryan was made for happiness, for adventures, for fun. He grabbed my hand. "Let's go."

And it was the best thing I could have done. The lead weight in my chest that had been making it hard to breathe disappeared as Ryan joked around with the man who ran the rink. He shooed him away so he could help me lace up the hired skates.

"Too tight, too tight," I complained.

"Sorry. They have to be tight." He gave the laces a vicious tug. "Are they digging into your ankles?"

"Yes!"

"Good." He pulled me to my feet and held me for a moment as I wobbled on the blades. "Easy. You're not even on the ice yet."

"I'd just forgotten."

"It'll come back."

The man held the gate open and Ryan steadied me as we stepped onto the ice. With his arm around me, I slid forward a few meters, trying and failing to find my balance.

"Whoa there, Bambi."

"How are you making it look so easy?" I complained.

"Skill. Talent." Ryan let go of me and skated around me in a small circle. I grabbed him as he passed and he drew me out toward the middle of the rink, skating backward.

"Come on, Jess. You just have to trust yourself."

I followed his lead, concentrating on what I was doing, and it was a few minutes before I realized that I was starting to enjoy it, to skate by myself, the exact movements I needed coming back just as Ryan had said they would. He whooped and cheered, rushing in to support me when I wobbled, letting me go when I could manage on my own. And once I was more confident, he skimmed to a stop in front of me and held out his hands.

"Skate with me?"

"I thought that's what we were doing."

He shook his head. "Like this."

And then I was in his arms, and we were carving a route around the ice, moving at a speed I could never have managed on my own, turning and spinning in lazy loops that sent my hair flying around my face. I was breathless and laughing when Ryan swung round in front of me, his blades cutting the ice as he stopped. He pulled me into his arms for a hug. I put my arms around his waist, holding him close, needing his support to stay upright. His head rested on top of mine for a moment, the two of us stock still in the middle of the ice.

"Jess." His voice was soft. It came from low in his chest, and there was a tremor in it. I leaned back to see him, trying to catch my breath, to say something mocking that would remind him we were friends and nothing more, and that it was only because we were friends I was skating with him. Then Ryan looked past me and said my name again. This time there was a warning note in it. He stepped away from me and I turned, almost falling. He grabbed my shoulders and steadied me, then let go again as if I was burning to the touch.

Because Will was standing under the trees, watching us,

and for once, all the darkness in him was visible in his face. He kept it hidden beneath a reasonable manner, but he had all his father's temper, and more. We looked at one another for what seemed like minutes before he shoved his hands in the pockets of his long dark coat, turned, and strode off through the square.

I'd been shocked into immobility. Now I skated to the edge of the ice, not too proud to grab the hand Ryan held out to me, and hobbled over to the bench. I needed to talk to Will. I would have been running after him already if the laces of the skates hadn't been so tight. I broke a nail and then another, sobbing as I fought with the right boot.

"Let me help." Ryan started to work on the left boot.

"I can manage," I said, yanking on the lace.

"Obviously not." He unravelled the knot with infuriating ease and pulled the skate off.

I dragged the other one off, the laces still half knotted, and handed it to him. "Work your magic. I'm sorry. I have to talk to Will."

"Jess . . ."

I was shoving my feet into my boots. "What?"

"Just"—he gave me a lopsided smile—"let me know how it goes."

I ran then, heading in the same direction as Will. He'd gone out of the park by the lower gate, taking the road that led along the seafront toward the wooded headland marking the edge of Port Sentinel. It was where my cousin Freya had fallen to her death, where Will and I had argued, and come together, and almost died. I didn't know for sure that he had gone that way, but I knew Will—or I thought I did. He would want to

162

stay away from everyone. He would want to let his anger burn unseen until he had it under control. I would get pure ice when I saw him next, the withdrawal of affection that was so much more devastating than shouting or slammed doors.

I was out of breath by the time I reached the treeline and peered up at the sandy path that ran up to the cliffs. I couldn't see him anywhere, and then it started to rain, a squall that had swept in from the sea. The tree trunks were black with moisture and slick when I reached out to steady myself on them. My legs were tired, the muscles complaining after the skating and running and now the steep hill. All I could hear was my own breathing and the scrape of my boots on the hard earth.

I reached the cliffs more quickly than I had expected. The bench loomed up in front of me and I grabbed onto it, remembering other times when we'd sat together, staring out to sea. Today the water was as hard and green as jade. The boom and swish of the waves far below sounded sinister. My hair hung around my face like damp string as the rain soaked through the shoulders of my coat.

I hit the back of the bench with my fist, welcoming the pain. Whoever named heartbreak got it so right. It felt as if my heart had shattered into a million tiny shards. I could feel the ache of misery building inside me, along with an edge of anger. Will could have waited to speak to me.

He could have trusted me.

I took out my phone and called his number, listening to the phone ring once, twice, and then cut off. So he wasn't going to talk to me. *Perfect*. I started back down toward town, moving fast, barely keeping my balance at times when the path was steep or rutted with roots. I had to look down at my feet, picking a careful but speedy route through the hazards. The last part of the path lay round a bend, so I had no warning before I crashed into him. I caught my breath as he grabbed hold of me, and it took a second for me to realize that it wasn't Will who held me, but his father.

15

Dan held my shoulders for a second, then let go. "Jess, what were you doing up there?"

"Looking for Will."

"Did he go up that way?"

"I thought he did." I was trying to breathe shallowly. Being able to see plumes of my breath in front of me was off-putting. I didn't want Dan breathing on me and I didn't want to breathe on him.

He frowned down at me. "Did you have a row?"

"How did you know?"

"Your eyes are red. And I'd have expected the two of you to be joined at the hip while Will's in town. But no Will." He tilted his head to one side. "And the two of you seem to spend most of your time fighting."

"It was a stupid misunderstanding," I said.

"It always is."

I dropped my head to try to hide my face, which was flaming. I didn't know which was more annoying—him commenting on our relationship, or him being right.

"Anyway," Dan said icily, "that's enough small talk. Don't you have something you want to say to me? An apology, perhaps?"

My stomach flipped over as if I'd stepped into an unexpected hole. "You got the diary."

"I got the diary." When I dared to look up, Dan was staring at me curiously. "Why did you think you should have it?"

"I thought it would make more sense to me than you. I know the people she was writing about."

"So you took it."

I bit my lip. "Mrs. Poynter wouldn't even let you search Gilly's room. You wouldn't have had it anyway."

"I'd have got it yesterday at two, which was when we took the cottage apart. So some time ago." Dan shook his head. "I thought you were sensible, Jess. I thought you were cleverer than that."

"I'm sorry," I said, meaning it. "Will's already had a go at me about it, if that helps."

"It probably wasn't so bad, coming from him."

I shivered. "It was bad." It had been like flying full tilt into a sheet of plate glass. The comedown from where I'd been to where I ended up was nothing short of brutal.

And now I'd made it all infinitely worse by skating with Ryan. Which . . . I knew it was innocent, but it didn't look it. Even I could see that. And even I could see that it hadn't been fair on Ryan, either.

I was starting to wish the unexpected hole had existed so that I could lie down in it and never get up again.

"Tell me about the diary," Dan said abruptly. "You read it. I read it too. It meant very little to me. Would you care to translate it for me?"

"I didn't understand everything," I admitted, "but from what I can tell, she had a brief relationship with Max Thurston."

Dan's eyebrows snapped together. "I didn't know about that."

"I think it was supposed to be a secret. And then . . . they broke up."

"Because?"

"She . . . um . . . did something with someone in the disabled toilets at school."

"Yes," Dan said. "I understood the 'I HAD SEX' part, believe it or not. Who was it with?"

"I still don't know," I said. "I'm trying to find out. But Max was furious. He dumped her."

"So they were finished when she disappeared."

"Yes, but—" I really didn't want to drop Max in it. On the other hand, I had my doubts about him. Dan was a senior police officer, so I thought I could trust him to make up his own mind about whether Max was really a suspect. "He was still hanging around. Wanting to talk to her. And I had the impression that she didn't want to see him. She went to great lengths to avoid him."

"His name again?" Dan had taken out a notebook.

"Max Thurston." I watched him scrawl it at the top of an empty page.

"Address?" He wrote it underneath the name. "I haven't come across him before. He can't be a troublemaker."

"Or he's lucky," I said.

That got me a glance with a gleam of amusement in it. "Is that it? He was hanging around too much?"

"Mm. And a couple of other things. Like he borrowed a car." I told him about what Ryan had told me, and how I'd seen Max at the library. "He'd just come in from outside because there was rain on his jacket. He sneaked in, behaved weirdly enough that I noticed him, and then ran out again."

"Making you his alibi."

"That was what occurred to me. And he didn't return the car until the following morning. So where was he, and what was he doing?"

"Sounds like the kind of thing I should ask him," Dan said. "You can point him out to me later."

"Later?"

"I've asked people to volunteer to search for Gilly. Not because I think they'll actually find her, but I want the pictures for the news. People trudging through a field—that kind of thing. We'll get more coverage from the national media that way. If I really thought you were going to run across Gilly's body, you wouldn't be anywhere near it."

It hit me like a sledgehammer. "Her body? Do you think she's dead?"

"It's a possibility." Dan looked down at me gravely. "I know you think of this as a bit of fun, Jess, but with every hour that passes there's less and less chance of Gilly coming home safely."

I swallowed, trying to come to terms with it. It was stupid, but I really hadn't considered that she might be hurt or injured.

168

I really believed she'd run away. That was what I'd been told, after all. I put it out of my mind to think about later, and focused on the other thing Dan had said that interested me.

"I wouldn't have thought you'd care about the national media."

"I care about finding Gilly Poynter," Dan said soberly. "I don't like having a missing teenager on my turf, especially right before Christmas. I want a happy ending and I want one soon. So we're all going to pretend to look for Gilly in some attractive Devonshire countryside, and her dad is going to make an appeal for her to contact her family, and we'll see if I get my Christmas wish or not."

Assembly time for the search party was three o'clock and it looked as if everyone in Port Sentinel had turned out for it. I trudged through the crowds in my rain boots, recognizing neighbors and school friends and people who worked in the local shops.

The search area was across a massive muddy field. At the edge of the field there was a belt of woodland that stretched over the top of a hill, with a small quarry on the far side. The helicopter had already been over the area we were searching with heat-sensitive cameras, and the search-and-rescue dogs had hunted through the dense patches of undergrowth where she might have been lying, unseen. We weren't going to find anything, but I could see the value of what we were doing all the same.

There was a knot of people I knew near the front—Darcy and Claudia, who had her arm linked with Immy's. Beyond them I saw Abigail and Louise Manning, and a little further away stood Nessa, muffled in a long gray coat but with her leather jacket underneath. I made my way over to her.

"Are you OK?"

"Yeah," she said quietly. She was looking past me, though, and I knew from her expression what I was likely to see when I turned round: Max Thurston in a Puffa jacket. I quite wanted to talk to him, to ask him about the car, but for two reasons I didn't dare. One: he was standing shoulder to shoulder with Ryan and I didn't want to go anywhere near him. And two: Dan Henderson had warned me in no uncertain terms that if I did or said anything to alert Max to the fact that he was a potential suspect, he'd put me in prison.

"For something. Anything I can think of," he'd said, and I knew him well enough to realize that he meant it.

"Do you think we'll find anything?" Nessa asked me, bringing me back to the present.

"Oh—honestly? No."

She nodded, a little color coming into her cheeks. "I thought not. I don't want to. You know."

"I do."

As if she felt she'd said too much, she turned and walked off a little way, and I took the hint. Besides, I had finally seen Dan Henderson, who was holding a clipboard in one hand, a megaphone in the other, and looking thunderously irritated by the clamoring reporters who surrounded him. I caught his eye and he swept through the ring of journalists, coming to stand very close beside me so I could speak to him without being overheard.

"Is he here?"

"Yeah." I gave Dan a description of what Max was wearing and where he was standing, and he nodded, not looking anywhere near him.

"Thanks." He walked off without waiting for a reply, and I was glad he hadn't prolonged our conversation. I didn't want to attract too much attention for helping the police. I didn't look round to see if Max was watching, either. It was all I wanted to do, but I stared out at the horizon instead. The light was going to start to fade soon and I hoped the cameramen would get the pictures Dan wanted.

"Jessica."

Oh crap.

I turned and found Dad trudging toward me through the mud. It wasn't his natural habitat—a city street would have suited him much better.

"Dad, what are you doing here?"

"I thought I'd come and help." He looked past me. "Is your mother here?"

"Is this your way of trying to impress her? By pretending to be a decent human being?"

Dad's mouth tightened. "You won't give me any credit, will you?"

"You haven't earned it," I pointed out. "Anyway, I don't know if Mum's here or not. I haven't seen her."

He scanned the crowd. "Well, if she's not here, I might go."

"Dad," I protested. "Even for you, that's cynical."

"One person more or less isn't going to make any difference," he said, which was true, but not the point. He scowled. "Look at him. He loves this, doesn't he?"

I looked in the same direction, to see Dan Henderson

171

addressing a group of uniformed officers, issuing instructions. "Dan? It is his job."

"Playing the hero." Dad snorted. "He's all talk. He always was. As if being a police officer makes you an automatic candidate for sainthood."

Privately, I thought that being a police officer was a lot more important than helping rich people to manage their wealth, but I didn't say as much to Dad. It wouldn't have gone down well.

Dan glanced over in our direction and saw Dad. He gave him the full death stare, and I had to resist the urge to duck for cover, even though it wasn't aimed at me. Dad muttered something under his breath and turned away, very casually, as if he hadn't just backed down from a staring competition he was never, ever going to win.

"If you see your mother, could you mention to her that I was here? Drop it into the conversation. Don't say I said to tell her."

"Right," I drawled. "She'll never think that's a strange thing for me to tell her."

"Remember, Jessica," Dad said icily, "it's in your interests too."

"If you say so." I watched him walk away and sighed. No matter how low I pitched my expectations, he still managed to disappoint me.

One of Dan's officers came over and shouted, "OK, everyone, can you line up beside the other searchers, please? We want to get started. Leave a gap of no more than two feet between you, and try to keep up with the people on your left and right. Please don't change your positions once you've taken up your place in the line."

I started to walk toward the line and saw Ryan approaching, on a course that would put us side by side. Instinct told me that was a bad idea. I changed direction, dodging behind a group of hill-walkers who were properly dressed and wearing broken-in boots I rather coveted. As they moved into the line, I fell in beside them. I glanced along the line to my right, checking that Ryan was a safe distance away. Then I looked to the left and felt my heart stop, because Will was about the same distance away on the other side. I stared at him, willing him to look round, to make eye contact with me, to acknowledge that I was there in any way. He gave me the benefit of his beautiful profile instead, ignoring me as thoroughly as I had been ignoring Ryan.

"Any room for me?" It was Mr. Lowell, pink-faced in a knit cap and a hideous purple jacket, pushing into the line beside me. *Oh great.*

He seemed pleased to see someone he knew. "Jess, good of you to turn out."

"I was thinking the same about you."

He shrugged. "It's the least I can do. Poor Gilly. I hope we find her."

I didn't dare reveal the truth about Dan's plan to him, so I just nodded.

He rubbed his hands together. "Cold, isn't it?"

I agreed that it was indeed cold. The camera crews had set up on the other side of the field, near the treeline. Dan was striding up and down, alternating between his megaphone for barked instructions to the assembled crowd and his radio. The police officers sprang into action, pulling people into line.

"Do you know Inspector Henderson?" Mr. Lowell asked me. "I saw you talking to him."

"Oh—he's a neighbor." I really didn't feel like going into detail about our exact relationship, especially since I didn't know. My boyfriend's dad? My *ex*-boyfriend's dad? "He was just saying hello."

A search dog wandered down the line on a long lead, sniffing the ground and people's shoes as his handler walked behind, chatting to the search party. It was a spaniel with long floppy ears, and it was just about the cutest thing I'd ever seen in its little police jacket.

"A dog," Mr. Lowell observed. If he kept up this level of insight, I was going to have to fake a faint, because I wasn't sure I could stand it.

The dog came closer to us, trotted past, and then doubled back to sniff our feet. I laughed. Mr. Lowell took a short, panicky breath and stepped away a little.

"I don't like dogs."

"I think it's friendly," I said.

As if the dog knew that Mr. Lowell was uneasy, it followed him, whining a little. The handler caught up with it, looping the lead around his hand.

"Come on, Bertie. What are you playing at?"

Bertie rose up and put his paws on Mr. Lowell's thigh, his tail wagging. He barked.

"I've got sandwiches in my pocket," Mr. Lowell said. He had his hands curled up to his chest as if the dog was going to snap at him any moment. "Ham sandwiches. That's probably it, isn't it?"

"Could be," the police officer agreed. "You probably think these dogs are infallible but they're not machines. Bertie gets distracted now and then. He goes chasing after foxes and rab-

174

bits and all sorts." He pulled on the lead. "Come on, Bert. Back to the car, mate."

Bertie's tail swished happily. He jumped up at me, his claws scrabbling on my jeans, then allowed himself to be dragged away. I felt hot with secondhand embarrassment. Everyone was looking at Mr. Lowell, laughing at how terrified he'd been. It was attention I could have done without.

Mr. Lowell rubbed at his leg. "Mud everywhere. That's annoying."

I looked at the field before us. "I think we'll get more muddy before we're finished."

"You're probably right." He came back to stand in the line, still worrying at the mark on his trousers. "All part of the experience, isn't it?"

"Yeah," I said. "Absolutely." *Life on the edge.*

At long last we started walking, covering the ground more slowly than I could have imagined. The earlier rain had cleared away and the sky was blue, shading to pink where the sun was starting to set. To the left, in the distance, an enormous cloud of starlings lifted up from the ground and began to perform incredible acrobatics, pure black against the pastel winter sky. They spun and twisted into different shapes that seemed choreographed, always on the verge of making something recognizable, if they would only hold still long enough for me to be able to see what it was.

"Amazing, isn't it?" Mr. Lowell said. "It's called a murmuration of starlings. Lovely word."

I nodded and went back to staring at the ground in front of my feet, stepping carefully so I didn't trip on the uneven earth. I thought about Gilly, and Max, and whether Dan would

175

talk to Max then or later or never. I thought about Ryan and what I should say to him. And I thought about Will, when I could bear to.

The search party was extremely well disciplined, probably because Dan was too terrifying to defy. It wasn't until we reached the trees that the line began to break as people encountered different obstacles, moved sideways and found themselves separated from their previous companions. I took the opportunity to drop back and hide from Mr. Lowell, not feeling remotely bad about it. I watched him disappear among the trees, the lurid jacket making him easy to spot. *Danger: Boring in Progress.* I waited for a minute, then moved off in the opposite direction.

And stopped. I could hear something in the distance.

Something that made me catch my breath, then start running as fast as I could.

16

In the still winter air it was easy to follow the sound of raised voices. I scrambled over a fallen tree and narrowly avoided sliding into a hollow full of dead leaves as I ran toward them, saving myself with an awkward, twisting leap. I rounded a little copse of birch trees and finally saw them, not ten meters away, facing each other, anger radiating off them like heat. And it wasn't the first time I'd seen Will and Ryan fight, but it was the first time I'd seen them do it and mean it. Just as I saw them, Ryan said something I couldn't hear. Whatever it was, Will stepped forward and shoved him hard in the chest. He fell back a couple of paces, then came at Will with all the frustration and anger he never showed me. If I'd ever wondered whether Ryan really cared about me, I could see it then, and it made me feel worse than ever. He shoved Will in exactly the same way as Will had hit him, and I heard Will grunt as the air exploded out of his lungs. It was his turn to put some distance between his opponent and himself until he'd recovered. Ryan smiled thinly at him, watching him get his breath back.

"Your problem is that you don't trust her."

"My problem is *you*." There was something terrifying in how calm Will sounded, an absence of emotion that would have had me running scared if it had been directed at me. As I knew only too well, you can dislike your father as much as you want but you can't duck your genetic inheritance forever, and Will's was surfacing at just the wrong moment.

"Then deal with it. Because I'm not going anywhere."

"Stop it, both of you." I ran up and tried to get between them. I might as well have been a buzzing fly. Neither of them so much as looked at me, too busy staring at one another. Then Will backhanded me out of the way, gently but firmly.

"Hey," I protested.

He didn't look away from Ryan. "I don't want you to get hurt."

"Stay out of it, Jess," Ryan said.

"If you're fighting over me, please stop," I said.

"It's not about you." Ryan glowered at Will. "It's about the two of us needing to sort some things out."

So the ceasefire they'd agreed the last time Will was home from school had come to an end, I gathered. That hadn't lasted long.

"I need to talk to both of you, separately." I looked from one to the other, not seeing any sign that they were listening. "This isn't the way to solve anything." I might as well have been speaking Mandarin. It was like being in a dream where your voice doesn't make any sound and you can't run. I felt weak, helpless, and pretty much desperate to stop them. I looked around, but the rest of the search party had broken up, drifting away in groups, so we were alone.

And then they moved. It was like dogs scrapping. One moment it was all raised hackles and growling, the next they had launched themselves at one another. It happened too quickly for me to see who threw the first punch, and maybe they'd both lunged at the same time. Certainly they both seemed completely committed to the task in hand—which was tearing the other person apart. It wasn't a pretty fight. It was punching and shoving and gouging eyes. It was a kick to the thigh that wrung a string of curses from Will. He tried to hide the fact that it was hurting him, but he limped from that point on and I could tell he was trying to guard it. Ryan saw it too, and concentrated on that side of his body, driving him back against a tree. He tried to smack Will's head off it and got a solid punch to his chest for his trouble. That gave Will enough space to push off the tree, bent low, his shoulder catching Ryan in the exact spot where he'd just hit him. Then he pulled back and hit him with a jab to the stomach, bringing Ryan to his knees. He bent over, wheezing, holding onto himself.

"You're going to really hurt each other," I said, desperate. "Will, stop."

His chest was heaving, his face battered. "Jess, you don't understand. This has been coming for a long time."

Ryan nodded from where he knelt on the ground. One of his eyes was closing and he had a trace of blood under his nose. He still looked as if he had plenty of fight left in him, though, and even as I watched he started to get up again. "Just go, Jess. Let us do this."

I turned away from them and ran. I wanted to cry—I

needed to—but I couldn't let myself. There was only one thing I could think, and I knew it would cause as many problems as it solved. But the alternative was unthinkable.

I burst out of the trees and stopped, searching across the huge field for the familiar figure I needed, hoping he was still there. It took a minute, but eventually I spotted Dan Henderson's dark head and started to run toward him. He was deep in conversation with two women, both in trouser suits. The police radios they carried gave away what they were: detectives. They were nodding as Dan spoke, concentrating on what he was saying, so when I slithered to a stop beside him, the three of them looked round in surprise.

"Dan," I gasped. "You have to come."

"What is it? Gilly?"

"Will."

His eyebrows snapped together. "Jess, I'm a little busy . . ."

"Please." I took hold of his arm and pulled. "Please."

There must have been something in my face that told him it was urgent. He thrust the clipboard at one of the detectives and followed me. I went unerringly toward the place where the boys were fighting, tracing the route I'd taken on my way out, ticking off the landmarks as I passed them. It was getting dark now under the trees, the bushes losing their shapes, submerging into the shadows. Dan was surefooted, and faster than I might have expected. He grabbed my arm and more or less dragged me over the places where I might have stumbled as I told him what was going on up ahead. It didn't take much explanation, which was lucky, because I didn't have the spare oxygen for that.

"Of all the times to pick. Stupid little—" He bit his lip, not saying what he was thinking, but I could fill in the blanks myself.

As soon as Dan saw them through the trees, thumping one another in an increasingly weary way, he abandoned me. I could make my own way toward them and take my time about it, it seemed. He ran straight at them, silent until he got to within a few meters. Then he let rip with a roar that sent the birds rocketing out of distant trees.

"WILL! What the HELL do you think you're doing?"

The two of them sprang apart, panting, as I caught up. I stopped at the edge of the clearing, to one side so I could see Dan's face as well as the two boys. As soon as they were interrupted, Ryan slumped to the ground, his hands braced behind him, as if he'd just finished a long race. His chest was heaving and he let his head fall back, wincing in pain. Will managed to stay on his feet, but with an effort. He staggered, reeling with exhaustion. He had a cut on his eyebrow that had bled down his face and he was soaked in sweat despite the winter chill. He was gasping, the air sawing in and out of his lungs with a rasp. He squinted at his father out of the eye that wasn't covered in blood, then looked past him to me.

"Good one, Jess." It took him two breaths to say it.

"What was I supposed to do?" I was on the verge of tears again.

"Don't blame her." Dan shook his head, disgusted. "You have to let me down, don't you? Every time."

"Dad. That's not—"

"This—today—it wasn't about you and your girlfriend, Will. It was about a missing teenager who might never be found." He stopped, letting the words sink in. "Never. And she's my responsibility now. Because she's gone, and her parents are waiting for me to bring her back, alive or dead. If she is alive, she might not be the person she was before she left. If she's dead, that's it. End of story. Thanks for sixteen years of hard work, Mum and Dad, but that's all you get." Dan paused again, but this time I had the impression it was because he was struggling for composure. "And this is a big day for me. I'm in charge here. I've got the whole world and their cameras watching me, waiting to see if Gilly will be home by Christmas. The very least you can do is stay out of the way, even if you can't actually do anything useful."

I saw Will flinch, but he didn't say anything.

"Do you want to tell me why you and this idiot are hitting seven kinds of crap out of each other?" Dan demanded. "Do you want to explain to me why that's more important to you than Gilly Poynter? Because I would dearly love to hear an explanation."

"Dad," Will said again, and it was painful to see how nervous he was. "I was just—I didn't mean—"

Ryan struggled to his feet, brushing dead leaves off his jeans. He came to stand beside Will, shoulder to shoulder. "It was me too, sir. It was both of us. We were fighting because we had a stupid argument."

"About what?" Dan jerked his thumb in my direction. "Her? Do you really need me to tell you she's not worth it? Don't make the mistake I did. A pretty face doesn't matter. They'll all lie to you. They'll all let you down. Jess isn't any different."

I felt my face burn. Will's whole body jerked and Ryan grabbed hold of his shoulder, muttering something. Will's hands were bunched into fists and I could see it was the end;

182

he'd had enough. It wasn't that Dan had insulted me, it was that he was systematically tearing down everything that mattered to Will. He would trample all over him if Will didn't stand up to him.

"Yes," Dan said, and I could hear the anticipation in his voice. "Go on. Hit me. See what happens then. I've been waiting for this for years. Show me what you've got."

Will put his head back, blinking hard, trying to keep from crying.

"You can't do it, can you? Because you're your mother's son." Dan shook his head. "You look like me but there's nothing of me in you."

"Thank God," I said, unable to stay silent any more.

Dan twisted round to look at me. "I think you've done enough, young lady."

"She didn't do anything." Will shook Ryan's hand off his shoulder, but it wasn't aggressive. It was just that he didn't need the support any more. "If you want to fight me, Dad, hit me. We might as well get it over with. Let's face it, the only way you'll ever beat me is if someone else gets there first."

"Are you challenging me?" Dan asked, his voice deceptively quiet.

"Yeah. If that's what you want. If that's what you have to do." Will shook his head slowly. "But I'm not going to hit you first. And you're not going to win. So you decide what you want to do and I'll play my part. And then maybe you can get over making a couple of bad decisions a long time ago and get on with the rest of your life instead of trying to torture me for mistakes you made." He took a deep breath. "You've made me hate you, but I'm still not going to hit you."

Dan stood there for what seemed like a long time, staring at his son. "Well. Maybe you're not all your mother after all."

Will gave him a look full of loathing and walked past him, then past me without so much as blinking in my direction. Ryan followed, still wincing. I couldn't tell if he was trying to catch up with Will or not. The last time they'd fought, they'd been best friends afterward—just as they'd been all those years ago, before they argued. Blood brothers. I didn't know what to expect this time, except two conversations I needed to have and would rather have avoided.

Dan turned and watched them go, and I couldn't read the expression on his face at all. Eventually he remembered I was there.

"Was that what you were hoping would happen?"

"Almost none of it."

He grinned at me, incredibly. "You should have known better than to ask me to help. I could have arrested both of them."

"Maybe that would have been better than challenging your only son to a fight."

"They're not fighting any more," he said softly. "Now which one are you going to put out of his misery? Or are you going to string it out a bit longer?"

"That's not—" I stopped myself. "I don't want to play this game. And you have work to do."

"I do."

"So thank you, but I don't want any advice from you."

"I think you need it."

"I'm sure you do." I hesitated, knowing it was risky to go on, like running toward a cliff. I decided to do it anyway. "You know, I'm pretty sure you're going to find Gilly."

"Thanks for the vote of confidence." Dan waited, knowing there was more coming.

"I heard it in your voice when you talked about her. You care about her. You'll find her, whether she's alive or not." *Over the edge.* "But if you're not careful, you're going to lose your son."

The seconds stretched out. "Is that what you think?" he said at last.

"It's what I know." And then I walked away, leaving him standing on his own in the darkening forest.

17

The field was gray in the fading light as I started to trudge across it. I felt tired in every inch of my body, and in my brain. I wanted to lie down and sleep forever. But I couldn't allow myself to do that. I had to try to fix the things I'd broken.

It was a long walk back. Most of the searchers had already left, packing themselves away into their cars and driving off into the gloom. I'd expected to see someone I knew so I could ask for a lift, but there were only strangers kicking off muddy rain boots and folding themselves into their cars, and I didn't really feel like begging a favor from a stranger. A long way off, I saw Will's ancient Ford Capri, which he'd nursed back to life. I was much too far away to attract his attention, even if I'd thought that was a good idea. I pressed myself into the hedge to make absolutely sure he couldn't see me, and even as I watched, he pulled out and drove away. I kept walking, picking up speed now. A country road was no place to be walking on a dark winter evening. I passed a black Golf GTI that was coated in mud, and jumped out of my skin when the driver beeped the horn and rolled down his window.

"Want a lift?" Ryan sounded exactly the same as ever, as if the scene in the woods had never happened. If his face hadn't been in tatters, no one would have guessed what he'd been doing half an hour before.

"Thanks." I went round and got into the passenger seat. It was the first time I'd ever been in Ryan's car and I looked around, curious. The back seat was piled high with assorted crap, including old trainers and school books, and the floor at my feet was covered in crumbs. "Wow. Showroom condition."

"Not a priority." Ryan gave me a sidelong grin. The eye that had been closing was now swollen shut. He started the car and swung out into the road, then started laughing.

"What?"

"Nothing. It's just that my whole body hurts, and laughing is better than groaning."

"Are you OK to drive?"

"Probably."

I was staring at his hands as they held the steering wheel. They were reddened and slightly swollen. "I really wish—"

"What?"

"That you hadn't done that."

"Sorry," he said shortly. "It wasn't only about you, if it helps."

"What was it about?"

"We just don't get on."

"So I noticed."

"Yeah. Well. I said some things to him I probably shouldn't

187

have said, and he said some things to me that weren't all that nice—and I mean it. I am sorry."

"I'm not blaming you. I blame myself." I squeezed my hands together between my knees. "I like you, Ryan. I like being around you. You make things so easy for me. But I shouldn't be here in this car, and I shouldn't have gone skating with you."

"Because it makes Will jealous?"

"No. Will needs to deal with that himself." I took a deep breath. "Because it hurts you. It's selfish of me. And I need to stop."

"Do I get any say in this?" Ryan asked.

"No." I smiled at him. "Because you have zero sense when it comes to girls."

"To you, you mean."

"I doubt I'm unique."

"I've never met anyone like you," Ryan said simply. He was concentrating on the road and it made it easier to hear him say it, to respond honestly instead of with a change of subject or a smart remark or a roll of my eyes.

"I wish I deserved the way you feel about me."

"Who says you don't?"

"I do." I tried to swallow the lump in my throat, but it wouldn't move. "I'm a terrible, terrible person to be with. Will and I—we're just tearing each other apart, bit by bit. You should be glad we never got together."

"What's the problem between you?"

"I don't know." I looked down at my hands. "We fight all the time."

"If you want my opinion," Ryan said, "you keep pushing him away. Maybe you need to work out why."

"It's not because I don't love him," I said quickly. "I do."

"Yeah, but you just said it yourself. You know you're not perfect so you don't think you deserve to be loved. You won't let yourself believe that he really cares about you, or that you're worth it."

I blinked, wondering how it was that Ryan saw so much while I understood myself so little.

"Do you remember when we were skating earlier, and I told you to trust yourself?" Ryan looked at me again, checking I was paying attention. "And then it all went a lot better, didn't it? You flew."

I remembered.

"So, do that. Trust yourself. Trust in how you feel. Because if you don't trust yourself, how can you trust anyone else?"

"You're not just a pretty face, are you?"

"You wouldn't believe how long I've waited for someone to notice that." We had arrived at Sandhayes. Ryan pulled up outside the gates. "You need to talk to Will. Sort it out, or break up with him. I know what I'd prefer you to do, but that doesn't mean it's the right choice for you."

I shivered. "I don't know what to say to him."

"You'll work it out." He gave me the lopsided grin that was all he could manage with the damage to his face. "I just want you to be happy, Jess, preferably with me. But unless you get Will out of your system, that's not going to happen."

"I don't think I can get him out of my system, though." I stared out through the windscreen. "Even if we broke up, I think it would break me."

"I wish someone felt like me the way you feel about him," Ryan said quietly.

"But you have a hundred girls chasing you."

"It's not the same," he said. "It's not real. It's a game for them as much as for me. I think that's one reason why I can't forget about you, even though I should."

There was no easy way to say it. "Maybe if you actually chose someone based on their personality rather than purely on looks you might find someone who was capable of caring about you."

"Ouch."

"Sorry."

He sighed. "You're right. You can't be the only attractive and intelligent girl in town."

"I'm definitely not." I put my arms around him and hugged him, leaning awkwardly across the gearstick. "Thanks, Ryan."

"Anytime."

I started to get out of the car and kicked something metallic that had slid out from under the passenger seat. "What was that?"

"Some rubbish, probably."

I bent to see, using my phone as a torch. "Oh. Lip balm." It was in a little tin with pink roses all over it.

"It's not mine," Ryan said. "In case you were wondering."

"Whose, then?"

"Yolanda's? Some other girl?" He gave me a one-shouldered shrug. "There have been girls in this car before. I know it's hard to believe."

"Do you think . . . could it be Gilly's?"

He leaned back in his seat. "I have no idea."

"Because Max borrowed this car, didn't he?" Ryan nodded.

I was thinking fast. "Let's leave it where it is in case someone comes back for it."

"Oh no, it's really going to bother me if my car is untidy." Ryan grinned again.

"Try to cope." I got out and watched him drive away. He probably would leave the lip balm where it was, and he probably wouldn't think about what it meant if it did belong to Gilly. I'd need to tell Dan. At least I'd learned the hard way not to touch it, or take it away with me.

I looked up at the house and made a snap decision. Instead of going in I went round the back, letting myself through the gate into the garden. It was dark, but I knew the way well enough, down to the back wall beside Tilly's studio. I clambered up the wall and sat on the top for a minute, looking at the back of Will's house through the trees in his garden. There were a few lights on and I matched them up with the rooms I knew: Karen's room where she spent her days. I could see her through the window, sitting up in bed, the curtains pushed back. The flickering shadows in the room told me she was watching television. The next room along was Will's, but the light was off. The bathroom, on the other hand, was lit up, and I saw a movement behind the frosted glass.

I jumped down from the wall and went through the garden, picking my way carefully. It was hugely overgrown, Dan not being remotely interested in anything to do with mowing lawns or pruning trees. I picked up a handful of small stones as I went. The kitchen light was on but there was no one inside, I saw, and beyond it all was darkness. I stepped back and aimed for the bathroom window. The first stone hit the ledge.

The second bounced off the glass with a satisfying thud. So did the third.

Will opened the window and looked out, apparently neither surprised nor pleased to see me. "What do you want?" he said in a low voice. His hair was wet.

"Can I come in?" I hissed.

"Now?"

"That's what I was thinking, yes." I moved back a step so I could check on Karen: still safely absorbed in whatever she was watching.

Will didn't answer me straightaway. This was exactly why I hadn't texted him or called first. I'd thought it would be a lot harder to say no to me when I was standing in front of him.

But maybe not impossible.

Eventually, after a few seconds that felt like centuries, Will sighed. "Hold on." There was a pause while he came down to the back door. I heard the sound of the key turning in the lock and then it opened. Will shivered as the cold air struck his skin. The only thing he was wearing was a bath towel wrapped around his waist. Bluish red marks bloomed on his torso, legacy of the fight. Washing the blood off his face had helped, but he still looked rough, and tired, and irritable. "Hurry up," he said when I didn't move.

"Yes. Sure." I went in past him, thinking I knew how to pick my moments.

He shut and locked the door, then went back upstairs and I followed, staring at his back. The skin was red, with grazes here and there from being slammed against the trees, and a really horrible purple-black line of bruising halfway across his spine. It hurt to look at it and to know what he'd done to Ryan

192

in return. He led the way to his room, where he grabbed a pair of jeans off the back of a chair.

"Wait here."

I sank down on the end of the bed, not daring to do anything else. He went back out and I heard him shut the bathroom door. The music from Karen's television was blaring. I hadn't been in Will's room before. Sandhayes was a more comfortable place for both of us to be, especially since both Karen and Dan detested me. From where I sat I could look around at Will's impeccable bedroom, as neat and obsessively tidy as he was in all things. Ryan's room probably looked as if a bomb had hit it, but Will's belongings were carefully arranged. I leaned back to gaze through the window at the lit windows of Sandhayes in the distance. I wondered if he stared at my house the way I stared at his.

Footsteps: Will, returning. He was wearing the jeans now, but his torso was still bare. He threw a tube of antiseptic to me. "Since you're here, do you mind? I can't reach the cuts on my back."

"Sure." I made room for him on the end of the bed and he sat with his back to me, his elbows on his knees. I tried not to notice how broad his shoulders were.

"How did you get back?" Will asked. "Did Dad drive you?"

"No. Ryan."

Will nodded, as if that was what he'd expected. "I waited for you for a bit but I didn't see you."

"I wasn't ready to talk to you."

"But Ryan was fine."

I stopped smudging the antiseptic on. "He was, actually. He was easy to talk to. I told him I didn't like the two of you fighting and he apologized. And then I apologized to him for putting him in the middle of our problems."

Will's head dropped a fraction. He didn't say anything.

"So what now?" I asked. "Are you and Ryan going to fight every time you meet? Or just ignore each other?"

"Neither. We talked. Afterward. I had to thank him for standing up to Dad."

"It was only fair. It wasn't right that Dan was blaming you for what happened."

"I knew he would." Will looked back at me. "Thanks for getting him to come along. I owe you one for that."

"I couldn't think of anything else to do. I thought you'd kill each other."

He looked away again. "Possible, but unlikely."

"Ryan wouldn't tell me why you argued. He just said it wasn't all about me."

Will sighed. "I started it. I told him to leave you alone."

I concentrated on smoothing on the antiseptic, and on remaining calm. "Because you don't trust me not to cheat on you."

"No. I knew you'd think that, and no. Absolutely not."

"Why, then? Why does it matter? I don't understand why you have to fight over it if you know I'd never do anything behind your back."

"It's because of lots of things." Will drew in a breath sharply as I touched one of the deeper cuts. I jumped back, and he said, "Keep going."

"Then keep talking."

"It's because he's had it easy for years. His parents give him whatever he wants, and mine can't or won't do the same. You saw his car. It was new when they bought it for him. Mine cost fifty quid and I fixed it myself."

"Hey, Port Sentinel is full of people a lot richer than Ryan. That's not a good enough reason to hate him."

"I don't hate him. But I fought my way through school here. He was friends with everyone. He was good at everything, but no one minded that he was clever because he was popular. I got my books stolen and thrown into the toilets and ripped and ruined until I beat up the three biggest bullies, one after the other, and made them leave me alone."

"I didn't know that."

"You knew I was the policeman's son. And you knew that people hated me for it."

It was true, I had known that.

"And you know Ryan and I were friends before he turned his back on me. I tried to help him and he used it against me."

Will was talking about something that had happened years earlier, when he'd told his dad Ryan was going to get beaten up, and Ryan had hated him for it.

"I thought you'd got over that."

"We did. That's the thing. We'd put all that behind us. But it keeps coming back." Will rubbed his eyes, his voice blurry with tiredness when he said, "He's not used to losing. He hates the fact that I've got you, so that's enough reason for him to want to punch my lights out. And I hate the fact that life is so easy for him. He's got everything he ever wanted." He twisted round to look at me. "I've only got you. So I told him to leave you alone."

"I understand, I think," I said carefully. "You think he's overprivileged. But he's popular because he's nice to people.

He's just been telling me what's wrong with our relationship and how to fix it. He's a good person."

"It's easy to be good and nice when you don't have to fight for what you want."

"Everyone has to fight for what they want," I said flatly. "Life isn't easy for anyone. The rich people have problems. The beautiful people have problems. No one gets everything they want. You should be proud of what you've achieved without any help or support from anyone."

"I am."

"Well, Ryan's never going to have that. He's never going to feel like he's got where he is on his own merits. But he's probably not going to let it torture him, unlike you." I put the cap back on the tube of antiseptic. "You're done."

"Thanks." Will stood up and pulled on a T-shirt, wincing as the cotton brushed against his skin. "Sorry."

"For fighting? You should be. It was stupid."

"Yeah, I got the impression that was how you felt."

"I'm sorry too."

"You are? You didn't do anything wrong."

"Except for stealing the diary. And skating with Ryan. And telling your dad about you fighting."

He sat down on the chair, leaning back, then sitting upright with a hiss of pain as the grazes made their presence felt. "OK. Well, I'm guessing Dad gave you a hard time about the diary. You really have a problem with poking your nose into other people's business."

"Other people's problems are easier to solve than my own," I said. "Your dad was OK. I learned my lesson, though, anyway."

"Skating with Ryan . . ." Will sighed. "If it had been anyone else, I wouldn't have been such a dick about it. So don't apologize for that."

"Which leaves Dan."

"Which leaves him." Will rubbed his head ruefully. "Do you know what the worst thing is? I hate him, but I still want him to be proud of me."

"I know," I said. "I get it."

"Do you?" He looked away, listening to the music jangling from down the hall. "I hate both of them. Mum gets at me all the time, trying to make me pick her side of whatever argument they're having. And Dad despises me. I wish I could just go and never come back. But Mum wants me here and I can't turn my back on her when she needs me."

"She seems a bit better," I said, thinking of how she'd looked in the doorway when I'd seen her with Dad.

"She's seemed worse than ever since I came home. She can barely do anything for herself." He sounded worried, and exhausted, and guilty, which was exactly how Karen wanted him to feel.

"You can't live your life for your parents. They're not your responsibility. You said that to me, remember?"

"Yeah, and I still believe it. But this is different. It will end. She'll die, and Dad will move on, and I'll get out of here." Will stood up, restless, and turned away from me. "I just hate waiting for her to get sicker. I hate hoping for her to get worse, just to end this."

I stood up too, and leaned my head against his shoulder. I put my arm round him so my hand was on his heart. "I wish I could help you. I wish I knew what to do to make it better."

"Just be you."

"Yeah," I said quietly. "I've always worried that's not enough."

"It's enough for me." Will turned round and traced the line of my cheek with a finger.

I went up on tiptoe to kiss him, very gently, careful of his bruises, then stepped back.

"Now let's get out of here before your dad comes home."

18

I was working in the Christmas market the next afternoon, and it was busier than on any other day I'd been there. It was the day before Christmas Eve and the shoppers were out in force. We'd sold out of handmade cards and wrapping paper, and the customers were focusing their attention on the prints and small sketches that had sat, unloved, on the shelves up until now, which meant that the daily takings had jumped enormously. I was happy to be occupied, to be useful, to be thinking about something other than my love life or Gilly's disappearance.

So it was a shock to look up halfway through the afternoon and see a face I recognized on the other side of the market. I recognized him from the news I'd watched the previous night: Gilly's father. Dan had persuaded him to appear at a press conference in front of all the cameras and journalists who'd been filming and photographing the search. The camera flashes had made him blink and stutter as he sat at a table with a picture of Gilly behind him. He had spoken briefly, with lots of long pauses, and had seemed to be on the verge of tears all the way through his statement. I'd have recognized him as being related to Gilly even without having seen him on television: he had the same small features and curling hair, although his was graying and going thin on top. It was strangely unsettling to see her features divided between her parents, to recognize her in both of them, and neither.

There was no sign or mention of Gilly's mother during the press conference. I didn't know if that was because she'd refused to be involved or if she just hadn't been invited to attend. She wasn't the most approachable person. I could imagine the public being less than moved by an appeal from her. Gilly's dad, however, had been perfect. He'd talked about how much he loved Gilly, and how much he missed her, and Tilly had had to leave the room. I forgot, now and then, that she was still grieving for her own daughter, whose place I had taken in Sandhayes but whose shoes I could never, ever fill. Gilly's disappearance was a huge news story, especially since it was coming up to Christmas. Everyone wanted to see her safe and well and back with her family.

Mr. Poynter was standing with a young girl, maybe ten years old, who was holding his hand. She looked very like Gilly too, and slightly scared by the throngs of people who were pushing past them.

"Can you manage without me for a bit?" I asked Mum. "It's important."

"Of course," she said, because she was too nice to say anything else and she realized that it mattered to me. I knew she was struggling to keep up with the customers as it was. As if she heard me thinking it, she looked at me pleadingly and added, "But don't be too long, Jess."

"I'll try." I ran, bolting out of the back door of the hut and jumping down the steps to the ground. I hurried round to the front, hoping that Gilly's dad and sister would still be where I'd last seen them. For a heart-stopping moment I couldn't find them, but then the crowds parted and I saw Mr. Poynter's bewildered face. I kept my eyes fixed on him as I crossed the square, muttering apologies as I trod on feet and knocked into people's shopping. I caught up with them just as they turned to head for the gate.

"Mr. Poynter?"

He turned, looking wary. "Yes?"

"I'm a friend of Gilly's." I introduced myself. "I saw you on the news last night."

"Lots of people did." He sounded edgy, as if his newfound celebrity wasn't something he'd ever wanted.

"It was very good. Very moving."

Mr. Poynter was holding his daughter's hand so tightly she made a small noise of complaint. "Sorry. I just . . . Can I help you?"

"I was wondering if I could talk to you for a minute about Gilly."

"You don't know anything about where she is, do you?" He was polite but desperate, hoping against hope that I might have some answers for him. I felt a squirm of guilt: all I had were questions.

"I've been trying to find out where she's gone," I said. "I was supposed to meet her last Friday."

"At the library," Mr. Poynter said, and I realized that he'd been briefed by the police. He knew exactly who I was and what I had to do with Gilly's disappearance.

"Could I talk to you about it? Just for a couple of minutes? It really won't take long."

He looked down at his daughter. "Now's not a great time."

"I understand," I said quickly, and I did. It wasn't a nice thing to discuss in front of Gilly's sister, who might not even know she was missing. "Maybe later."

"I don't know where I'll be later." He thought for a second. "Violet, do you want to skate?"

"You said it was too busy."

"Well, it looks a little quieter now."

"Can I?" She jumped up and down. "Can I really?"

"Come on." He looked at me. "If you don't mind."

"Not at all." I looked around and spotted Darcy by the skating booth, tying her laces. "I have a friend who could help Violet skate, if you like."

"That would be good, wouldn't it?" Mr. Poynter shook his daughter's hand encouragingly. "That sounds like fun."

"Yep." She bounced all the way to the skating rink, where I grabbed Darcy just before she stepped onto the ice.

"Nice skirt." It was red and flared, and she'd teamed it with a blue jumper and yellow tights. "Bright, aren't you?"

"As a button. And this is a proper skating skirt. I made it myself. The pattern is from the 1950s, when people really knew how to dress." She attempted a twirl, but it didn't totally come off since she was already wearing skates but wasn't on the ice.

"Can you skate?" I asked, suddenly dubious.

Darcy grinned. "I insisted on having lessons after the

Winter Olympics in 2006. I was glued to the women's competition. All I wanted was sequins and white boots."

"Understandable." I laced my fingers together imploringly. "Could you do me a huge favor?"

Darcy could. Darcy was delighted to take Violet onto the ice and hold her hand while she skidded and wobbled and laughed. Violet was entranced by Darcy's outfit, her skating ability, and the way she'd done her hair (two-tone curls snaking down over one shoulder). Darcy was entranced by being found entrancing. It was a match made in heaven.

All the way at the other end of the happiness spectrum, Mr. Poynter and I leaned on the barrier and talked in low voices. He occasionally called encouragement to his beaming daughter and managed to smile at her, but his eyes were sad and his forehead was wrinkled with worry.

"I hope you don't mind me asking about Gilly," I said.

"No, I don't mind talking about her. I'll talk to anyone if it just brings her back to me in one piece." He attempted to laugh. "Not that I'm expecting you to do that."

"I was just wondering . . . when was the last time you heard from Gilly?"

"Weeks ago." His face was drawn. "The start of November. She called me and we talked for a bit."

"November? That's a while ago," I said, trying to say what I was thinking diplomatically. "Nothing since?"

"We argued. She wanted to come and live with me and her sister." Mr. Poynter rubbed his head. "I wish—I wish I'd handled it differently."

"Did you say no?"

"I told her to wait until the end of the school year—or at least until January. I told her it wasn't a good idea to change schools midterm."

"Did she say why she wanted to move?"

"She wasn't getting on with Marian."

"Marian?"

"Her mother."

There was a shock. "Did they usually get on?"

Mr. Poynter shook his head. "I don't know how she could bear her. Marian is poisonous."

"Oh," I said. "Right." That was more or less the impression I'd formed too, but I didn't want to say too much, even with that opener.

Mr. Poynter gave me a guilty smile. "Marian and I split up four years ago. It wasn't a pleasant divorce."

"Most of them aren't all that great," I said, thinking of Mum and Dad. "Why did Gilly stay with her mum?"

"She chose to. She wanted Violet to stay with me and she wanted to make sure her mother was all right. She couldn't stand the thought of her being on her own, even though . . ."

"Even though?"

"Even though she was a very difficult person to live with." He sighed. "I wasn't happy about her being with Marian."

"But when she said she wanted to leave . . ."

"I was trying to do what was best for her. I wanted her to be happy, and of course I wanted her to come back to me, but I knew it would cause huge problems with Marian. And then there was the issue of finding a school for Gilly. I said I'd look into it. I told her she'd probably have to wait until September next year, and she burst into tears, so I said I'd try to find somewhere for January. I did too." He paused for a second, and when he spoke again it was with real force. "But I wish I'd just said yes. She told me I'd let her down and I argued with her about it. But she was right."

I recalled the diary entry, the one that read as if she'd been crying when she wrote it. *Why do people have to let you down?* It fitted with the timeline.

"And that was the last conversation you had with her?"

Mr. Poynter nodded. "I tried to call her again, but it was impossible. Her phone was off. No matter when I tried to call her, I just got her voicemail. I left hundreds of messages but she never replied."

"She said she'd lost her phone."

"I wondered if Marian had taken it away to punish her for something."

"Mrs. Poynter is quite strict, isn't she?"

"Yes," he said quietly. "Very much so."

"I'm surprised Gilly had a phone at all."

"I gave it to her and paid for it. That was how I made sure I'd get to speak to her. There is a landline in the cottage, but when I rang, Marian cut me off as soon as she heard my voice."

"Did Mrs. Poynter know Gilly had the phone?"

He nodded. "She didn't like it, but she couldn't really complain. It was nothing to do with her. I paid all the bills. But I can imagine it would have given her great pleasure to have a reason to take it away. She would have been pleased that it punished me as well as Gilly. She tried everything she could to come between us as it was."

"Was confiscating the phone the sort of thing she would do to punish Gilly?"

"I think so. Gilly never told me much. She rang me when she could, and I left messages for her when she didn't answer the phone straight away, and that was that. I assumed she always had it, but maybe that wasn't true." Mr. Poynter sighed. "I should have asked more questions about how things were. I didn't want to know. I wanted to believe that she was all right even though I knew she probably wasn't."

"You could have come to see her," I said. Bristol wasn't a million miles from Port Sentinel.

"I wish I had." He was gripping the side of the rink so tightly his fingertips were bleached white. "But I didn't."

It was no wonder, I thought, that Gilly had fallen so hard and so fast for the mysterious X. Everyone else was trying to make her fit into their little boxes. X had set her free.

I don't even know who I am anymore.

I feel like this is the person I was always meant to be.

And if what they'd told me was true, Gilly had cut off her best friend, her ex-boyfriend, her parents—everyone—to devote herself to X.

And had regretted it, I thought, remembering how the diary entries had spiraled down to a dark place where despair and fear were her companions. Where she had been living in fear for herself, and for others. What I couldn't tell was whether she was scared of X or of someone else.

Because of all the people I knew who'd been around Gilly, I could think of only one who made me truly, instinctively nervous.

"Mr. Poynter, I know this is a strange question and I don't mind if you don't want to answer it, but do you think . . . is it possible that Mrs. Poynter could have harmed Gilly?"

He turned and looked at me and his eyes were haunted. "Why do you say that?"

"It's just a thought I had. She was one of the last people who saw her. So I just wondered if it was possible. In your view. Knowing them both, I mean."

Mr. Poynter nodded slowly. "It's what I thought from the start. It's what I told the police. If they're looking for someone who wanted to threaten Gilly, they should start close to home. Because if Marian found out that Gilly was planning to leave, I don't know what she would be capable of doing to her."

19

I walked into Port Sentinel's police station later that evening with the usual feeling of foreboding. It was Dan's domain. You challenged him there at your peril.

I was too familiar with peril of various kinds to take the hint. And I'd spent the hours since I spoke to Gilly's father wondering what I should do. Now that I'd made up my mind, I wasn't about to back away just because it involved talking to Dan.

"Can I speak to Inspector Henderson, please?"

The woman on the reception desk looked pitying. "He's a little bit busy, dear. I can take your details."

"It's about Gilly Poynter."

She raised her eyebrows, but took out a piece of paper. "What's your name, dear? I'll let him know you're here."

She was a large, comfortable sort of older lady, and it took her a little while to get up and put in the code to the keypad that unlocked the door behind the counter, while I simmered with impatience on the other side of the desk. The door led into the rear of the police station, and it wasn't long before Dan yanked it open and beckoned to me. I ducked under the counter and passed through into the business end of the police station, a place I found completely fascinating. Previously I'd spoken to Dan in his office, but he kept me in the corridor this time, just inside the door, as if he couldn't even spare the minute it would have taken to go down the hall. He looked tired and cross. His shirtsleeves were rolled up and his tie was pulled down.

"What do you want?"

Good start. "To talk to you about Gilly." I was half expecting him to throw me out then and there, but he was still listening. I went on, "I was talking to Mr. Poynter and I have an idea about what might have happened—"

Dan held up a hand. "Unless you have actual, solid evidence, I don't want to hear it. I'm too busy to listen to a wild theory."

"It's not a wild theory," I said. "It's based on fact. Completely."

"I'm a bit beyond theories, Jess. I've been interviewing a suspect all day and I'm about to charge them with kidnapping."

"Gilly's mother?"

Dan frowned. "Obviously not. Max Thurston."

"You're charging him? Has he said he did it?"

"No. He's not telling us anything. His parents got hold of a solicitor who's annoying the life out of me and won't let him say a word in case we use it against him." Dan shoved his hands into his pockets and leaned against the wall. "I just want him to tell me where I can find Gilly. It's in his interests to talk. He's in a world of trouble and he needs to give us all the help he can to get out of it."

"Why do you think he did it?"

Dan looked down at me as if I was insane. "You know very well. He's the ex-boyfriend. He borrowed the car. All he can tell us is that he drove around for a while that night, with no particular destination in mind. That's not an alibi, and neither is seeing you at the library, whatever he may have thought. And we've got his phone records. He got a call from the landline at fourteen Pollock Lane at six minutes past four on Friday. It lasted fifty-three seconds. Immediately after that he sent a text message to Ryan Denton's phone asking to borrow his car. Ryan didn't respond until forty-three minutes past four. And you know that he agreed to lend Max the car. We've taken it away for forensic examination, and if there is an eyelash that belongs to Gilly Poynter in it, we will find it."

"But kidnapping . . . What if she went willingly? If she rang him and asked him to help her . . ."

"Then she'd better come to the police station and tell me that."

I saw his plan. If Gilly was alive, arresting Max might be enough to bring her out of hiding. If she wasn't—well, Max was as good a place to start as any. Until they found her, alive or dead, they wouldn't be sure what had happened to her. Dan was groping in the dark just as much as I was, even if he had all the resources of the police and I only had a gut feeling that he was wrong.

Dan straightened up. "I'd better get back. They'll be waiting for me."

"Please, just give me five minutes," I begged. "It's not that long for them to wait. It might even help."

He sighed. "Five minutes. Not a second more."

210

"OK. Good." I gathered my thoughts. "Right. I was talking to Mr. Poynter earlier, and he told me that Gilly's mother was capable of harming her."

"He said that to me too."

"And?"

Dan shrugged. "Bitter ex-husband. It's not all that unusual for them to point the finger at their partner when a child goes missing."

"You mean you didn't take it seriously?"

"I didn't say that." Dan glared at me. "I take everything seriously. I looked into it and I didn't find anything to concern me."

"She took Gilly's mobile phone. She cut her off from her friends, her dad—she was keeping her a prisoner. You read the diary. Gilly just wanted to be normal like everyone else and 'M' wouldn't let her do anything."

"Speaking as a policeman who has to deal with the teenagers in this town, I wish there were more parents like that."

I kept a grip on my temper with difficulty. "But don't you see? She was controlling Gilly. She would have been furious if she'd found out that Gilly was planning to leave Port Sentinel, Mr. Poynter said. She could have harmed her. I told you she was out of it on Friday night."

Dan's eyebrows drew together. "You did. How does that fit in? Because she got wasted from guilt after hurting Gilly?"

I shook my head. "I found a mug with some sort of powder in the bottom in the kitchen, and she was slurring her words, half asleep. I assumed the two things were connected. But what if *Gilly* was the one who was drugged. What if Mrs. Poynter was faking?"

Dan sighed. "The residue in the mug was gone by the time we searched the house so we'll never know what it was. And we weren't in a position to test Mrs. Poynter's blood so I can't confirm that she was drugged. You'll have to let that go."

"It's just that she came upstairs while I was looking around Gilly's room. She'd been practically comatose in her chair, but she made it up the stairs to see what I was doing, and they're steep. I fell over and I was stone-cold sober."

"So I should hope," Dan said automatically. "But you don't live in that house. She does, and she's familiar with the stairs. You'd be surprised what people can manage through sheer muscle memory."

"OK," I said, "but what about the tissues in Gilly's wastebasket and the blood I saw on the wallpaper?"

He held up a hand. "Let me stop you there. We collected the Poynters' rubbish and went through it. We found the strips of wallpaper and tested them. It wasn't blood. It was coffee."

"How could I confuse coffee with blood?"

"You said it was dark in the bedroom. Blood looks black in the dark."

I shivered at the very thought. "And the tissues in the bin?"

"The blood was Gilly's. There wasn't a lot of it." Dan rubbed his left eye with the heel of his hand and yawned. "We're still waiting for it to be analyzed further, but it looks innocent enough. If she'd been stabbed or injured in some other way, we'd have found blood in the house, on the furniture or the walls or the floor, and we didn't."

"But Mrs. Poynter had cleaned up. The whole house smelled of bleach when I went round to get my notebook."

"Bleach isn't enough. We look at the cracks in the plaster

and the gaps between the floorboards. If there was any blood shed in that house, it was on a small scale."

I changed tack. "That doesn't mean nothing happened. If Gilly was the one who was drugged, she would have been passive. Her mother wouldn't have needed to hurt her. Before she disappeared, she'd been lying on her bed. She might have been unconscious."

"Or she was waiting for her ex-boyfriend to turn up with a borrowed car and take her to her dad's house. Except that she never got there, so Max has some explaining to do." Dan peeled himself away from the wall again. "Which is where you came in, I think."

"But—"

"I've listened to you, Jess, and I've told you what we've found out. It rules Gilly's mother out. I know she's not the most likable person, but that doesn't make her a suspect."

"Gilly was frightened. Don't you remember what she said in her diary? *I was scared before, but now I'm terrified something bad is going to happen.* She felt trapped. She wouldn't let me anywhere near her house. She didn't feel safe there."

Dan sighed. "Jess, ninety-nine percent of the time, when a teenager goes missing it's because they've run away from their parents. And if you listened to them talk about their reasons, you'd think the parents were evil incarnate. Almost always, they're not. They're doing their best to guide and protect their children from doing stupid, impulsive things."

"I just—"

"I've listened to you and I've explained to you that we investigated Mrs. Poynter as best we could. We don't have any reason to suspect her. We do have some excellent reasons to suspect Max Thurston. And now I really have to go." Dan reached past me and opened the door that led to the reception area. I went, without even trying to argue.

For one thing, I had nothing left to say. I'd tried my best to persuade him. I could go and confront Mrs. Poynter, but I shrank from doing that. As a course of action it hadn't worked out all that well for me in the past.

I walked down the steps of the police station, not knowing where to go. There was a bench just outside it and I sat down, shoving my hands into my pockets to keep them warm. It was dark, cold, and town seemed to be deserted. The forecaset for the night was terrible—gales, a high tide, driving rain. It hadn't started to rain yet, thankfully, but the wind was catching the tops of the trees, tossing them about, and my hair blew into my face. Behind me somewhere, Max was facing an increasingly frustrated Dan. If Dan was right, it was no less than he deserved. But I couldn't understand why he'd been so obvious about giving Ryan the car key back, or why he hadn't had the car cleaned when Ryan would have suspected nothing, or why, if he knew where Gilly was, he had been wandering around town like a lost soul ever since she disappeared.

Unless he'd harmed her.

I tried to imagine it, and couldn't. But I remembered Max trying to put the blame on Nessa. I remembered the look on Gilly's face when she cut herself; how Max had apparently been standing right behind me; how his could have been the voice that had prompted her to break the glass. I remembered him standing outside the classroom at school, waiting to talk to Gilly, and how frustrated he'd been. I remembered the look on Gilly's

214

face when she doubled back to talk to Mr. Lowell: desperation. You would have to be feeling desperate, I thought, amused in spite of myself, to want to talk to Mr. Lowell instead of—

And the smile died on my face.

Oh. My. God.

The moments clicked through my mind like images in a slideshow.

She would rather work with a girl . . . Take it from me, she feels strongly about it.

I knew what X wanted me to do and say, so I did it.

I'm such a coward.

Gilly's good at history. She's going to study it at university.

All that extra work for history is a giant pain in the ass. I know I should be grateful to Mr. L for taking an interest—I wouldn't even have a computer if he hadn't said I needed one—but I just can't deal with all the reading and the extra essays.

I always wanted someone to love me. I thought it would make everything better.

Now I understand that you should be careful what you wish for.

I got up and ran back into the police station, colliding with the reception desk in my haste. The woman looked up in surprise, and then she frowned. Whatever Dan had said about me, it hadn't been too complimentary, I guessed.

"Please, I *really* have to speak to Inspector Henderson again."

"He's busy."

"It's hugely important. Massively. I really need to see him."

"I'm sorry, dear, I can't let you disturb him."

215

I bit my lip, then ducked under the counter and made for the door. There was a keypad beside it and I tapped in the code I'd memorized when she went through it the previous time.

"Where are you going? You can't touch that." The receptionist was getting up, too slow to stop me. I slammed the door in her face and took off down the corridor, heading in the opposite direction from Dan's office. One of the female detectives I'd seen talking to Dan earlier came out of a room carrying a folder.

"Hi," I said. "Have you seen Inspector Henderson?"

"What—who are you? What are you doing back here?"

"I need to see him." I glanced back to see the receptionist thundering toward us and I turned back to the detective. "Please. I need to see him right now."

"Come with me, please. You're not allowed back here." The receptionist grabbed hold of my arm.

"Please." I hadn't taken my eyes off the detective's face. "I know what happened to Gilly. I know who took her."

The detective seemed to make up her mind. "Hold on, Becky."

She walked down the hall and knocked on a door. There was a pause and then it opened.

"Sir, there's someone here to speak to you."

Dan looked down the hall and his face changed from surprise to thunderous anger in a split second. "I thought I told you—"

"It wasn't Max," I said, pulling my arm out of the receptionist's grasp. "It was Mr. Lowell, our history teacher. He's X. He's the one she was sleeping with."

Dan strode toward me, his jaw clenched with rage. "Jess, this isn't a game. That's a serious accusation to throw around."

"I know. But it's true." My arm ached where the receptionist's fingers had dug in, and I rubbed it. "He was controlling her. He made her refuse to work with Max when he picked her name. He was giving her extra history lessons when she wasn't even that interested in the subject. Her mum thought she was brilliant at it, because Mr. Lowell told her that, so she was allowed to go for extra tuition with him. He was the reason she got a computer. Where they had sex at school—that's right beside the staff room."

Dan was shaking his head. "Come off it, Jess."

"She couldn't tell anyone about it. It was a huge secret. They weren't a normal couple and people wouldn't understand, she said." I played my trump card. "And he was part of the search party yesterday. He was standing right beside me. One of the search dogs barked and jumped up at him. He said it was because he had food in his pocket, but what if the dog was trying to say that he smelled of Gilly?"

Dan closed his eyes for a moment. The anger had faded out of his face, to be replaced by utter fatigue. "Right. For the record, I think you are insane. But I am prepared to go and speak to Mr. Lowell. I'm going to go and see if he's at home, first of all. If he is, and he can explain everything you've just told me, I do not want to hear one more word about him or anyone else being responsible for Gilly's disappearance."

"OK," I said, weak with relief.

"What about Max Thurston?" the detective asked.

Dan checked his watch. "We have a couple of hours left

217

before we have to charge him or let him go. No harm in leaving him a bit longer. It might persuade him to start talking."

She nodded.

"Can I come with you?" I asked.

"Not a chance," Dan said. "You're going home, and that's where you're going to stay. If you were a dog, I'd suggest your owner got you microchipped."

I grimaced. "We could go to Mr. Lowell's house on the way."

"It isn't a fun outing, Jess. It's my job."

"I know that. Look, just please let me come with you to Mr. Lowell's house."

"And say what? That you're doing an internship with me? I don't think so."

"I can stay in the car."

"Then what's the point?"

"I don't know," I said, desperate. "Maybe I might see something useful. Please."

Dan sighed. "Let me find out where Lowell lives. If it's on the way, I'll deal with him first, then you."

"OK." I was crossing my fingers as the detective disappeared into the room she'd come out of originally and looked Mr. Lowell up on the computer. Don't let anyone ever tell you that crossing your fingers doesn't work, by the way, because it turned out that Mr. Lowell lived at a point that was almost exactly halfway between the police station and Sandhayes.

I beamed at Dan. "So I can come."

"And stay in the car."

"Fine."

"And this is the last of it. You're not involved in this little adventure anymore. The end."

"Right."

"Promise me you won't try to get involved anymore."

"I promise," I said, glad beyond words that I hadn't uncrossed my fingers yet. *I promise to stay out of your way, maybe.*

Because until Gilly Poynter was safe and well, I wasn't going to make any other promises at all.

20

Orchard Grove," Dan said. "Tell me if you see any sign of an orchard because I've never spotted one around here."

Orchard Grove was the development of small houses where Mr. Lowell lived. They were designed for low-to-middle income workers who were priced out of Port Sentinel's historic houses and mini-mansions, because the millionaires still needed nurses and teachers nearby. The builders had crammed the properties together, so although Mr. Lowell's house was technically detached, there was only a narrow alley between it and the house next door. The houses were brick, with bright white pointing. Some of them looked nice, where the owners had planted the front garden and put ornaments in the windows and added a bit of individuality to their homes. Mr. Lowell's front garden was a patch of grass beside an empty driveway.

"No car," I said. "No lights on. He's not in."

"I'll ring the bell anyway to make sure." Dan pulled up

across the end of the drive, with two wheels on the grass. I watched him walk up to the front door, his head bent against the wind that was blowing in off the sea, stronger now than it had been earlier. The blinds were down. The house looked abandoned.

He knocked and waited, then knocked again. After a minute he crouched down and yelled through the letterbox, "Police. Answer the door, please."

It had precisely no effect. Dan took a narrow flashlight out of his pocket and shone it through the mail slot. Then he let the flap fall back into place, straightened up, and turned to call across to me, "No one's home. I'll have a look round the back, and then we're out of here."

I wanted a closer look, but I waited until he'd disappeared round the side of the house. I slipped out of the car and hurried up the drive. There was nothing to see through the front window—the blind fitted too snugly for that, no matter how hard I tried to peer in. But there was always the mail slot. I knelt down, as Dan had, and lifted the flap to look inside.

And the beam of a torch caught me full in the face, blinding me. "What are you doing?"

I almost didn't hear the question, I was so busy scrambling backward, acting purely on instinct. I let go of the letterbox flap with a clatter. My heart was pounding. When Dan opened the door, I stared up at him reproachfully. "You scared me."

"You should have been in the car. Why aren't you in the car?"

"I was curious." *I mean, duh.* "Why are you in the house?"

"The back door wasn't latched properly." Dan slid seamlessly into a singsong voice, as if he was reading from his notebook.

221

"I was concerned there might have been a burglary. After ascertaining that there was no sign of such a crime, I was making the premises secure."

"Did you find anything strange?"

"Nope."

"No sign of Gilly? Or a struggle?"

"No. The rooms downstairs are tidy. Nothing's strange or out of place. I haven't been upstairs, but I don't have a reason to go at the moment." He flipped his flashlight up in the air and caught it. "You were wrong."

"I can't have been." I stood up and tried to look past him. "If you let me—"

"Absolutely not." Dan pushed me back with the end of the torch. "Back in the car. Next time, I'm going to lock you in."

"Wait!" I'd caught a glimpse of something over his shoulder, something gray-blue and familiar. "Look, there, behind you. On the stairs."

He looked. "A scarf. Brilliant. Do you want to arrest it or should I?"

"That's Gilly's scarf."

"Are you sure?" He lifted it off the newel post with the end of the torch and inspected it. "How can you tell it's the one she had? Any marks, distinguishing characteristics?"

"It looks like hers."

"It's just a scarf. It might be Gilly's, and we can have it tested to see if the DNA on it matches hers. But it doesn't prove anything except that she was here."

"Don't you believe me?"

Dan was never going to make it that easy for me. "I believe that Gilly was here. But it's not enough."

I did a little dance of frustration. "What more do you want?"

"A clue?" He folded his arms. "A sign that all is not right? Because at the moment, everything we know can be explained away with the greatest of ease. According to you, Gilly was in the habit of coming here for her history lessons. Leaving something here isn't, in itself, enough to link her with him after her disappearance."

"Did you ask him when he last saw her?"

"I wasn't aware he was relevant to the inquiries we were making and he didn't volunteer." Dan smirked at me. "Not so easy to find the bad guys, is it, when you're not just blundering in and almost getting yourself killed?"

I ignored the reference to some of my previous adventures in detective work. "One way to find the bad guys is to look for them. You're in his house. Are you allowed to search it? Properly, I mean?"

"For what? Gilly?" He tilted his head back and called, "Come out, come out, wherever you are."

We both listened to the silence for a moment. "Obviously she's not here," I said. "But she *was* here. And there might be something that tells us what happened. If she was tied up, or hurt. Signs of a struggle, like you said. Traces of blood—"

"That's enough." Dan cut across me, shaking his head.

"It's just what you said to me about Mrs. Poynter's house."

"Well, I probably shouldn't have said it." He scanned the narrow hallway. "I'll have a look upstairs. Quickly, mind you. And then I'll have a word with the neighbors, who'll be just delighted to come to the door on a night like this. Get back into the car and wait for me."

223

"Seriously?" I was shivering. "It's freezing in the car with the engine off."

"I'm not leaving it running so you can stay warm."

"Why don't you let me wait here, inside the house? I won't touch anything."

Dan groaned. "This is such a bad idea, I have no idea why I'm saying yes."

"But you *are* saying it." I hopped inside before he could change his mind, and slammed the door on the wind. "Thank you."

"Don't thank me—and stand *there*." He pointed at the doormat. "Don't move off that spot."

"OK."

"I mean it, Jess. If there is anything to recover from this house, I don't want to have to explain in court why I let a sixteen-year-old girl wander around all over the evidence."

"I understand." And I would stay where he'd told me to stand. But there was nothing stopping me from leaning as far as I could to see into the living room, which was just off the hall. "Can you put the lights on? It's really creepy in here in the dark."

Dan flicked all the switches with the end of his torch.

"Don't you have gloves?" I asked, curious.

"I'm not putting them on until I have a reason to need them."

I watched him run up the stairs. Part of me hoped he would need the gloves because I was right and Mr. Lowell was the one who'd kidnapped Gilly. Another part of me just wanted to be wrong.

Once I was sure that Dan was fully occupied upstairs, I did my best Michael Jackson impersonation and leaned over as far as I could without falling. I'd promised not to touch anything, and I would keep my promise, but I could still look.

The living room was sparsely furnished, with a big television and a gray L-shaped sofa. There was a desk against the wall opposite the door, and I strained to see anything on it. Mr. Lowell was tidy and the desk looked neat. It was made of a large piece of glass resting on two trestles, and there was a filing cabinet underneath the glass. The computer was switched off, as far as I could tell. A printer sat underneath the desk, and I could see the light glowing green. So he'd been using the computer just before he left, I thought, and he'd printed something, and it was the last thing he needed so he shut down the computer quickly and headed for the door. And he'd forgotten about the printer.

I really hoped it was the kind that printed the last page out again when you pressed a button.

Dan was coming back down the stairs. He gave me a suspicious look, and I pointed down at my feet.

"Never moved."

"All right."

"Did you find anything?"

"Nope. Everything was just as you'd expect to find it."

I sighed, frustrated. "What about his computer?"

"What about it? Jess, we shouldn't even be in here. I'm bending all sorts of rules, and there's no sign of anything having happened here. No struggle. No fight. No blood."

"But maybe that's because she wanted to go away with him.

225

Or she thought she did." I pulled a face. "I can't say I get it. Even as teachers go, he's not all that great. She could have done a lot better."

"We need to go."

"Before we do, check his desk," I said. "Look, the printer is still on. What was he printing?"

Dan glanced at it. "He was replacing the ink. The old cartridge is in an envelope in the kitchen, ready to be sent back."

Mr. Lowell was an avid recycler, with a paper bin in his classroom and a dressing-down for anyone who didn't use it. The recycling habit obviously ran deep. "So do you think he was planning on coming back?"

"I should have said so. He hasn't cleared the place out. There's cash upstairs, and his passport. All of which makes me think you are entirely wrong about him. If he was doing a runner, it was a massively incompetent one."

"He couldn't come back with Gilly," I said. "She'd tell everyone what they'd done. So if he's coming back, maybe she isn't."

Dan sighed. "Or he's innocent and had nothing to do with Gilly's disappearance. Will you let it go?"

"Will you check the printer? See if you can print the last pages again."

Dan went into the sitting room and knelt down beside the printer. He fiddled with it for a bit, then shook his head. "I think replacing the cartridge wiped its memory. He must have switched it off and on again."

"Shame."

"To say the least." Dan checked the bin, then opened and closed the desk drawers. "We need to go."

226

"Can I come and look first?"

Dan glowered. "Don't touch *anything*. Point, if you have to."

I crossed the room. "What's in the basket?"

"What? This?" Dan started leafing through the in-tray on Mr. Lowell's desk. "Bills. Insurance documentation. Nothing interesting."

"No, that." I pointed at the shallow basket on top of the filing cabinet. "Is that paper?"

"Looks like." He picked the basket up and set it on the seat of the chair. "Blank."

"Check the other side. It's printed paper that he's reusing as rough paper, I bet. He does it in class too."

Dan fanned the pages out on top of the desk. "E-mails. A quote for painting the hall. Earth-shattering stuff."

"What about that one?" I was looking at one near the end. The printing was so faint in places that I could only read a little of the subject line: . . . *osit rec . . . for . . . ttage from 3/12 . . .*

Dan had picked it up and was peering at it. "I can't read this. The ink is streaky."

"That'll be why he changed the printer cartridge," I said patiently.

"What do you think? Deposit received for something cottage from the third of December, maybe?"

"Could be. Can you read any other words?" Frustratingly, he was holding it so close to his nose that I couldn't see anything.

He put it flat on the desk and switched on the lamp over it, blocking my view again. I managed to see *Swifthoo . . . Cott . . . Swifthook Cottage?*

"It seems to be an e-mail confirming that he rented a cottage

227

from now until the new year," Dan said. "He paid the deposit in cash."

"Where's that?"

"I'll have to look it up. This says it's three miles from Leemouth. From what I can see of the address, it's in the middle of nowhere."

"Just up the coast? Why would he want to rent a cottage for a month just a few miles from his house?"

"I don't know, Jess. Maybe he wanted some peace and quiet over Christmas." Dan put the paper back in the basket and guided me to the door. "And now we're leaving. You'd better hope Lowell doesn't find out we were here. I can make something up about a report of a burglary, but explaining your presence would be a lot harder."

"I won't say anything."

"Now it's time I took you home."

"But—" I said.

"You have your uses." Dan put a heavy hand on my shoulder and propelled me toward the door. "Those uses are now at an end."

I was prepared to argue the point, but I didn't get the chance. The police radio coughed into life in Dan's hand.

"All units, all units, begin Operation Eggshell immediately."

"What's that?"

Dan was looking grim. "It's an evacuation order for low-lying coastal areas. The Met Office have told us to expect a storm surge this evening and the coast guard were monitoring the height of the tide. The evacuation is far more risky and upsetting than a bit of flooding, if you ask me. I've lived here all my life and I've seen plenty of storms, and none of them caused anything like the kind of damage they're predicting." He shoved me out of the house and slammed the door behind him. "But it's still my job to manage the evacuation, so let's start with you."

21

As soon as Dan dropped me off at Sandhayes, I ran upstairs to my computer and looked up *Swifthook Cottage, Leemouth*. According to the map, it was a long way out of Leemouth, in an isolated spot right on the coast. I clicked the link advertising it for rent.

A charming seaside cottage practically on the beach! This one-bedroom pretty holiday home is perfect for honeymooners, sleeping two in shabby chic comfort. Private and secluded location, not overlooked by neighboring houses. A short drive to the shops and restaurants of Leemouth. Open-plan living room, bathroom, fully fitted kitchen, mezzanine bedroom.
NB Access via unpaved road and footpath.

The shops and restaurants of Leemouth consisted of one takeaway fish-and-chip shop, a village shop, a post office, and a pub that served food in the summer. The cottage was properly in the middle of nowhere. I flipped through the pictures, which were blurry and taken with a phone. They failed to hide the fact that the cottage was rather more shabby than chic, full of mismatched furniture. It was an old single-story building with a shaggy thatched roof. In summer, I could see how it would be a perfect holiday spot, but in winter it looked as if it would be bleak. The beach was a small cove, surrounded by dunes. It was hard to get to, and at this time of year no one would bother to make the journey. I had to hand it to Mr. Lowell: Swifthook Cottage seemed to be the perfect place to hide something.

Or someone.

I sat back in my chair, frustrated. I just wanted to go and see if I was right. Dan was far too busy with the evacuation for me to have another go at persuading him to come along with me, which meant I was stuck.

I turned off the computer but stayed in my chair at the desk, chin on hand, thinking. I had promised not to get involved.

Anyway, I didn't have a car and I'd need one to get to Swifthook Cottage.

I'd done my bit by pointing Dan Henderson in the right direction. What I'd told him would bother him, I knew. He wouldn't admit it to me, but he'd make it his business to get to Leemouth at the earliest possible opportunity. And I had enough experience of getting into trouble to know that you could run out of luck, generally when you least expected to.

Gilly had run out of luck a long time ago. Even before she met Mr. Lowell, she'd had to cope with her mother and her mother's problems. She was used to keeping secrets. She was an easy target for Mr. Lowell. He'd seen that she was isolated and he'd made sure she stayed that way. I had no doubt he'd told her to dump Nessa as a friend. He'd told her to get rid of her phone. He'd controlled everything.

The rain was whipping against the windows and drumming on the roof right above my head. The wind made the house creak like an old sailing ship in a gale. If it was this bad up the hill, I couldn't imagine what it would be like down on the seafront, with the waves smashing into the promenade. On a normal day the beach was completely under water at high tide. It would be flooding onto the road tonight. Anyone further down the town would have to hope the council had put out enough sandbags to keep the waves at bay.

And the same went for every beach along the coast. If it was going to be high tide in—I checked—two hours, Swifthook Cottage would be in trouble.

Who did I know who had a car? Hugo was the obvious answer, since he was actually in the house. His little yellow Fiat, Miss Lemon, was his pride and joy. Even though Hugo wasn't all that devoted to helping others, he found it hard to resist an opportunity to go for a drive. I went to find him. He was lying on his bed, headphones on, eyes closed. I found a rolled up pair of socks on his floor and threw them at him.

He opened an eye. "What do you want?"

"Take the headphones off."

"What?"

I mimed it instead of shouting, and very reluctantly he lifted them off.

"What is it?"

232

"Can I ask you a huge favor?"

"You can ask. I reserve the right to say no."

"Can you drive me somewhere?"

"I knew getting a car was a bad idea," Hugo said. "I should have just signed up for my taxi license and made it official. Where do you want to go? Darcy's house? If it's just round to Will's, I'm not doing it. You can walk."

"In this weather?"

Hugo groaned. "Don't make me get out of bed for a two-minute drive."

"I'm not. I don't want to go to Will's. I want to go somewhere a bit further."

"Where?"

"Leemouth. Well, just outside it."

Hugo narrowed his eyes. "Explain, please."

I sat down on the edge of the bed and did my best to tell him what had been going on with Gilly's disappearance, and where I thought she might be. He was shaking his head well before I got to the end.

"No way. Absolutely not. Even if Miss Lemon worked in wet weather, which I'm not a hundred percent sure she does, there's no way she could make it along an unpaved road, particularly if it's muddy. It's been raining for hours. She'd get stuck in a puddle."

"What about taking me to Leemouth? I might be able to get a taxi from there."

' "Might' is right. You won't. No way. Not on a night like this, and possibly not in Leemouth ever. You've been there, haven't you?"

"Once."

"So you know what it's like. It dreams of being a one-horse town. They're saving up for a Shetland pony."

"Yeah, I don't want to live there. I just want a lift."

"To do something typically crazy and dangerous. In the first place, I don't know if you've noticed, but it's a little bit wet out. It's too risky to drive around on country roads when the weather's like this. No nonessential journeys, it said on the news."

"I love how you're taking the warnings seriously when I want to go somewhere. If you were the one who had a reason to go out, nothing would stop you."

"That's possibly true. I'm not ashamed."

"You're never ashamed."

Hugo grinned. "It's a wasted emotion."

"You're not normal."

"Normal is overrated." The smile faded. "Come on, Jess. What are you going to do if you find the cottage and she's there? Break in? Make a citizen's arrest? I think your Wonder Woman costume must be cutting off the circulation to your brain."

"I just don't want to sit around while someone I know is in trouble."

"Sorry. The answer's no." Hugo put his headphones back on. Speaking a little bit louder than he needed, he said, "Not from me, anyway. And good luck finding someone else to take you on a night like tonight."

There was absolutely no point in trying to persuade him to change his mind. Hugo had spoken. I went back to my room and paced about, too tense to settle down. I did know someone else who had a car. The obvious person to ask, in many ways.

I just didn't think I had a hope of convincing him.

"I thought you'd say no."

Will was leaning forward, peering through the windscreen and the water that was cascading down it. "I probably should have."

"But you love me too much to say no."

He gave me a look. The bruises had darkened on his face. He looked tough and capable and, at that moment, amused. "I know you too well. You'll go on your own and get yourself into trouble."

"Well, whatever the reason, I'm glad you're here." I put my hand on his thigh and squeezed it. "All I want to do is see if Gilly's there. If she is, I'll call your dad and tell him. If she's not, no harm done. We go home and no one is any the wiser."

"It sounds so easy when you put it that way."

"It should be easy."

"Should be." Will was driving slowly, coaxing his car through the enormous puddles that were gathering on the roads. We were on a typical Devon lane, so narrow there was only room for one car at a time. The bends in the road and the high hedges on both sides cut your chances of seeing an oncoming car to almost nothing. There was an occasional passing place to let cars coming in the opposite direction go by, but otherwise there was nowhere to go if something unexpected loomed up. I was trying to keep the terror off my face, but I definitely felt scared. The engine stuttered and Will pulled a face.

"If we don't break down."

"Is that likely?"

Instead of answering me, he laughed, and I found myself thinking I didn't really mind if we got stuck in a ditch somewhere as long as I was with him.

Assuming it was on the way back from not finding Gilly. I could taste the worry I felt about her. It was like metal in my mouth. I wanted to find her, but more than that I wanted to check that she was nowhere near the coast, nowhere near Mr. Lowell. Safe somewhere.

Happy, even.

I wished I believed that was likely.

"It's high tide in less than an hour."

Will nodded. "We're nearly there."

"I don't want to be too late."

"We won't be. You said it was an old cottage. It'll have survived a few high tides in its time."

I realized that I was leaning forward with my hands clenched on the edge of the seat and made myself relax a little. "So there's no need to panic."

"There's never a need to panic," Will said, calm as ever. He steered the car round a sharp bend. "We'll just— Oh *shit*."

I whipped my head round in time to see a confusion of branches, and fractured but all too solid wood filling the road. *A tree*, I thought, brilliantly, before we were on top of it.

The car lurched sideways, skidded, collided with something massive and—after what felt like forever—stopped. It was leaning at an uncomfortable angle, so I was higher up than Will. Everything in the car that wasn't actually attached slid to the right with a slither and a rattle.

"God," Will said. "Are you OK?"

"I think so," I said shakily, trying to work out what hurt and why. My head had snapped forward and back again so my neck ached, and I could feel a burning sensation across my chest where the seat belt had dug into me. I'd put a hand out to brace myself against the dashboard and my whole arm felt bruised from the force of the impact. "Are you all right?"

"Yeah." Will leaned across and popped open the glove compartment to get a flashlight. Then he opened his door and slid out. "I just need to check if the car survived."

I sat and waited for him to return, staring out through the windshield at the fallen giant that blocked the entire road. Will had tried to steer round it, but there was nowhere to go. We'd ended up almost sideways across the carriageway, and there was no way I could get out on my side. I undid my seat belt and clambered over the seats.

A noise behind me made me jump, and I twisted in my seat to see that Will had opened the boot. He saw me looking and held up a reflective triangle. "Just getting this. I need to put something in the road to warn other drivers about the car."

"Is it OK?"

"It will be. But I can't move it. It's caught on a branch and I don't want to try to push it off in case I rip the engine out."

I nodded and watched him walk away, disappearing round the bend. I probably didn't breathe again until he was back in sight, talking into his phone with one hand over his mouth to cut the noise from the wind to a minimum.

When he'd finished, he poked his head through the open door. "The cops are sending a recovery vehicle, but it won't be soon. They sound a bit frazzled."

"I'm not surprised. I bet this has happened all over the place." I slid out to stand beside Will. I was shivering by now. We were sheltered from the worst of the rain and wind by the car, and it wasn't the cold that was making me shake.

Will wrapped his arms around me. "It's OK. We're fine. The car will be all right."

I leaned into him. "I know. It was just . . ."

"Yeah." Will rested his chin on top of my head. "Scary."

"I'm being a wimp. Sorry." With an effort I stood upright, on my own. "I'm sorry for getting you into this."

"All in a good cause." He sighed. "The bad news is that we're not going any further in the car."

"Is there any good news?"

He nodded. "We can walk from here."

22

Will was right. The turning for the cottage was just beyond the fallen tree. It was little more than a track, and I doubted whether the car would have got more than a few meters further. Grass grew along the middle, and I tried to walk there rather than on the sticky black mud on either side. I bent my head against the wind and rain sweeping in from the sea, following the light of the torch that Will shone on the ground in front of us. The high hedges gave us some protection from the weather, but it was still brutal, still terrifying in its power. I hadn't yet seen the sea, though I could hear the surf booming and crashing ahead of us, and the rain tasted of salt.

"Car." Will ran the beam of the torch over the back of a VW Polo that was pulled up by the side of the road. It was empty, the windows fogged with salt. The wheels were clogged with mud.

"Mr. Lowell's," I called back.

When we turned the next corner, we were facing the sea. The beach was basically gone, the sea thundering into the dunes. Every wave seemed to reach higher and higher again. We were still twenty meters from the edge of the surf, but I didn't feel as if that was far enough. There was no barrier between the sea and the land, nothing to hold the water back. It cut into the soft sand of the dunes, and every time it retreated it stole more of them away.

I climbed onto the nearest dune to get a better view, and the wind almost took my breath away. I blinked against it, battling to stay upright, and saw a light glowing not far from where we stood. The night was so black I couldn't pick out anything else—not the ridge of the roof or the white walls of the cottage—but there were no other buildings near the beach.

"I think the cottage is that way," I yelled over the sound of the waves, and pointed. "But we'll have to go across the dunes."

I followed Will as he picked out a route, staying low, looping around to come up behind the cottage. Once we reached it, the solid mass of the building provided a little shelter from the tearing wind. There were no windows this side, which sort of made sense, because who wanted to look at the rolling featureless dunes when there was the sea to stare at?

"What do we do now?" Will asked.

"Look through the windows? Try to see if Gilly's inside, and if anyone else is?"

"And if she is?"

"Call your dad."

He grimaced. "Wait here."

"What? No. I'm not waiting. You go left and I'll go right."

"You'll get blown away."

"I can cope with a bit of wind."

"OK. Don't say I didn't offer." Will headed off to the left without waiting for me to reply. I went left, gasping as the wind caught me full in the face. There was a window halfway along the side of the cottage, and I worked my way toward it, stumbling a little on the tufted grass. A generator hummed, providing the electricity for the cottage, and cover for me if I made any careless noise. The light was shining onto the ground, so I didn't want to get too close: I'd be easy to see if I wandered into it. I pulled my hood forward and crept along until I was just beside the window. Then, slowly, I inched to the left until I could see a section of the cottage's living room. It was just as dingy as I'd suspected from the Web site, although to be fair I probably wasn't seeing it at its best. The light came from the bare bulb in the middle of the ceiling. It shone harshly on the stack of furniture that was blocking the door. I couldn't tell if it was a barricade against the weather or intruders.

There was a loud boom as a particularly big wave hit the beach. I watched in horror as water swelled up under the door, seeping up through the floorboards, spreading out across the floor. I was so busy staring at it I forgot I was supposed to be keeping a low profile. I stood on tiptoe to get a better view, and then froze as Mr. Lowell walked into my line of sight, like an actor walking onto the stage. He stood with his hands on his hips, staring at the door and the water oozing back toward the sea. His face was turned away from me, but it would only take a glance in my direction for him to see me. I started to sink down, moving slowly. He looked just the same as usual—he could have been standing in his classroom, not in a cottage in the middle of nowhere. As I watched, he said something over

241

his shoulder, and I stood completely still again as Gilly came into view.

I suppose I'd expected her to be tied up, if she was there at all. I'd thought she would look desperate. She was just the same as ever. Her feet were bare and bluish with cold. She looked small, and tired, but not frightened. Resigned, if anything. She put her hand on Mr. Lowell's back and spoke to him, her face close to his. I thought she was trying to persuade him of something, or comfort him, and it was so intimate it made me feel as if I was intruding.

But then, too quickly for me to do anything to hide, Gilly looked straight at me. Her eyes widened in shock, but she didn't give me away. She stroked Mr. Lowell's shoulder a couple of times and said something else, still with her eyes fixed on mine. She tilted her head to the right and I got the message: *Come to the other side of the cottage.* Then she turned and walked away from Mr. Lowell, out of sight.

I ran, slipping and sliding on the rain-soaked grass. As I rounded the corner of the cottage, I collided with Will. He tried to hold onto me but I wriggled free. "I saw her. I saw Gilly."

"Are you sure?"

"Positive."

"Then come on." He reached out for me. "We need to call Dad."

"You do it. I have to talk to her." *And maybe rescue her.* I was thinking of the water sliding up through the floorboards, the cottage creaking as its foundations weakened.

Will took out his phone and checked. "No signal. Damn."

I checked mine. "Me neither."

242

"I'll have to go back to the road." He looked up. "But I don't want to leave you."

"You won't be long." I kissed him. "I promise I'll be careful."

I didn't wait for him to reply, but ran, hurrying in case Mr. Lowell got there first; in case Gilly changed her mind; in case there was anything I could do.

She was waiting at the bathroom window, which was small, high up, and had a bar across it for good measure. Her fingers were curled round the bar and her face was strained in the light that streamed from behind her. I got a toehold on a pipe and levered myself up so I could see into the room. She was standing on the edge of the small bath.

"Jess! Oh my God, Jess . . ."

"Are you OK?" I tried to keep my voice low. It was hard to hear over the noise of the storm, but shouting didn't seem like a good idea. "Are you hurt?"

"No—nothing like that."

"What are you doing here? Did Mr. Lowell kidnap you?"

"No! Not exactly." Gilly bit her lip. "It's complicated. I wanted to get away from my mum and he was able to help me."

"So you want to be here with him?"

"Of course. But it wasn't supposed to be like this. It was supposed to be one night, but then . . ."

"Then he wouldn't let you go."

Gilly's eyes were wet. "We can't go back to the real world. No one understands there. They'd arrest him. Throw him in jail. Stop him from being a teacher any more. All because he loves me." She shook her head. "It's so unfair."

"It's the law."

"Well, it's wrong." She moved her hands on the bar, trying

243

to get a better grip. It was old and rusty, the surface pitted with corrosion, and it rattled as she pulled on it. "But I want to leave now. I want us both to leave. I keep telling John it's too dangerous to stay." *John.* She must have seen the shock on my face. "He's not evil, Jess. He really loves me."

"He's your teacher."

"I know that."

"And he's keeping you here. No one knows where you are, Gilly. Everyone is worried. Your dad is beside himself."

She took a moment before replying. "And Mum?"

"Absolutely. She is too." A white lie. In her own way, she probably was.

"She hit me, you know. She threw a mug of coffee at me, because she was angry with me. That's how I got this cut on my cheek."

Which explained the bloody tissues in her room and the coffee stain on the wall, I thought.

"That's why I had to leave. I'd had enough." Gilly shut her eyes briefly. "This has all been a huge mistake."

"Kidnapping you? Locking you up here? It's a bit more than a mistake."

"John didn't mean any harm. He just loves me." She shrugged. "I know it's hard to believe."

What I believed was that Gilly had decided to take Lowell's side—that she couldn't or wouldn't see that he was abusing his position of trust and putting her in danger. "I believe he cares enough about you to risk everything. But does he care enough to let you go? It's too dangerous to stay here, Gilly. The tide is rising, and—"

"John says it will be fine. John says I need to trust him. The cottage has been here for a long time; we'll be OK."

I opened my mouth to answer her—and gasped as two arms went around me, holding me tightly, pinning mine to my sides. "What the—?"

"Stupid girl," Mr. Lowell breathed in my ear.

"You shouldn't have tried to interfere." It was Gilly who said it. She was looking out of the window and her eyes were cold.

"Let go of me." I tried to struggle. "Leave me alone."

"You'll tell them where we are." Gilly looked at Mr. Lowell. "Bring her inside. Then we can decide what to do with her."

I blinked. "But, Gilly—"

She slammed the window on me without acknowledging that I'd even spoken.

"Come on."

"Let go." I kicked and wriggled, making Mr. Lowell grunt with effort as he dragged me to the door. I didn't help him, but I couldn't stop him, no matter how hard I tried. He shoved me up against the building with one hand while he opened the door with the other. I hit it at an awkward angle. The door frame caught me high on one cheek and across my mouth, and I tasted blood.

"Sorry." He actually sounded it, and I felt a flicker of hope that soon dimmed and died. Before I could suggest he let me go, he pushed me through the doorway, and I sprawled on the floor, on tiles that were gritty with sand and sticky from salt. I was in the small kitchen at the back of the main room, I realized, with the bedroom overhead in a kind of gallery. The ceiling was low and the kitchen itself was dark, but at least the water wasn't coming through the floor where I was lying. Over by the door it surged up through the cracks with every wave.

For a moment no one said anything. Then Mr. Lowell slammed the door and locked it. "Well? What now?"

"I don't know. Let me think." Gilly padded up and down, her feet whispering on the floorboards. "We need to get out of here."

"With her?"

Gilly looked down at me. "She'll slow us up. Leave her here."

I sat up gingerly, my head ringing. I couldn't understand how Will and Ryan had been able to stand up and talk after hitting one another. I was reeling after one blow to the face. "I came here to help you."

"I didn't want your help. I don't want it. That's so typical of you, Jess, trying to be a do-gooder, blundering in where you're not wanted. Just like at the party."

"I didn't know what was going on."

"But it didn't stop you interfering," she flashed. "And then everyone was talking about me. Speculating. And I had to get rid of Nessa again, because she tried to worm her way back into my life, and bloody Max was hanging around, hoping I'd confide in him and be stupid enough to let him get close to me a second time. As if I would be interested."

"He's been arrested," I said. "For kidnapping you."

Gilly laughed. "Poor old Max. I bet he's feeling sorry for himself."

"Justifiably." I glanced sideways at Mr. Lowell. "Why did you call him before you disappeared?"

"I needed to get away and I knew he'd help me. I'd had enough of my mother. I tried to make it look as if she'd taken an overdose of her sleeping pills but she didn't drink enough

246

of the coffee. She got angry instead, and she threw it at me." She shot a look at Lowell through her eyelashes. "I didn't want John to have to get involved, but I needed to get away before she woke up and worked out what I'd done. She'd have noticed all her pills were gone and then she would have killed me. I'm not exaggerating. It was her or me. Of course Max let me down."

"He tried," I said. "He did his best. He just got there a bit late."

She rolled her eyes. "Typical."

"I can understand you cutting Max off. He wasn't a great boyfriend and he was a terrible ex. But why was Nessa so bad?"

Gilly wouldn't look at me. "She was too intense. She wanted to know everything I was thinking, all the time."

"She was worried about you." Quite rightly, as it turned out.

"She wanted to own me."

"That's not true," I said. "She cared about you."

"In all the wrong ways. She just wanted to take advantage of Gilly," Lowell said. "She had her own agenda."

I turned to look at John Lowell properly. "Is that what you told her?"

"It's the truth," he said quietly.

"It's really not. And what about *your* agenda? What about picking on a vulnerable girl and persuading her to trust you? What about making her lie to her friends and family?"

"I didn't plan any of this." He glanced at Gilly and smiled. "I fell in love. So did she."

"I was the one who seduced him." Gilly sounded defiant. She padded past me and wound her arms around Lowell's neck, pressing her body against him. "He couldn't resist me."

"You were scared. You wrote that in your diary."

247

"I was scared that he would leave me. I was scared he'd go to prison."

"He *should* go to prison," I said. "He deserves to."

"It's no one's business but ours. We know how we feel," Gilly said coldly.

Lowell turned his head and kissed her, his tongue probing her mouth, and I felt like throwing up. It wasn't just the unwanted public display of affection. It was fear. Apart, Gilly and John Lowell had been weak, damaged people. Together they were dangerous, egging each other on, wrapped up in one another to the exclusion of everything else. And I didn't believe that Gilly was the one who was really in charge. Lowell wasn't saying much but he was watching her, and listening closely. I felt as if she was really speaking to him, not me, to prove that she thought the way he did. He'd filled her head with doubt and hatred for the people who loved her, and made her think it was her own choice to push them away.

"OK. I get it," I said. "It's true love and she made a move on you and there was nothing you could do about it. What are you going to do now? Do you know the whole country is looking for Gilly? Do you know how much trouble you're in?"

"Don't listen to her." Gilly turned Lowell's face to hers, using both hands. "She's trying to freak you out."

"She's right, though. You've no idea. There were hundreds of people looking for you yesterday."

"They'll forget."

I laughed. "How long are you planning to stay here? Weeks? Months? Did you even think this through?"

Gilly bit her lip. "It wasn't supposed to happen this way."

"We'll work it out," Lowell said. "Don't listen to her."

248

Gilly turned to answer, but whatever she said was drowned out by a wave that battered the front of the cottage. The furniture that was piled up against the door shifted, pushed back by the force of the water that sprayed in as if it was gushing out of a fire hydrant.

"We need to get out of here." Gilly looked at me. "What do we do with her?"

"Tie her up." Lowell went over to a drawer in the kitchen and pulled out a rope. "The clothesline should do."

"Why do you need to tie me up?" I got to my feet and backed away from them. I fetched up against the stairs—little more than a ladder, really, that ran up to the gallery above.

"Because we don't want you chasing after us. We don't want you interfering in our business." Mr. Lowell smiled at me and I felt completely chilled. "You've been very rude about me, Jess. And very rude to Gilly. You can't expect me to ignore that."

Gilly looked at him adoringly, but there was the tiniest hint of doubt in her eyes. "I love you."

"I love you too." He started to move toward me and Gilly grabbed hold of his arm.

"Do we—do we have to do it this way? Can't we let her go?"

"It's so like you to be forgiving," he said, patting her arm. "But there's a time for forgiveness and a time for punishment. Trust me, I know what to do."

Another wave hit the cottage, and I felt the force of it travel through the old wood, shivering under my feet, and against my hand as I braced it on the wall.

"This building can't stand much more," Gilly said. "Let's go and find the car. We need to go somewhere else. Anywhere. It doesn't matter where we go."

"But, Gilly—" said Mr. Lowell.

"If we stay here, we die. And I'd rather die than lose you, but I haven't lost you yet." She kissed him again, and I took the opportunity to duck into the kitchen, making for the back door. Not that I stood a chance of reaching it without being noticed.

"Where do you think you're going?" Lowell caught hold of my hair and yanked me back to the stairs. I struggled, but Lowell was too strong and too quick. Gilly held my hands through the treads of the ladder and Lowell lashed the clothesline around them, so tightly that my wrists started to ache almost immediately.

"You can't do this to me," I said, desperate.

"We already have." Gilly turned to Lowell. "The key, John."

He took it out of his pocket. "We wouldn't want to leave the door unlocked."

"No, we wouldn't." Gilly flashed a triumphant grin at me. "Bet you wish you'd minded your own business now."

Anger flared, drowning out the fear for a moment. "I'm certainly wondering why I bothered."

She led the way to the side door, which Lowell unlocked. The two of them stepped out into the night, heads bent against the wind, and Lowell slammed the door. I heard the key scrape in the lock, and then nothing but the keening of the wind, like hundreds of ghosts crying a warning I didn't need to hear.

I already knew I was in trouble.

23

First things first. I twisted to see my watch. Still half an hour until high tide. Which meant that the storm was only going to get worse for the next half-hour, and there was basically no chance the cottage was going to survive without serious damage.

Which meant I had to get out of there. I didn't want to think about how long it would take Will to call his dad, or whether he would come back. There was every chance he would run straight into Gilly and John Lowell on his way back to me, and every chance that he'd try to stop them. And he didn't know any more than I had that Gilly was the dangerous one. I could imagine him tackling Lowell and getting blindsided by Gilly.

I could imagine them hurting him.

I put the tearing anxiety about Will to one side. There was nothing I could do to help him while I was trapped myself, and there was no point in waiting to be rescued. It was up to me to free myself.

I looked at the ladder first. The rest of the cottage was little more than a shack, but the ladder was new, made of solid wood reinforced with steel treads.

Luckily I wasn't depending on the ladder to be old and rickety. On my side trip into the kitchen, when Gilly and Lowell thought I was trying to get to the door, I'd managed to pocket a small rusty knife from the drawer she'd left hanging open. I'd slid it into the pocket of my jeans before Gilly grabbed me.

So all I had to do was get it out.

The next couple of minutes were not elegant, involving me struggling and swearing as I tried to contort myself in order to reach the knife handle. Lowell had tied my hands in front of my face, high up, so I had to climb up the lower treads of the ladder to reach my pocket, and as my hands went numb, they became increasingly clumsy. I was terrified of dropping the knife—I'd never be able to pick it up again if it fell on the floor. Slowly, painfully, I drew it out of my pocket, holding it in my left hand because the rope was slightly looser on that side and that hand had more feeling in it. With extreme care, I slid the blade under the edge of the rope and began to saw at it. Another bit of luck: it was a very old piece of rope and the plastic threads sheared easily under the pressure of the knife. I caught myself with the point of the blade a few times, cutting my skin, though I barely felt it. The cottage was like an icebox, but I was sweating.

Halfway through . . . two thirds of the way . . . I started to try to pull against the rope, hoping it would give way, but it was stubborn. The waves thundered against the walls, louder than anything I'd ever heard, and the knife slipped again, and I redoubled my efforts, sobbing under my breath, and at long last the few final strands parted. I yanked my hands free, care-

252

less of the rope burning my skin, and took a couple of precious moments to flex my fingers, letting the blood flow out of my hands again. They were stiff and almost useless as they were, and I needed them to work.

The door at the front of the cottage gave a loud, ominous creak under the weight of water pressing on it, and I ran to the side door Lowell had locked. I was hoping it was the kind with a latch that could open it from the inside, but of course it wasn't, and no matter how I had tugged on it, I couldn't even rattle it in the frame. I turned out the kitchen drawers looking for a spare set of keys, but of course there wasn't one—I hadn't expected there would be. That would be too easy. Leaving the jumble of cutlery and random clutter on the counter, I turned my attention to the windows, trying one after another, but they had been painted shut many times and it would have taken hours with a chisel to force them open. I didn't have either.

Which left the bathroom window. I ran in, hitting the light switch as I went. Nothing happened, and behind me the living room went dark. I paused to listen, and realized that the hum of the generator had stopped. So I could barely see, as well as everything else. *Terrific.*

I had to clamber onto the bath to open the window, just as Gilly had. It went halfway up and jammed. But I remembered Gilly's face looking through it; I knew it could open wider, and I was determined it would. Behind me, a crash was the sofa floating loose from the pile of furniture by the door. It was rattan, and it swung around the living room on the surging water like a mine, colliding with heavier pieces of furniture. I was glad I had the bath to stand on because the water was slopping around the bathroom floor too. I worked harder on the window,

253

and was rewarded with a shriek as the sash shot up the last few inches.

Which left me free, except for the metal bar that ran across the middle of the window, a deterrent to thieves—who would have had to be desperate to even think of burgling that shack. I rattled the bar, and shoved it, and jumped down from the bath to splash through the ankle-high water, hoping to see something solid to hit it with. I found an old plank, rough to the touch and slippery with seawater, and wedged it into place, and it promptly broke. I couldn't move the bar in the least, even though I remembered it was rusty and old. I just couldn't get the right angle, no matter how hard I tried, and it was wet from the rain and I started to cry. It was possible that I might be able to weather the storm in the bathroom, that I could get high enough to stay clear of the water, assuming the whole cottage didn't fall down on my head. But I wanted to get out, and I was so close to being free.

A shout in the distance made me jump. It sounded a lot like my name.

"Over here!" I held onto the bar again, this time for support as I yelled, "Hey! Over here!"

I saw a powerful flashlight bobbing in the blackness, and strained to pick out the person holding it, dark against the darkness. And another flashlight, this one reflecting yellow on a high-vis jacket. Light from the second torch briefly caught the first person, who was well ahead, and I recognized Will's dark head. Will and—I squinted—his father. Will was about ten meters away, high up on the next dune, battling against the wind as he ran along the top, his dad behind him. I stared for a little while, trying to work out what they were doing and why they hadn't come to get me—until I realized what was wrong. While I'd been trying to free myself, the water had swept in around the cottage, and now it was making a very effective moat.

Will got to the point closest to the window, where it was still possible to stand on dry ground, and half ran, half skidded down the side of the dune. He dug his foot in at the last moment, his arms windmilling as he tried to stop himself tipping into the water. He regained his balance at last and shone his flashlight at the window. "Are you OK?" He had to shout over the sound of the water and the wind.

"I've been better." I tried to keep the quavering self-pity to a minimum as I shielded my eyes from the beam. I was trying to keep some of the night vision I'd built up. "I can't actually get out."

Will looked along the side of the building. "That door . . ."

"Locked."

Dan jogged down more sedately and stood beside Will, looking ridiculously like him—a little broader, a little more solid, a little grayer. A lot more irate, obviously. "Where's the key?"

"In Mr. Lowell's pocket."

Dan swore fluently for twenty seconds while Will and I listened and, in my case, learned. "I've just put it in an evidence bag."

"You caught them, then."

"I saw the Polo driving toward us. Dad rammed them off the road," Will explained. "He scared Mr. Lowell into telling us where you were and what they'd done. But we didn't know we needed the key"

"Ah." I tried to make light of it, as if it wasn't the worst news they could have given me. "Then I'm stuck."

255

"You can't stay there." Will pulled off his shoes and dropped them behind him. "Hold on. I'm coming to get you."

"What the hell do you think you're doing?" Dan shouted. He grabbed Will by the arm. "You can't go over there without a life jacket. A lifeline. It's suicide. The coast guard are on their way, and—"

"I can't wait. *She* can't wait."

"I'll go."

"No, Dad—"

"Don't argue with me." Dan said it in a tone I'd never heard from him before. "I can't let you do it."

I heard a window go on the other side of the cottage, blown in by the force of the water. It swirled between me and the two men like the contents of a witch's cauldron. The water was full of debris—branches, bits of the cottage, God knows what—and it surged in and out with terrifying force.

"I'm going." Will dragged his jacket off over his head without even unzipping it.

"You can't go over there. I forbid it." Dan held onto him, desperate. "Let me go instead. It's my job."

"I'm stronger than you. I'm a better swimmer."

I looked over my shoulder as a huge wave smashed against the front of the cottage. Something structural and important gave way and the whole frontage splintered, sagging as the planks broke under the weight of the water and the roof.

Out of time.

I scrambled up to stand on the window ledge, bracing myself against the roof with my hands. I stamped on the rusting bar as hard as I could, smashing it again and again, until one end gave way with a screech of tortured metal. I kicked it another few times, pushing it out of my way. Then I wriggled through the tiny window and sat on the sill. Dan and Will broke off their argument when I shouted, cupping my hands around my mouth.

"How long for the coast guard to get here?"

"Any minute," Dan said.

It would have been comforting if the next sound hadn't been a splintering crash.

"The roof's going," Will shouted. "Get out of there!"

As he said it, a big section of the roof behind me gave way. The timber came down with terrifying force and I jumped, hurling myself away from the building, acting on instinct. The water seized hold of me like a giant animal, the force of it dragging me sideways, off my feet, and I struggled to lift my face out of it, to keep my bearings, to know where I was even if I couldn't reach safety. Dry land was only four or five meters away from me, but it might as well have been a thousand, because I wasn't in control of where I went. A wave slapped me in the face, and seawater rushed into my mouth and nose, making me choke. Under the water, pieces of the disintegrating cottage buffeted me and I tried to grab onto something—anything—that would help.

What I managed to grip, in the end, was a solid figure who loomed up in the murky water: Dan, who had ended the argument with his son by jumping into the water.

Which was all fine and dandy, but it just meant that there were now two of us struggling against the flood. However, being bigger and stronger than me, Dan was better able to resist the force of the waves. He braced himself, chest deep in the water but holding steady, and pulled me up so I could finally find the ground with my feet.

Will waded in ankle-deep, reaching out as his dad shoved me toward him. I stretched out my hand and our fingers brushed . . . And I slid sideways with a cry. Will's reactions were catlike: he lunged and caught my arm and tore me out of the water to fall against him. And then his arms went around me, and he held onto me so tightly an angel's hair couldn't have fitted between us.

"I've got you."

I was soaking wet and shivering. I wanted nothing more than to press myself against him, but I twisted round to see Dan wading toward us. It wouldn't be long before he was safe too, and then—

The wind gusted savagely. A beam from the shattered roof came free, slid down, tipped end over end as it fell and hit Dan on the back of the head. He pitched face-first into the waves. The water surged back and Dan went with it, not moving, not struggling. Not conscious.

The jolt that ran through Will's body was pure shock. "Dad!"

He shoved me away, dropping the flashlight, and ran straight into the water before I could stop him, swimming with the current, his arms scything through the sea. I grabbed the torch and shone it on the yellow of Dan's jacket as it disappeared into the darkness. I saw Will catching hold of him just before they went out of range of the flashlight beam.

Oh God.

I ran up to the top of the dune, looking for the coast guard, who were supposed to be on their way. Nothing pierced the darkness. Behind me, there was only more darkness, not police officers rushing to our assistance.

We were on our own.

New plan.

From higher ground, I could see the two of them together, Will struggling to keep his father's head out of the water. The current was taking them round to the right, where there was a line of rocks that cut out into the sea. Beyond that they would be gone, out of range.

Bodies to be recovered, not people to be rescued.

Not if I had anything to do with it.

Practically the first thing I'd learned when I came to live in Port Sentinel was that it wasn't safe to walk on rocks in the surf. They were slippery and uneven, and the waves were unpredictable. It was difficult in fine weather and daylight. On a stormy night, walking on the rocks was basically lethal.

So I ran along them instead, into the darkness.

The surf was breaking over the top of the rocks, spray blasting me, and the wind pressed my soaked clothes against me as I ran and, occasionally, jumped. My lungs were bursting, my heart thumping so hard it hurt. I didn't have time to be careful: I was racing the waves. I couldn't let them win. Every so often I shone the torch into the water for a second to check on the two of them, hoping that Will had realized what I was doing.

I reached a narrow spine of rock and had to make a decision about which way the current was taking them. If I picked the wrong one, I would be too far away from them to help. Right looked easier. Left looked more likely. I went left, and didn't let myself think about whether I'd got it right or not.

Toward the end of the line of rocks, they got lower and sharper, and balancing was harder. I stopped on the last rock that was flat enough to kneel on.

This was where we would win or lose.

259

The water was spinning them around like a waltzer when I managed to spot them amid the chaos of the surf. Will was watching me, the strain on his face obvious. Dan's head was lolling.

And I knew that Will would never let go of him. He'd die with his father rather than allow him to drown. In spite of everything, Will still loved his father. He wouldn't be able to live with himself if he abandoned him.

Will made a huge effort and struck out through the water toward the rocks. I knelt down, wrapping one hand around the front of my rock to anchor myself, and now it was my turn to stretch out my hand to him. He was so close . . .

Just as the pair of them came within reach, a nasty curling little wave caught hold of them and spun them round, pulling them away. I could have waited for them to come closer again, but somehow I knew it was the only chance I'd ever have. Instead of Will's hand, I caught the back of his sweatshirt and pulled, gritting my teeth, as the water dragged the cloth through my fingers and the muscles in my shoulder screamed. All I could do was hold on—individually they each weighed more than me; the two together were too much for me, and there was nothing to hold onto and no way on earth this was going to work.

The water swirled back, and for once it was in our favor. I pulled as hard as I could as it floated them up and over the rock. Will reached out and grabbed onto the nearest spur with his free hand, and I held onto him as if my life depended on it, which it basically did. If Will drowned . . . I couldn't let myself even think it. I ignored the ache in my muscles, the fact that the rock was shredding my skin where I clung to it—everything except holding onto him. The wave receded, leaving them behind, and I sobbed with relief as Will scrambled up out of immediate danger. Somehow he still had his arm around his father. It took him two or three attempts to haul him up to where we were, because Dan was a dead weight. Eventually, with my help, he got him more or less out of the water and laid him on his back, tilting his head back so that his mouth was open. Dan's eyes were closed.

I'd never seen anyone look less alive. Will knelt beside him and put his hand on the side of his neck, his face tight with concentration.

"Will," I gasped. "Is he—?

"He'd better not be." Will bent over his father and slapped his face. "Dad? Don't you dare, Dad. Not now."

A powerful light shone on us. I looked up and saw the coast guard's boat cutting through the waves toward us, ready to help us, to rescue us, to save us.

Just a little too late.

24

There were many, many places that would have been more pleasant to be than the Hendersons' house—the rim of an active volcano, a plague-stricken village, a war zone . . . in fact, it was hard to think of anywhere I would have *less* liked to be.

I sat very quietly beside Will on the windowsill, trying to look pleasant and unthreatening, as Karen Henderson watched me from her wheelchair. Her narrow face was implacably hostile, as usual.

But I was there for Will, not for her, and he had his fingers laced through mine, and I wasn't going anywhere.

We were in a room I'd never been in before, and for good reason: it was Dan Henderson's bedroom. He lay on the bed, motionless under a white sheet.

"How are you feeling?" his wife asked. She sounded as if she was talking to a child.

Dan shifted, irritated. He had a bandage on his head and

his skin was gray, but being ill didn't make him any more willing to suffer fools gladly. "I wish people would stop asking me that."

"It's only natural. You almost died. You both did." She shot a venomous glance in my direction. "You shouldn't have been there in the first place. If it wasn't for *you*, none of this would have happened." The second *you* was meant for me.

"You're not the first person to point that out," I said. Will's fingers tightened on mine—I hoped because he was supporting me. Possibly it was a warning. *Please don't fight.*

"Jess saved us," Will said quietly. "You should thank her."

Karen snorted and looked away. No chance.

"It worked out well," Dan said. "John Lowell is going to prison for a very long time and when he gets out, he'll never work with young people again. Gilly—well, if there was ever someone who needed help, it's her. She very nearly killed her mother. She was bloody lucky she didn't succeed. And she was even luckier that she can blame John Lowell for some of the things she did, like leaving Jess to die. She's being charged with attempted murder. Her lawyers are going to point the finger at Lowell all the way through her trial, and honestly, I don't mind if they do. She's a victim too. None of this would have happened if he hadn't set out to separate her from her friends, her family, and everyone else she trusted. He manipulated her. He has to take some responsibility for what she did, and what she became. As it is, she's going to be spending time in a young-offender's institution until she's eighteen and then I'd guess another few years in an adult prison and by the time she comes out she should be a lot wiser about what she does."

"I feel sorry for her," I said.

263

"That's generous of you, considering." Dan sighed. "I hope she'll get some help in prison. The best thing for her is to be away from the media attention, anyway. The story has been all over the papers and not everyone is sympathetic to her. You'd think it was all her idea and that Lowell was the innocent one."

There was a clatter from downstairs: someone opening the front door.

"Hello? Where is everyone?" It was my aunt's voice. She had a key to the Hendersons' house and she had been practically living there for the past week, while Dan was in hospital.

"Tilly." Dan's face softened. "Someone go and tell her to come up."

"I'll go. I want a word with her." Karen spun her chair round and wheeled herself out into the hallway. Tilly got on quite well with her because she simply ignored her little digs and complaints. She was probably the closest thing Karen had to a friend. It didn't surprise me that Karen wanted to talk to her alone—probably to complain about me, and how ungrateful Dan was. It should have come as a shock to no one that he was a terrible patient.

Will looked at his dad. "Wishing you were back in the hospital?"

"A bit." Dan raised an eyebrow. "Hospital's not fun, but at least there are always nurses to look at."

Grim. I made my expression completely neutral as Will shook his head, mortified.

"Dad . . ."

"Sorry." He didn't look it. Dan was getting back to his old self, despite the skull fracture, the chipped scapula, the cracked ribs, the torn ligament in his back that meant he wasn't

264

allowed out of bed yet. Not to mention the near-drowning. He'd been lucky to survive.

We'd all been lucky.

"I am grateful," Dan said, as if he'd been thinking along the same lines as me. "But you should have let me go, Will. You could have been killed, and what good would that have done?"

"I couldn't." Will's voice was flat. "Sorry."

"I thought you hated me."

"So did I." The three words hung in the air. Will wasn't going to say anything else. That was all Dan was going to get. That was all he deserved.

Dan looked at the ceiling, blinking hard. "Jess told me I was going to lose you."

I felt Will tense. "Did she?"

"And it made me think I probably haven't been a very good father. I did what I thought was right."

"How," Will said carefully, "could it be right to try to make me hate you?"

"Because I want you to go. I want you to get out of this town and not look back." Dan wasn't looking at either of us. "I don't want your mother to make you stay. I don't want Jess to. I want you to be free."

Will's hand tightened on mine again. "Because that's what you didn't get to do. What if that's not what I want out of life?"

"Then I've failed," Dan said simply. "You're better than that, Will. Too nice for your own good, if anything. I didn't think you were tough enough to go unless I pushed you. I couldn't let myself mind about you hating me. That was the choice I made."

It wasn't what I'd have chosen myself, but that was Dan all over. *The end justifies the means.*

Will sounded very tired when he spoke again. "I can't leave Mum. Not how she is. You know that."

"You have to go to university." There was a warning note in Dan's voice.

"I'm deferring my place."

"This is exactly what I didn't want to happen," Dan snapped. "You'll waste your life just like I have. These aren't your obligations, Will. You didn't ask to be born. This is about me and your mother, not you. Don't let her drag you into the middle of it."

Tilly threw open the door and bounced in, beaming. "Dan, you're back! How are you feeling?"

"My head hurts and I'm hungry."

She tilted her head to one side. "Soup? I made vegetable soup. You'll love it. It's got lentils in it."

Dan's face was a picture. "I hate soup."

I couldn't help it; I started to giggle. Will grinned, then started laughing too. Dan glared at the two of us, and it made it worse.

"Sorry," I said, gasping for air, "but you're such a grump, Dan. Who hates soup?"

"I do." He was starting to smile, though.

"All soup?" Tilly asked. Her eyes were huge, pleading.

"Pretty much." Dan sighed. "All right. I'll try the lentil soup."

She clapped her hands. "I'll go and heat it up."

As Tilly clattered down the stairs, there was a ring at the door, and I heard her answer it.

"I wish everyone would just leave me alone," Dan said. "No more visitors."

"No soup, no visitors. Got it," I said.

"More painkillers."

"In half an hour," Will said, checking his watch.

"Oh, come on."

"No, Dad."

Dan leaned his head back on the pillows and breathed deeply through his nose. Relying on other people was pure torture for him. As if to compound the agony, Karen pushed open the door and propelled herself back into the room.

"I hope you didn't miss me while I was gone," she said archly, and was ignored. "Who rang the doorbell?"

"No idea," Will said. "We didn't see. Tilly let them in."

As he said it, Tilly opened the door and came in, her face blank with surprise. She tried to sound cheerful, though. "Look who's here."

Mum walked in, closely followed by Dad—*Dad?* She looked over at me, and I couldn't read the expression on her face at all: shock, mainly, and anger. Dad was looking noble, which was a bad sign.

What have you done?

Karen looked up at Mum with pure loathing, but her face changed when she saw Dad. It was—but it couldn't be—terror I saw.

"I'd better go," she said, and started to wheel herself toward the door.

"Stay." Dad's voice was firm. "You need to be here, Karen."

"What's going on?" Dan demanded. He was struggling to sit up in bed, evidently feeling at a disadvantage lying down.

"How are you feeling?" Mum asked, and instead of exploding at her, Dan grinned.

"Like hell. But grateful to your daughter for getting me out of trouble."

"She has her moments," Mum said, trying and failing to hide how proud she was. Then her face went serious again and she looked behind her to Dad, obviously nervous.

What's going on?

Dan looked past her and frowned. "Why are you here, Chris?"

Dad seemed to be roughly as cheerful as someone walking to the scaffold. "I have something to tell you. Something you need to know."

"Stop," Karen said, her voice faint.

"Dan, I had no reason to like you, but you put yourself in harm's way for Jess. She told me what you did." Dad swallowed. "And I'm grateful. So I want you to know the truth, no matter what happens." He looked across at me. "I'm sorry, Jess."

"Why? What are you talking about?" I was already sitting on the edge of the windowsill. Now I stood up. "What do you mean by the truth?"

"I'd like to know that too," Dan said.

"I need to go." Karen's face was red. "Will, take me out of here."

He stood up too, but hesitated beside me, not sure what to do.

"Leave her where she is. You should be here as well." Dad took a deep breath. "You all know why I came to Port Sentinel. I wanted to persuade Molly to come back to me. I wanted me and her and Jess to be a family again. I knew she was happy here and would never come back to London. I thought we could make a new life together here instead, and maybe I could make amends for the things I've got wrong."

268

Dan snorted. "As if."

"I didn't get the chance to prove I'd changed," Dad said with dignity. "But I did get to talk to Karen. We have a lot in common, Karen and I. We've both suffered from the fact that you and Molly regretted breaking up in the first place, and getting married to other people."

"This is ancient history," Dan said. "I'm not hearing anything new."

"I'm getting there," Dad snapped. "Just let me explain. We never got a fair chance at making our marriages work. There was always a shadow between me and Molly, and I know Karen felt the same about you, Dan. But we got on with it, and we had children, and watched them grow up." He took a deep breath. "And as they got older, we both became aware that the day would come when the children were old enough to be independent, and when that happened, the chances were that we would find ourselves separating—getting divorced."

"So you thought you'd get in first and cheat on Mum with girls who were at least ten years younger than you," I said, unable to bear the self-pity any more.

"I handled it badly. I'm not saying I didn't." Dad sighed. "Anyway, I set Molly free. And as I'd expected, once we'd split up she came down here."

"That wasn't because of Dan," Tilly said. Her voice was tight with anger. "That was after Freya died, so she could support me."

"Nonetheless, she was back where she grew up. Where you were, Dan."

"Nothing happened." Dan looked at Mum with a smile I'd never seen on his face before. "She wouldn't, and I couldn't, and you are lucky, Chris, that I'm stuck in bed because if I was fit, I'd be showing you what I think of you for even suggesting Molly and I would get together again."

"But you did sneak around," Will said. "You saw each other a lot. I saw you together, Dad, in your car."

"Look, I'd be lying if I said we hadn't thought about it. We loved each other very much, once upon a time. That doesn't go away. But we'd both moved on since then. We'd changed."

"We were just friends," Mum said. "The only reason we didn't want anyone to know we were meeting was because we didn't want to upset Karen. Dan thought she wouldn't like it"

Karen laughed, and it was a horrible sound. "Of course. No one wants to upset poor Karen."

"Karen had her suspicions," Dad said. "When I came down here, she confided in me. She wanted me to keep an eye on the two of them, because she was housebound." He paused, probably for effect—in spite of himself he was enjoying being the center of attention. "Or should I say, she *seemed* to be housebound."

"What do you mean by that?" Dan asked. His eyes were watchful.

"Christopher," Karen said, "I hope you're not going to suggest—"

"She's lying," Dad said, cutting across her. "She pretended to be ill. She told you she had motor neurone disease, but she's faking."

"The doctor said—" Will began.

"She saw Molly at Freya's funeral. It was then that she started developing symptoms. She picked a disease that pro-

270

gresses in unpredictable ways. She found one that couldn't be diagnosed easily, with symptoms she could fake easily enough. Your doctor referred her for tests. She went to London for them and you couldn't go, could you, Dan? You had work, and she didn't want you there anyway. And then she came back and said it was bad news. She was dying. So how could you leave her? You'd have to be some sort of monster. Even if the love of your life had come back and was living in her old house, practically within touching distance." Dad waited for someone to speak, and when they didn't, he laughed. "Don't you believe me? She was convincing, I grant you. She fooled enough people to get by, and hid from anyone who might have spotted the truth, and you threw yourself into your work, Dan. You didn't have a clue that she might be tricking you. You just wanted her to get on with dying so you could get on with living."

"That's a flaw in the plan," Dan said. "How were you going to manage the dying part, Karen?"

She was as white as the bedclothes. Her fingers made little plucking movements on the blanket she had thrown across her knees.

"A miraculous recovery, I imagine," Dad said. "A misdiagnosis. Wonders will never cease. Let's all live happily ever after."

"He's lying," Karen ground out.

"I'm not." Dad smiled grimly. "She told me everything herself. She wanted me to help her. She wanted Molly to be safely out of reach, and preferably out of Port Sentinel, before she revealed she wasn't dying after all. She knew that was the only thing that was keeping Dan by her side. She thought he would leave as soon as he heard she was healthy—but a brokenhearted

271

Dan might stay." Dad turned to Karen. "I have every reason to keep your secret, Karen, except that it makes me sick to my stomach. I can't stand it any more. Dan needs to know the truth."

"I can explain," Karen said in a low, terrible voice. She looked up. "Will, I can explain."

For the first time I looked at Will, and my heart twisted. He looked stunned. Devastated. In the space of ten minutes, everything he believed had been turned upside down. He walked out of the room like a sleepwalker, stumbling a little, away from the sound of the tearing sobs that were shaking his mother's thin frame.

"Jess, go after him," Dan said. "Make sure he's all right."

As if a spell had been lifted, I found I could move again. I heard the front door bang and I ran down the stairs. A car engine started: Dan's Range Rover, parked on the drive. I pulled open the door in time to see Will reverse into the road and accelerate away, his expression set. I ran out, too late to stop him, too late even to see him drive away. I listened to the engine sounds change as he went up through the gears, faster and faster, trying to outrun something he couldn't ever leave behind.

25

The door was open. I knocked on it tentatively. "Hello?"

"Jessica? Is that you? Come in."

I managed two steps before I had to stop, blocked by a stack of cardboard boxes and a roll of bubble wrap. I looked around, wrinkling my nose. Dad's flat was even more depressing when he was halfway through packing. Every item of furniture was covered in books, magazines, clothes, and rubbish. What I could see of the living room was filthy. Gray curls of dusty fluff littered the floor and there were dirty marks on the walls where the furniture had been.

"Over here," Dad said from somewhere behind the sofa, and I edged round the bubble wrap so I could see him. He was sitting in a ring of papers, and if he was trying to sort them out, it didn't look as if it was going very well.

"How's it going?"

"Fine, I think." He looked around at the general mess, as if that was how he'd planned to pack, as if he was actually ahead of schedule. "They're coming to pick up the furniture to put it into storage in half an hour. I have to hand the keys back at midday."

"That's not actually a lot of time." I was trying to find somewhere to sit. I settled for the arm of the sofa, having removed a mug, and a plate that had once been used for toast. "You're going to need to clean it properly. They'll charge you if they have to do it. You might even lose your deposit."

Dad waved a hand. "I don't care about that. Let them sort it out if they care so much. I'm glad I'm leaving, honestly."

"Because New Year's Eve is the perfect time to move back to London," I said.

"I don't care about that, either. It's time to go."

"Are you going to miss me?" I wanted to know what he'd say.

"Of course."

Let's try that line again, I imagined a director saying. *This time, try to put some feeling into it.*

"Well, things will definitely be different without you." I was being diplomatic. I meant *better*.

Dad stood up, brushing some of the dust off his jumper. "You know, I'm glad I told Molly and Dan the truth. I'm sorry if it makes life more complicated for you."

I shrugged. "I think it'll be OK."

"Even if they get together?"

"Well, as it turns out, Dan has been having an affair with one of his detectives. So I think that's his first priority." It was the one who'd helped me at the police station, in fact. She was very pretty, and I was inclined to think he'd done well.

Dad raised his eyebrows. "Is your mother devastated?"

"She knew." I looked at him pityingly. "Remember when

she said they were friends? Friends talk. He's been crying on her shoulder ever since she got back to Port Sentinel."

"Poor Molly."

"Hardly," I said, thinking of the conversation I'd had with Nick Trabbet earlier, when he'd asked me, in an uncharacteristically tense voice, if I thought Mum would like to go on a date with him.

I was pretty sure she would.

I folded my arms. "Dad, you have to leave Mum alone. She's got a new life now. It doesn't include you. Go and make someone else happy." *If you're even capable of that.*

"I don't like letting her go."

"She's already gone."

Dad nodded slowly. "You're one of them now."

"Them?"

"Your mother's family. You belong here, don't you?"

I didn't answer him straight away. I looked out to sea, to the Sentinel Rock that stood just beyond the harbor, the rock that gave the town its name. The storm hadn't done anything to damage it. It looked just as solid as ever. White birds wheeled around it and the steel-gray waters lapped at it. It hadn't changed. It might never change.

"I think I do, now. I think this is my home." I stood up.

Dad looked even more disappointed. "You're leaving? I thought you could help me pack."

I looked around at the chaos he'd created. "I think you're doing fine on your own."

After Dad's flat I needed some fresh air. I walked along the seafront, on the storm-battered promenade, muffled in my coat and scarf. It was cold out, but not raining, quite, and there were lots of locals around, inspecting the broken steps and missing pavement the council had yet to replace. People greeted me as I passed them—neighbors, friends from school, regular customers in the shop. I saw people I recognized but didn't yet know, and picked out the strangers, the blow-ins, the ones who were looking around with that surprise and delight that I remembered from my first day in Port Sentinel. It was pretty, even with the gray clouds hanging low enough to brush the steeples of the churches. Port Sentinel was small, gossipy, and occasionally dangerous, but it was home now.

I was about halfway along the promenade when I saw Will. He was walking toward me, not hurrying, but there was something about the way he was moving that told me he was looking for me. I stood where I was and waited for him to reach me.

"Hi."

"Hi, yourself," he said, stopping before we were close enough to touch. "Heading home?"

"I just wanted a walk."

"I can walk with you."

"Now I'm more interested in standing still."

Will took his hands out of his pockets and caught hold of me. He tipped my face up to his, tangling his fingers in my hair, and I kissed him with all the passion and love that I felt, that I knew he felt too. He'd been staying at Sandhayes since he found out about his mother, while Dan and Karen battled over splitting up once and for all. Tilly put him in the little room opposite mine, and everyone made a magnificent job of ignoring the creaking floorboard in the middle of the landing that announced, every single time, when he was sneaking into my room in the middle of the night. (Hugo didn't ignore it, but I ignored Hugo, so that worked out in more or less the same way.) We'd spent hours together, wrapped up in one another, talking and not talking. Planning out the future. Teasing one another about the past. We'd been dragging so much baggage around with us since we met—Freya's death, our parents' romantic history, Karen's illness, and Ryan's feelings for me—and it had caused us nothing but trouble. For the first time it was all about us—just us. No one else. And it was like all the best times I'd spent with him, but all the time. We knew each other so well. We knew the worst of each other, as well as the best. And I loved all of Will, even though he had his faults. Maybe because he had faults. I couldn't pretend to be perfect, and I knew he loved me all the same.

Sometimes I just looked at him, because that was all I wanted to do. That sweep of dark eyelashes. The straight line of his nose. The curve of his lips. I stared at them again, fixing them in my mind. *This is how he is. This is how he looks. This is who I love.*

"Nick is going ask Mum on a date." I had to tell someone.

"Really?" Will looked genuinely delighted. "Are you pleased?"

"Of course."

"Will she say yes?"

"Of course," I said again.

He put his arms around me and held on to me. "I wonder what Dad will think."

"He'll think it's good news."

"If it was you," Will said, "I wouldn't. That's why I could never believe they were just friends. I can't imagine not loving you."

"We're not like them."

277

"No, we aren't." He smiled down at me. "If it was you, I would want you back, no matter how much time had passed. No matter what had happened."

"You'd have to let me go in the first place. Or leave me behind," I couldn't help adding. The shadow of him leaving was there all the time. He would go back to school, and then to university, and then on to who knew where. And I wanted to go my way too. I had my life to live. I had a dream that I couldn't even voice yet, that I hadn't even mentioned to Will—that maybe I could join the police myself. Become a detective, even. I didn't know how that would fit in with Will's life, or even if it would.

But the thought of not seeing him for even a day made me shiver.

"I'll never let you go." Will's arms tightened around me. His eyes were the softest shade of gray, like cygnet down. "Wherever I go, whatever I do, you'll be in my heart."

Something caught on my eyelashes and I blinked. The air was full of tiny white stars that danced around us: snow, turning the ordinary day into something magical.

Will was watching me, waiting, and I knew he needed to hear me say it.

"Wherever I go," I said. "Whatever I do."

He caught me up, lifting me off the ground, swinging me round as we kissed. If there were other people walking along the promenade, smiling at the two of us or rolling their eyes, I didn't care. I was lost in him, and he in me, and that was how it was supposed to be.